Ash Wednesday

Harold Eppley

Northfield Public Library
210 Washington Street
Northfield, MN 55057

Oconee Spirit Press LLC
Waverly, Tennessee
www.oconeespirit.com

Ash Wednesday. Copyright 2012 by Harold Eppley.

All rights reserved. No part of this book may be reproduced or transmitted in any form or by any means without written permission of the author. Printed in the United States of America.

ISBN 978-0-9840109-0-5

1.Clergy–Fiction. 2. Dustin (Penn : Imaginary place)– Fiction.

Characters, places and events in *Ash Wednesday* are the product of the author's imagination or are used fictitiously. Any resemblance to real people, institutions, organizations, businesses or incidents is entirely coincidental.

The text paper is SFI certified. The Sustainable Forestry Initiative® program promotes sustainable forest management.

Cover design by Kelli McBride

In loving memory of
Samuel Moffitt Eppley
(1935-2004)

Acknowledgments

I am a fortunate man and a grateful one, too. I am thankful for all who helped to bring the publication of *Ash Wednesday* to fruition.

Thank you to my dear friend Karen Church for being the first to read and critique an early draft of this novel and for telling me it didn't suck. Thank you to Nick Fisher-Broin, Kip Groettum, Brad Kmoch, Carole Greene, and the Bay View writing group for their encouragement and wise advice throughout the years it took me to complete this book. Thank you to Deborah Adams and the staff of Oconee Spirit Press for publishing great books and inviting mine to become one of them. Thank you to my talented wife and writing partner, Rochelle Melander, and to my children Samuel and Eliana for allowing me to obsess about my novel when I should have been paying attention to them.

I am grateful for family, friends and mentors who have supported my writing habit at every age I've ever been, most especially Helen Wasuck, Karen Bockelman, Ralph Smith, Steve Rye, Jen Andreas, Lisa Clark, Holly and Mike Carlson, Carolyn Clouser, Rebekah Eppley, and the one who introduced me to the wonderful world of literature, my mother, Linda Eppley. I appreciate my friends from western Pennsylvania for suffering and frolicking with me in God's country through four long winters and three gorgeous summers. Finally, I am grateful for all who still dare to call themselves Lutheran, especially members of Lincoln Park Lutheran Church in Milwaukee, Wisconsin. *I am reasonably certain that Jesus loves you more than he loves everyone else.*

Part One

Summer into Fall

One

Gerald Schwartz

Ten down, two to go.

Pastor Gerald Schwartz stifled a yawn and leaned back in an armchair covered with cat fur. Without moving his eyes, he snuck what he hoped was a surreptitious glance at his watch. He was feeling gassy from the four chocolate gobs he had consumed in the past half hour. He hoped he could refrain from emitting any embarrassing odors for another few minutes. Not that his current host would notice. Why, he mused, a chocolate-inspired expulsion might be sweetly refreshing compared to the stench of the unchanged litter box presently wafting about Mrs. Hawthorne's apartment.

"If you ask me—and nobody ever does—this entire country has gone to hell in a handbasket. It's not like it was when I was a child," said Mrs. Hawthorne. She had talked nearly nonstop for forty-five minutes. As her pastor, Gerald was privy to every detail of Mrs. Hawthorne's unremarkable life, from her battle against bunions to the length of her latest stool, and not the kind you sit on, either.

Gerald had dozed off for a good part of Mrs. Hawthorne's most recent monologue. For more nights than he could recount he had awoken from a deep sleep at three in the morning. He spent the hours until sunrise flailing against the mattress, unable to drive the demons from his head. Perpetually tired, he did some of his best sleeping while visiting his elderly parishioners.

"You know, Reverend, I don't believe I've told you about the time my brother saved me from drowning in the creek when I was just four years old."

Gerald knew better than to inform his host that she had already told him about her brother's heroics. He had heard the story so many times he could recite it by heart. During a previous visit he made the mistake of interrupting Mrs. Hawthorne to note that, enthralling though it was, the incident at Meyer's Creek sounded vaguely familiar. Perhaps she had mentioned it to him during one of his eighty-four other visits to her home.

She glared at him. "Pastor, are you implying my memory is starting to falter?"

So today, during the fraction of an instant when he customarily nodded his head and raised his eyebrows, feigning interest in the story that was to follow, Gerald interjected with the one segue guaranteed to bring Mrs. Hawthorne's chatter to an abrupt halt, "Shall we celebrate holy communion now?"

He said this while lifting a small black box from his lap. He placed it reverently on the coffee table next to a stack of large print *Guideposts* and *Hot True Romance* magazines.

"That sounds like a fascinating story," said Gerald, doing his best to sound sincere. "Perhaps you can save it for our next visit. Time is running short and I still have to bring communion to several other people."

Actually, just one more after this. No harm in telling Mrs. Hawthorne a little fib to move things along. He could hardly inform her that his true motive for making a hasty exit was to catch the end of the Pirates game. Not to mention the nausea he was feeling from the cat box odor and his need to take care of his gas problem.

"Who else do you need to see?" asked Mrs. Hawthorne. She watched her pastor fill a miniature silver chalice with the wine he carried in his communion kit.

"Miss Kirch and Mrs. Arnason, among others," he said, trying not to reveal his irritation.

"Gert Arnason? You just came from her house. She called me after you left."

There were no secrets in Dustin, Pennsylvania. Plenty of misinformation, but certainly no secrets. Gerald leaned toward his host and waved in front of her a round white wafer with an embedded cross. "Shall we stop our quibbling and proceed with our Lord's holy meal?"

"For goodness' sake, it's four already. Time for my story," said Mrs. Hawthorne, as she reached for her remote control.

"I'm quite certain your show can wait. The Lord comes first," said Gerald.

"Oh no, Reverend, I can't miss a single minute. Today we find out who the father of Melinda's baby is."

Gerald knew from experience that Mrs. Hawthorne would become belligerent if he tried to press the matter further. He would have to out-shout the actors on Mrs. Hawthorne's favorite daytime drama.

"FINALLY, PANTY LINERS THAT PROVIDE FULL DAY PROTECTION," blared a voice on the television. Mrs. Hawthorne was deaf in one ear and raised the volume so loud that Gerald felt his eardrums vibrate. He managed to finish the prayers during the commercial break. He was not as fortunate while reciting the sacred words of institution. Gerald glanced at the television, shocked to see a shirtless man and a mostly undressed woman engaged in a passionate kiss.

For the eleventh time this day, he said, "In the night in which he was be-trayed our Lord Jesus took bread—"

"OH GOD, TIFFANY, YOU LOOK SO HOT. I'M GOING TO MAKE TONIGHT SPECIAL FOR YOU."

"…gave thanks, broke it and gave it to his disciples, saying—"

"WHEN I'M WITH YOU MY INSIDES START TO QUIVER."

"This is my body given for you—"

"OH GOD, YOU'RE SO SEXY I COULD EAT YOU UP. HAVE YOU BEEN WORKING OUT?"

"…my body, given for you. Do this in remembrance of me."

"TAKE ME NOW! I CAN'T RESIST ANY LONGER."

Gerald peeked at Mrs. Hawthorne. She was watching the television. She closed her eyes and dropped her chin when she saw the pastor looking at her.

"Mrs. Hawthorne, I would appreciate your lowering the volume. I'm losing my concentration."

"And Tiffany's losing her virginity. Kids these days don't have any mor-als."

"Tiffany?"

"On my story. These kids jump in bed first chance they get. It wasn't like that when I was young. Charlie and me were both virgins till the day we got married. You know, I don't think you've ever heard about my wedding night. Up at the Timberland Lodge. It was the first time Charlie and me had ever been naked together and let me tell you—"

"Next time, Mrs. Hawthorne."

+++

Gerald leaned back in the crumb-covered driver's seat of his Buick. He had turned the air conditioner to maximum circulation in an attempt to dissipate the byproduct of Mrs. Hawthorne's baked goods. The Pirates were losing by two runs in the eighth. Eleven down, one to go.

He was not sure why, but communion calls to the homebound on the first and third Mondays of every month were among Gerald's least distressing pastoral duties. Mrs. Hawthorne was a self-centered compulsive talker. Lois "9 Lives" Warner worried incessantly about a variety of imagined ailments. And Mrs. Weidenbach blathered about the myriad talents of Gerald's beloved predecessor, Pastor Franklin. Yet Gerald was able to tolerate, occasionally enjoy, the parishioners who were unable to attend Sunday services at Abiding Truth Lutheran Church.

Ed Jacobson, the only man on his shut-in list, liked to talk baseball and ask the pastor questions about his medications. He mistakenly believed that Gerald's theological degree included the study of pharmaceuticals. Gerald felt sorry for Mr. Jacobson, who had lost thirty pounds in the eighteen months since his wife's death. Gerald had once peeked into Ed's refrigerator to see what he had been eating. Its sole contents were two cases of Rolling Rock and a jar of pickles.

Gerald and Ed occasionally bonded over their unexpected newfound status as bachelors. Gerald tried to steer clear of this topic, however. Ed was easily moved to tears when remembering his dearly beloved Annie. And Gerald still felt his jaw grow tense whenever he recalled how after 33 years of marriage Margaret inexplicably decided to divorce him.

The others on the homebound list were confined to their homes by a variety of maladies. Chronic arthritis. Parkinson's disease. Congestive heart failure. This did not include Lillian Sutherland, who said she "couldn't possibly have a visit from the pastor today" because she was "getting her hair done in Spooner's Grove." Last month, she had an appointment with her psychic palmreader on Gerald's visiting day.

Though she lived across the street from the church, Lillian had been on the official list of homebound members since spraining her ankle three years before. During her short period of convalescence, Lillian realized it was more convenient to have the pastor bring communion to her home than to make the 300-foot trek across the street for Sunday worship. Miraculously, despite her homebound status, Lillian was able to attend any church functions involving food or gambling.

For Gerald, the most comforting aspect of monthly visits to the home-bound was the immutable predictability of it all. He knew his parishioners by the unchanging spaces they inhabited. He knew there would always be exactly seventy-six angel statues on the mantle above Gert Arnason's fireplace, no matter how many times he counted them. Prudence Weidenbach's screen door would open only if he first pulled the handle up before pushing it down. Gerald found it inexplicably soothing that the faucet in Lois Warner's bathroom emitted an annoying squeal every time he turned on the water to rinse his miniature silver communion chalice.

Gerald also knew that Lillian Sutherland would soon be complaining because her pastor never came to see her. On Wednesday, Harriet Redgrave would stop by the church to chastise him for neglecting at least one of his pastoral responsibilities. And Monday morning, on her way to the library, Dorothy Moyers would peek in the parsonage window before dropping an anonymous letter into his mailbox. Gerald knew that if this year were like the past six, he would preside at seven times more funerals than baptisms. And to his chagrin, Irmalee Hackett, his organist, would play *In the Garden* at every one of them.

Gerald steered his Buick up Maple Street, avoiding the potholes while staying within the posted speed limit of 20 miles per hour. After signaling well in advance, he made a right turn onto the sprawling campus of the Valley View senior living center. Gerald drove around the lot twice. When he parked, the odometer on his car read exactly 178,000. He hoped his final visit of the day would be a short one.

+++

Miss Kristina Kirch had resided for the past three years in an assisted living facility perched at the top of a hill overlooking the town of Dustin. Valley View Manor bordered on a park, which had once been the site of Abiding Truth's annual Easter sunrise service. This tradition was discontinued in Gerald's third year after someone noted that cloud cover had prevented anyone from seeing the sunrise for the past eight Easters.

In recent years, the park had become a popular spot for teenage partiers and clandestine lovers. Broken beer bottles and used condoms posed hazards to the few children who dared to venture onto the dilapidated playground. Like most of Dustin, Summit Park had seen better days.

The view from the top of the hill was alternately spectacular and dismal, depending upon which direction a person looked. Directly to the west, a lush tree-covered valley spread like a blanket for miles before the land rose again, culminating in the rounded tree-topped peak of Mount Siebert. A lazy river snaked through the valley, bordered on both sides by the sprawling village of Pottersfield. On clear days, the view from here was one of the most awe-inspiring in all of Pennsylvania's Allegheny mountain range.

Yet a mere turn of the head revealed a completely different sight. A few miles to the southeast sat the unsightly remains of a coal mine. Though the mine had been abandoned for ten years, most of the houses surrounding it were permanently covered with an ashen-colored film. Next to the empty mine sat Ray's Salvage, sprawled out as an ugly reminder that death could be lurking around the next corner. This massive collection of mangled rusty automobiles, most of which had met their demise on the narrow winding roads leading into town, included a few that had carried some of Gerald's parishioners. Ashes to ashes, Dustin to dust. So went a not-so-funny local joke.

When Gerald first moved to Dustin and was still inclined to exercise, he would climb to the top of the hill as part of his daily prayer walk. He would look out across the valley toward Pottersfield and muse that this must have been how Moses, the great leader of the Israelites, felt when he gazed at the Promised Land from the top of Mount Pisgah.

In recent years, however, Gerald always drove to the park, and then only when he had to. Gerald rarely stopped to enjoy the scenery. The awe-inspiring vista served only to remind him that while Moses might have been moved by the view from Mount Pisgah, he never did make it into the Promised Land.

The door to room 128 was slightly ajar. Confident that his flatulence problem had been resolved, Gerald knocked three times. Waiting a full 30 seconds and hearing no response, he peeked inside the room. A shriveled, silver-haired woman in a wheelchair stared curiously at her visitor.

"It's your pastor, Miss Kirch. I'm here for our 4:30 rendezvous." Gerald lifted the black communion kit with one hand. He pointed to his white ministerial collar with the other.

"Oh yes, Pastor. Please have a seat." Her lips barely moved when she spoke.

Miss Kirch suffered from Alzheimer's disease, or so Gerald surmised from her behavior over the past two years. She had worked as a housekeeper at the parsonage during Pastor Franklin's tenure before moving to a farm-house near Somerset, where she cared for her ailing mother before returning to Dustin. Gerald heard that Miss Kirch had once been very beautiful and that she had inherited a large sum of money from her mother. As with most gossip that originated with Dorothy Moyers, he was inclined to doubt the veracity of the latter rumor.

Certainly the rumors Dorothy had spread about him were mostly untrue. He did not have too much to drink at the Wilmore/Sidman wedding reception. Admittedly, he had slurred a few words during the opening prayer, but that was due mostly to exhaustion.

And despite the unrelenting whisperings at the bimonthly women's guild meetings, Margaret most certainly did not leave him because she had fallen in love with another woman. She had moved to Harrisburg to live with her former college roommate Althea.

After thirty-three years of marriage, Gerald could attest to the fact that Margaret was heterosexual. Or more likely asexual. But she certainly was not gay, for God's sake. Still, last week, through the heating vent that led from the church basement to his office, Gerald had heard Edna Weinwright's booming voice declare, "Harrisburg is teeming with homos and colored people."

Between her thumb and index finger, Miss Kirch was caressing a small Celtic cross pendant, attached to a finely braided silver chain she wore around her neck. When she was not staring blankly out the window, she was usually fidgeting with something, a symptom of her progressing Alzheimer's. "So how are Gracie and the children?" she asked.

It took Gerald a few seconds to realize that Miss Kirch had mistaken him for Joseph Franklin, who had served as pastor of Abiding Truth for thirty-eight years. He died six days after his retirement in 1997, a month before Gerald's arrival in Dustin. Though Gerald had never met the man, he was well acquainted with his ghost. Seven years after his death, parishioners still spoke about Franklin with fondness usually reserved for Jesus, Elvis, or one of the Pittsburgh Steelers.

"Oh no, Miss Kirch," Gerald said, trying to conceal his irritation, "I'm Pastor Schwartz. I don't have any children."

Miss Kirch stared at him, her forehead wrinkled, her chapped lips pressed together.

"Or a wife," added Gerald, as though he had just remembered how alone he was.

"Oh, yes, you're the new guy," she said, sounding momentarily coherent. "From one of those big cities down the mountain. Johnstown, is it? Altoona?"

"Baltimore."

"Johnstown. Baltimore. They're all the same to me."

Gerald winced. Comparing his beloved Baltimore with a decaying mountain burg whose claim to fame was being devastated by a flood in the 1800s was like equating Languedoc-Roussillon Corbiere with Boone's Farm. Then again, on those rare occasions when Gerald's parishioners sampled "wine" it was bound to be Boone's Farm. And those who dared to set foot in a "big city" rarely ventured beyond Johnstown or Altoona.

"How are you?" Gerald asked. He knew how she would answer.

"Oh fine," she said, "same as always." Unlike Mrs. Hawthorne, who operated on verbal autopilot, Gerald could rarely encourage Miss Kirch to speak about herself.

As he glanced around at her sparsely decorated living area, Gerald sensed that something was different about her room. The cross-stitched wall hanging of the 23rd Psalm graced its usual spot above the television. A calendar from the Aschenbrenner Funeral Home was tacked to a bulletin board next to a copy of the week's meal selections.

Large X's were drawn through the first eight days of August, giving the impression that someone was counting down to an important event. Gerald knew there were no impending milestones for Miss Kirch. The calendar merely served as a reminder that she had made it through another day. If she could survive another eight hours a brand new X would await her in the morning.

A mother-of-pearl statue of praying hands sat on the bedside table. Behind the statue Gerald noticed a framed photograph. He rose and stepped across the room. "I don't believe I've seen this before," he said, as he lifted the photograph from the table.

It was a black and white portrait of a young woman who appeared to be in her early 20s. She was standing by herself on a beach with a large body of water in the background. The woman wore a one-piece bathing suit, modest by modern standards, yet tight-fitting enough to reveal her slim figure. She had dark, flowing hair, which rested on her well-toned shoulders. A shy smile revealed a hint of perfectly white teeth. Bright eyes the same hue as the water behind her sparkled, undimmed by age. The woman's head was tilted slightly to the right, revealing a finely braided chain around her neck with a small Celtic cross pendant attached to it. Gerald recognized it as the necklace Miss Kirch was wearing now.

He stared at the young woman's eyes, unable to look away for a few seconds. "It's you," he said finally.

Except for her necklace, the woman sitting before him bore little resemblance to the one in the photograph. Only a few of her teeth were remaining. Gerald guessed that she probably had not smiled for several years. Miss Kirch's hair was thinning and gray with bald patches, her shoulders slumped, her eyes clouded over. All signs of beauty had long since melted away.

Gerald studied the photograph. "You certainly were attractive," he mused.

Miss Kirch stared at him blankly and Gerald felt blood rush to his cheeks. Embarrassed by his uncharacteristic effusiveness, he stammered, "Y-you s-still are, of course."

"Thank you," she said, with the graciousness of a woman who had received the compliment before.

Gerald took a moment to regain his composure. "It's a remarkable portrait. When was it taken?"

"Long time ago."

She was staring at her shoes again. This was how it usually went—a few minutes of coherence followed by a return to her usual state of confusion.

"It's time for communion," he said, returning the photograph to the bed stand.

+++

Gerald sank into the driver's seat of his Buick and offered a quick prayer of thanks to Whoever Might Be Listening. Twelve down. Another month of homebound visits completed.

That night, after Gerald had finished his customary liter of wine and chased it with four shots of bourbon, a few handfuls of low-fat crackers, and a leftover piece of German chocolate cake from Sunday's fellowship hour, he took one last gulp of bourbon, lay down on the king-sized bed he and Margaret had shared for thirty-three years and fell asleep with his clothes on, waiting for the demons to come.

Two

Betty Mundy

The front door was unlocked, so she knew Clarence wasn't down at the Buckshot Club. He was either in the bathroom or lounging on the sofa with Spot the dog on the floor next to him, watching *Jeopardy*. She hoped he hadn't eaten the oatmeal raisin cookies she had left on the kitchen counter, which would ruin his appetite for lunch.

"That you, hon?" Clarence called from the living room. She heard the toilet running and a clamor that sounded like rock music blasting from the television.

"Sorry I'm late," she said. "The copier jammed again. How's the colitis?"

"I'd stay out of the bathroom awhile. I dried the dishes for ya. And Edna called. That woman sure talks loud."

Betty felt a rush of gratitude, one of those overwhelming moments she experienced several times a day when she realized how blessed she was. Clarence didn't have a job, watched too much television, and wouldn't come to church with her. But how many husbands helped with household chores?

"What did Edna want?"

"That committee they formed's meetin' tonight. She said ya oughta be there. They're up to no good, ain't they?"

"I'm going down to Pottersfield tonight. I'm helping Dougie and Allyson pick out wedding favors."

Betty brought Clarence his bologna sandwich on white toast with ketchup and a glass of two percent milk. His eyes were fastened on the 60-inch television screen, which dominated the Mundy's otherwise modest living room.

"What's that you're watching?" she asked. Betty could not believe how much they had paid for this so-called "home entertainment center." Personally, she could live without television and be perfectly content.

"It's that preacher from Dougie's church."

"You mean Pastor Weiss."

A man's baritone voice was filling the room. It almost sounded like a song the way he was speaking.

"Dougie always sits near the front, don't he?"

The camera was panning the congregation. Betty knew it was a large church. It was a few blocks from Dougie's new house and she drove by it every time she went to see him.

Clarence gulped from his glass of milk and made the irritating slurping sound Betty had long ago learned to ignore. "I like this guy. Ya can understand what he's talkin' 'bout. Ain't like Rev'rend Schwartz. That pastor of yers is always usin' big words. Makes a normal person feel stupid."

The camera zoomed in on the preacher. Suddenly it was like he was right there in the living room.

"Wow!" exclaimed Betty. "Allyson is right. Pastor Weiss is . . ." She turned her head so that Clarence could not see her face and whispered, "a good-looking man."

Clarence frowned. "That's not why I like 'im. He just talks good."

The pastor stood on a large open stage. He wore a dark formal suit with a crisp white shirt and a flashy red tie, which was much nicer than the one tie Clarence owned.

Three large screens were visible on the wall behind the stage. Two of them flashed profile shots of Pastor Weiss and the third, above the preacher's right shoulder, showed an outline of the sermon. The setting looked nothing like any Lutheran church Betty had ever seen. There was neither a cross nor an altar. When the camera panned the sanctuary, Betty caught a glimpse of the All-U-Can-Eat Communion Brunch Buffet.

A headline appeared at the bottom of the television screen: *Are You Buff Enough? Part 3.* Pastor Weiss was lifting a barbell over his head, barely breaking a sweat, his hair staying perfectly in place.

"Would ya look at that?" Clarence pointed at the television set and guffawed, revealing a mouthful of partly chewed bread and bologna. "This guy knows how to get your 'tention."

Betty sat down next to Clarence. Her lunch could wait.

"Today," said Pastor Weiss, "I will conclude my series about getting and staying in spiritual shape…"

Pastor Weiss had no Bible in front of him, not even a single note card. He appeared to have memorized every word of his sermon, and the way he looked into the camera when he spoke made Betty feel like he was speaking directly to her.

His voice filled the room. "Let me tell you something, friend. Other people may not understand You. Other people may not appreciate You. But I can tell you this—Jesus loves YOU. And He loves You more than He loves everyone else.

"It doesn't matter whether You're rich or poor, whether You're young or old, where You were born or where You went to school. What matters is this—of all the people in the world, YOU are the most important."

Betty understood why Dougie had chosen this church. If she weren't the secretary at Abiding Truth, she might consider driving down the mountain on Sundays to check it out. She could listen to Pastor Weiss all day. He had a way of making You feel good.

The camera panned the front rows of the congregation, where a number of young adults were seated. Betty could tell from the way they were sitting, still as statues, that Pastor Weiss had their rapt attention.

"There's Dougie!" exclaimed Clarence. "Looks like our son's a TV star."

She could only see the back of his head, the cowlick he'd had since he was five years old sticking up like a weed in a garden. It made Betty proud to see Dougie in church now that he'd moved out on his own. Of course, he had been making her proud for years. Dougie graduated third in his high school class and won a college scholarship. At Altoona State, he majored in something that sounded important. Since graduation, he had been working at Mountain View Hospital and earning twice as much as Clarence ever made.

Pastor Weiss was praying now and Betty was praying with him right there in her living room. When she peeked at Clarence she saw he had bowed his head and stopped chewing his bologna sandwich. She wasn't sure when the preaching had stopped and the praying had started. She just knew the pastor had her attention and she felt closer to God than she had all day.

Usually when Betty wanted to feel close to God she would slip into the sanctuary at Abiding Truth and stare at the portrait of Jesus that hung behind the altar. Fair-skinned with a flawless complexion, curly brown locks and a neatly trimmed beard—just looking into His eyes made her troubles melt away. He was God, of course, which explained why He was so good-looking. But He was human too. He could relate to all your problems. Yet He never sinned. He never harmed a living creature. He never blew wind at the supper table. He always covered His mouth when He coughed. He was perfect in every way.

"I like that guy 'cause he puts everything in black and white," Clarence said, as the closing credits rolled across the screen. He shoved the last of his sandwich into his mouth and washed it down with a gulp of milk. "So ya think that preacher's sexy, do ya?"

"Good heavens, Clarence. I never said that."

"Nah. But we been married so long, I can tell what yer thinkin'."

+++

Edna Weinwright was the kind of woman who could make any size room feel crowded. Nobody had invited her into the kitchen but there she sat in Clarence's favorite chair with her ample bosom resting against the table. Betty had told her she had lots to do but Edna was not good at taking hints. So Betty sat quietly and listened because she figured Jesus would want her to.

"I have nothing against Pastor Schwartz and I don't hold his divorce against him. Honestly, I don't know how he stayed married to that uppity snob as long as he did. Let her carouse Harrisburg with her lesbian friends. We don't need her type in Dustin."

"Mrs. Schwartz is a talented and colorful woman," interrupted Betty before Edna could bear further false witness against her former neighbor.

"Really, Betty, I swear you'd find something good to say about the devil himself. Sometimes a Christian's got to tell the truth no matter how much it hurts. Most Everyone thinks Reverend Schwartz isn't doing his job."

Betty knew that "Most Everyone" meant Edna and her compatriots Harriet Redgrave and Dorothy Moyers. "Really?" she asked.

"Since he's been pastor everything's gone downhill. He's never been friendly and nobody understands his sermons."

"Smart people are hard to understand. I mean, look at Rogie."

"What about him?"

Rogie—Roger, Junior—Edna's oldest son, was what people around Dustin called "backward." At the age of 37, Rogie lived at home and spent most of his time on a computer. Whenever you talked to him he would go on about some technical matter and you'd have no idea what he was saying. He had never even been on a date.

"All I mean is when Rogie talks it's hard to follow him. Because he's smart."

"I can follow him just fine. Besides we're talking about Pastor Schwartz."

"Pastor Schwartz is a brilliant man."

"Brilliant? He can't even match his socks. Last Sunday he walked around with his fly open."

"Clarence does that sometimes. All men do."

"He falls asleep at meetings. When Rogie gave his talk about switching to automated thermostats, Pastor was snoring away. That's downright disrespectful. Reverend Franklin would have never done that."

"Nobody's perfect. Not even Pastor Franklin."

"I'm not saying he was perfect, just that he did his job. Don't get me wrong, Betty. I was willing to stand up for Pastor Schwartz for a while. But frankly, when he refused to baptize my granddaughter that was the last straw."

"That's what this is about, isn't it?"

"It's about lots of things. How could he not baptize a sweet little baby? I've asked him politely and I've even begged him. Alfie's asked him. Priscilla's asked him. But he still refuses to do it."

Alfred's wife, Priscilla, was religious but not in a church-going sort of way. For the past five years she had been vice-president of the Berkson County chapter of Fetuses for Jesus, a group that protested at local abortion clinics. As far as Betty knew, the organization was fairly inactive since the closest abortion clinic was in Pittsburgh, 75 miles away.

"Pastor Schwartz has rules," said Betty. "He doesn't baptize children if their parents don't come to church."

She was tempted to add, "And it's been five years since your Alfred darkened a church door," but she knew it would be unChristian to rub salt in Edna's wounds. Pleasurable but definitely unChristian.

"My grandchildren are descendants of Horace Moyers, the very first vice-president of Abiding Truth. That ought to count for something."

"I'm sure it does." Betty resisted the momentary temptation to remind Edna that, according to the church register, *her* great-great-grandfather, Charles

Loretto, was the very first *president* of Abiding Truth, having won the vote 17-16 over Mr. Moyers.

"There's something else. Pastor's been drinking like a fish. Dorothy checked his liquor cabinet. She said he emptied three whole bottles of whiskey in just a week."

Though the Abiding Truth parsonage, located a block from the church, had been constructed in the 1940s as a private residence for the pastor, Edna, Dorothy, and others considered the property public domain.

"Don't you think it's wrong of Dorothy to snoop through Pastor Schwartz's personal belongings? A person should be entitled to some privacy."

"If he wanted privacy he shouldn'ta become a pastor. The parsonage belongs to the church. It's our Christian duty to keep an eye on it. We didn't even have a lock on the door 'til someone stole that stuff from the Franklins. My point is that our church is losing members. We have a duty to do something."

"I don't understand. Who do you mean by 'we'?"

"The pastor review committee. Harriet, Dorothy, and I are heading it up. Most of the council is on it. Except for Les."

Not surprising. Harriet, Dorothy, and Edna stuck together like a pack of wolves, each one of them a Moyers and proud of it.

Betty made a mental list of Abiding Truth's council members. Edna, of course, was vice-president and her husband Roger was president, at the beck and call of his wife. Rogie was the treasurer. There was Joyce Zyszkiewicz, the financial secretary; she was Edna's cousin, as was Dorothy. Roger's brother Dick, who owned the video store, was also on council. The only member of the governing board who was not from the Moyers or Weinwright clans was Les Cresco. And he never said anything at meetings. Who could blame him?

Pastor Schwartz once proposed that the congregation pass a rule allowing no more than two members of the same family on the council at the same time. He claimed it would prevent something he called "nepotism." But nobody understood what he meant. The measure was voted down unanimously.

"We don't expect you to join our committee," said Edna. "It's just—maybe you could tell us a few things. Like does he really spend his afternoons taking naps?"

"What are you talking about?"

Edna shifted in her chair and the legs creaked beneath her. "One time when Dorothy thought he'd be out making visits, she stopped by the parsonage and found him snoozing on the sofa. He sat up and scared the bejeezers out of her."

"I'm not at liberty to tell you how Pastor spends his time."

"Well, we'll find out. And we don't want Pastor knowing about it. I know you ain't gonna tell him. With Clarence laid off, you need your job. And the council can fire you, as you are well aware."

Clarence wasn't 'laid off.' He was on disability because of his heart. If Betty bit her tongue any harder she would put a hole right through it.

"What exactly are you planning to do?"

"Let's just say Pastor Schwartz's days at Abiding Truth may be numbered."

"The Bible says all our days are numbered—by the Lord. Not by some committee." Betty tried to give Edna the Evil Eye. She wasn't very good at it.

Edna countered with a scowl of her own. "I've been praying long and hard about this."

"Shouldn't you talk to The Bishop about this?"

"Last time I called Him they put me on hold. They played *Abide With Me* fifteen times 'til I hung up. We best take care of this matter ourselves."

+++

By the time Edna removed her plump backside from Clarence's favorite kitchen chair, it was nearly four o'clock.

"Is it my 'magination, or does that woman's ass get larger every time I see her?" Clarence said over dinner. They were finishing the last of the warmed-up venison casserole.

Betty stifled a smile. "She is getting a bit big for her britches," she whispered. Betty knew that Edna's life had not been easy. She had lost her baby girl and Betty could not begin to imagine how painful that must have been. Still, it was no excuse for acting like a bully.

As Betty stood up to clear the dishes the phone rang.

"Eleanor!" she and Clarence said in unison. Eleanor was Edna's younger sister. She and Edna had been feuding for close to twenty-five years now, ever since their mother died and left all the fancy silverware to Eleanor. Whatever opinion Edna had about a church matter, Eleanor had a different one. In fact, Eleanor generally waited to hear Edna's opinion before forming her own.

"Gonna get that?" asked Clarence, just as the answering machine recording began.

"Betty!" screeched Eleanor. "I can't believe you're not home. I need to know what Edna said to you. I know she was there all afternoon. Pick up now, I know you're there. She's up to something, isn't she? This thing better not cut me off. You know they make machines now that let you talk as long as you want. I know she's up to something. I know—"

Beeep.

Clarence was grinning. "Don't know 'bout you, but I ain't in no hurry to get one of them new answerin' machines."

+++

Fog shrouded the mountain as Betty steered the Chevy up the road toward Dustin. It was the end of a challenging day. Edna had been agitating enough, but this trying day had been capped by an evening in the company of Allyson Jenkins.

They say men fall in love with women who are like their mothers. Betty and Allyson both had curly hair and a fondness for ice cream but as far as she could tell, that's where the similarities stopped. Allyson had made it clear she had no intention of becoming a mother. That's what she said when Betty once worked the subject of grandchildren into a conversation. Betty had not dared to raise the matter again.

Betty was trying to like Allyson. She didn't even mind that the girl was Jewish. Betty had never met a real live Jew before. One of her uncles had married an Episcopalian and someone had told Betty that Jews are like Episcopalians, though she wasn't sure how.

Clarence would not say what he thought of Allyson. He wasn't one to share his feelings about anything, except the quality of refereeing at Steelers games. The girl was smart. Betty would give her that. Once she finished her residency at Mountain View Hospital she would be a certified lady medical doctor. Allyson's father was a surgeon in a large Philadelphia hospital. Betty knew it was a matter of time until Allyson would pressure Dougie into moving where her family lived, a full five hours away.

Allyson acted like anyone who was not born and raised in Philadelphia or New York City was beneath her. Last week at the Bridal Boutique in Pottersfield, Betty had suggested that Hershey's Kisses and bottles of bubble soap would make nice wedding favors. Allyson laughed and said, "Don't forget the moonshine and Wonder bread." Betty did not realize Allyson was insulting her until Dougie told his fiancée to lay off the "hillbilly jokes."

Tonight, Allyson had launched into a tirade about how you can't find decent seafood west of the Susquehanna. Betty told her about the deluxe fried shrimp combo platter at the Highland Café. And to be polite, she offered to take Allyson there one night.

Allyson smirked and said, "How nice! Does it come with little paper containers of tartar sauce and ketchup?'

"I'm not sure about ketchup, but you can always ask for a bottle," said Betty. Then she saw Dougie giving Allyson a dirty look.

Betty was aware that people made fun of her, but the way Allyson did it seemed mean-spirited. Betty had once overheard her ask Dougie, "How could you stand growing up in a town full of idiots?" Now that was an insult.

Granted, a number of stupid people lived in Dustin. Most of the Weinwrights and Dorothy Moyers' brothers and the man who blew up his house trying to heat gasoline on the stove. But smart people lived in Dustin, too. Sophie Oglesby was wise, in a quiet sort of way. Jane Herberger could call out the answers to *Jeopardy* in the form of a question faster than anyone. There were smart people and stupid people everywhere. Surely Philadelphia had its share of idiots.

Betty was still trying not to seethe when she realized that in the fog she had missed her turn-off. No bother. Like every other road on Mount Kiersey, this one wound around the mountain and would eventually bring her back to where she wanted to be.

Betty's miscue got her mind off Allyson and onto what Clarence called her "deep thoughts." These were those moments when she pondered her life and wondered what it was all about. Once when they were driving she asked Clarence if he ever thought about such things. He stared at her blankly and turned up the radio.

Fifty-three years Betty had lived in Dustin. There was no place she would rather be. Here she had friends she had known all her life, people with whom she could talk about anything, like Milly Vogel and Jane Herberger. No sight in the world could be more magnificent than the view from Summit Park. Of course, it was there that God worked The Miracle that had changed her life forever.

The Miracle. Sometimes Betty would go a day or two without consciously thinking about it. Yet it was always present, like the beating of her heart and the flow of air through her lungs.

August 14, 1981—the hottest day in twenty years. The kind of day when opening the refrigerator door felt like a sin because it gave you so much pleasure. Betty had planned to flop into the recliner and stay there awhile just as the telephone rang. Had it not been for that call, The Miracle might never have happened.

"Hey, sis. How you doing?"

"Is that you, Marian? It must be really hot there in Pittsburgh."

"I've got news. Clifton and I got married."

"Wow! Congratulations!"

"Thanks. I knew you'd be excited."

Betty and Marian had encountered their share of conflicts through the years. Still, Betty loved her only sibling and the two remained close even after Marian had moved off the mountain.

"I can't believe you're married! Wow! Have you told Mom and Papa?"

"You're the first to know. We got married last night. A quick civil ceremony. It was over in three minutes."

"I mean have you told Mom and Papa about Clifton at all?"

"Well, not yet. But I'm sure they'll like him. He's going to be a dentist and make lots of money. And Papa and Clifton have lots in common."

"They do?"

"Sure. They both like to hunt and drink beer. And Cliff was an all-star running back in high school. Papa should be impressed with that."

As far as Betty knew, every man in western Pennsylvania between the ages of 18 and 92 hunted, drank beer, and claimed to be a football star in high school. Marian would have to do better.

"There's more, sis. Cliff and I . . . we're going to have a baby."

Three seconds passed and Betty did not say a word.

"I mean, that's good news, right? It'll be the first grandchild."

"I'm sorry for not responding," Betty said finally. "Congratulations."

Betty hung up the phone and started to wail, overwhelmed by an unspeakable sadness. She could not recall how she ended up at the park that day. She remembered telling Clarence she had to go out, even though the car had no air conditioning. She passed the large rock near the lookout on which someone had painted VERA RULES! and wandered into the woods that bordered the park. She leaned against a white ash tree and there she prayed.

How could He do this to her? In the 12 years she'd been married she never missed church unless she was sick, never ate a meal without first giving thanks, never let a day pass without opening her Bible.

And here was Marian, just 21 years old. Marian, who had been smoking pot since she was twelve. Marian, who would jump off a cliff because her father told her not to—which was undoubtedly why she had married a Black man. Here was Marian, with a child in her womb, while Betty continued to waste money on trips to the fertility clinic in Greensburg. *Why can't You give me the child I ask for?*

It was then Betty noticed that an eerie silence filled the woods. The sky was a most peculiar shade of gray. Suddenly, a flash of lightning lit up the forest, shook the very ground on which she stood, scared the anger right out of her.

Betty later learned that lightning had struck the rock she had passed moments earlier. She could not recall how she made it home. When Clarence met her on the porch her clothes were drenched and she couldn't stop shaking. The rain had stopped. In the western sky, a rainbow shimmered.

One week later, Betty emerged from the bathroom bearing a positive home pregnancy test stick. The doctor at the clinic said he couldn't believe it. Betty was convinced that Dougie's conception was related to that bolt of lightning. It was a Miracle, and no one could tell her otherwise.

In the years that followed, her nephew Danny, with skin the color of chocolate, visited his relatives in Dustin every summer accompanied by his mother. His father, Dr. Clifton Jackson, refused to join his family on their annual pilgrimages up the mountain. He once confided to Betty, "There are places an educated Black man should avoid."

+++

It was almost ten when Betty got home. Clarence was sitting on the stairs with his pants off.

"Dougie called. But ya don't hafta call him back. Let's go to bed."

"What did he want?"

"He and the girl had a big fight after ya left. They called off the wedding."

"What?"

"They'll patch it up. Let's go to bed. I've been sitting here with a hard-on all night. Shouldn'ta turned on that Baywatch rerun."

"Poor boy. I better call him."

"It's just a lovers' spat. They'll make up."

Or maybe not. Perhaps God had answered her unspoken prayer—Dougie and Allyson had broken up. Now her son could find a nice local girl who would stay home, cook his supper, and raise his children the way God intends.

Clarence reached for Betty's hand. "Dougie'll be fine. C'mon," he said, with the urgency of a man who could not wait much longer.

She followed Clarence up the stairs and gave his sagging butt a playful swat. This was their life—meatloaf on Mondays, Wheel of Fortune after dinner, five minutes with Clarence on top then eight hours of sleep. When they went to the Tastee-Chill in Colton they always got vanilla soft-serves with hot fudge. A smiling cow ornament graced their front yard. Their Dalmatian's name was Spot. Many lived more exciting lives but Betty knew none had it better.

"I'll have to pray extra for Dougie," she said, when they reached the top of the stairs.

"I dunno how someone who loves Jesus so much can be so damn good in bed," said Clarence.

"Watch your language, Clarence Mundy," said Betty, pretending to be shocked.

But she knew he knew she wasn't.

Three

Gerald Schwartz

"Which vegetables are included in your garden salad?" asked Gerald as he peered up from his menu at the harried waitress.

"You know—lettuce," she said, yanking the menu from his hand. "Zat what you want?"

"Which kind of lettuce would that be?"

The waitress glared at him like some haggard mother tired of her child's incessant questions. "Let—tuce. It's green. Crunches when you bite into it. Grows in a garden."

Located along the interstate and frequented mostly by truck drivers on their way to somewhere else, the Highland Café was the only dining establishment within ten miles of Dustin.

"I'll assume that's iceberg," said Gerald. "And which other vegetables?" He reached for his confiscated menu but the waitress pulled her hand away.

"Croutons and bacon bits. Look Father, I don't mean to be disrespectful to a man of the cloth, but can't you see the place is crowded? Ya want fries with the salad?"

"No," said Gerald. Then remembering that he had to prepare a Bible study, a task requiring extra fortification, he called the waitress back and ordered a family-sized basket of onion rings.

Across the table from Gerald sat Allan Weiss, pastor of NEW CREATION!!! in Pottersfield. Though neither pastor was smoking, Weiss was shrouded in a gray haze that made Gerald feel as though he were conversing with a specter. They were seated in the restaurant's recently designated non-smoking section, which consisted of four tables without ashtrays in the corner of a large open room where all the other customers could smoke. Most of them were.

Like Gerald, Weiss was an ordained minister in the American United Lutheran Church. In Gerald's opinion, he looked more like a professional golfer than a clergyperson. Today Weiss had the gall to show up for their weekly dinner date dressed in a polo shirt and designer jeans. As usual, he reeked of cologne and sported a neatly coifed hairstyle which accentuated his boyish face and made him look much younger than his actual age of 35.

"If you want to relate to your parishioners, you've got to dress like they do," said Weiss between bites of his bacon-less BLT.

"A pastor ought to look like a pastor," said Gerald.

"In a black clerical suit? That's what Catholic priests wear. May I call you 'Father'?"

"No one calls me that."

"The waitress just did. I'm curious, Gerald—do you ever take your collar off? You don't sleep with it on, do you?"

Solitary by nature, Gerald had steered clear of most of his colleagues since his divorce. However, in an attempt to foster clerical unity, The Bishop had mandated that each pastor in the district partner and meet weekly with someone whose "theology and approach to ministry differs from one's own."

Worship attendance at Weiss's congregation had tripled in the four years since he had become their pastor. His sermons were broadcast five times a week on a local television station. Weiss attributed his success to a number of bold decisions. NEW CREATION!!! had enlarged and renovated their sanctuary to include theatre seating, a coffee bar, and other modern amenities. They introduced a "non-traditional" service which included a band that played retooled rock songs, sermons aided by something called "PowerPoint presentations," special lighting effects, and unorthodox communion practices. Weiss also convinced the congregation to change its name, removing the words "Lutheran" and "Church" from the title and adding fashionably excessive exclamatory punctuation.

Dustin was situated a mere 18 miles up Mount Kiersey from the sprawling valley village of Pottersfield but the two communities might as well have been on opposite sides of the continent. Unlike the many impoverished communities dotting the mountainsides of the Alleghenies, Pottersfield attracted a number of young professionals, including physicians and administrators who worked at the Mountain View Regional Medical Center in nearby Altoona.

Pottersfield boasted a main street with ten blocks of successful businesses ranging from antique shops to computer supply stores. The village was also home to the golden-domed Berkson County courthouse, a magnificent new library, and an 18-hole golf course. Weiss's parishioners enjoyed seasonal recreational activities, golfing in the summer and skiing in the winter. Most of Gerald's parishioners preferred to go hunting, both in and out of season.

Dustin's main street consisted of a row of vacant buildings. There were only four active businesses, the most successful of which was the Aschenbrenner Funeral Home. Karen's Korner Bar, the oldest business in town, attracted large crowds on weekends. The block south of Karen's included a general merchandise store the locals called *Bubby's*, though the hand-painted sign out front read *Guns 'N Gifts.*

A fourth business, *Dick's House of Movies*, owned by one of Gerald's parishioners, rented videos and DVDs. Dick's was commonly known to have a sizable collection of XXX films, available only to those who knew a password that provided access to a dimly lit room in the back of the store.

Six days a week and many nights a steady stream of coal trucks rolled down Dustin's main street, grinding gears as they went. They left behind a thin dusty coating which settled on the windowsills of the parsonage and irritated Gerald's sinuses. Since its own mine had closed ten years earlier, Dustin had become a place to pass through, a town enduring its insidious demise.

Gerald was about to inform Weiss that he did not make a habit of sleeping in his clerical collar—except for last night—but Weiss was on a roll.

"Traditional religious symbols don't mean anything to the new generation," said Weiss. "People under 30 find them highly irrelevant to their lives."

Gerald had heard that Weiss's salary was five times what he earned at Abiding Truth. Unlike most rumors, Gerald was inclined to believe it. Either that or Weiss had racked up an excessive amount of debt trying to maintain his affluent appearance.

"I prefer irrelevant to irreverent. And I dare say, God does, too," said Gerald.

"Do you actually enjoy listening to those German funeral dirges your organist cranks out week after week?" said Weiss.

"I don't attend worship to enjoy anything. I'm there to show my respect to God, not to dance around like I'm at a rock concert."

"We don't dance. We sway."

"The pipe organ is inherently majestic. It conveys a sense of the sacred—a quality which is sorely lacking in electric guitars."

Weiss started to hum.

"What's that?"

"'Take Me Out to the Ballgame.' I was thinking how sacred it would sound played on an organ."

"Oh, hell."

"Look Gerald, I know you don't like what I have to say. But the world is changing and the church needs to change with it."

Weiss smiled flirtatiously at the waitress as he handed her a twenty-dollar tip, twice the cost of their meals.

"Why, thank you!" she said, her previously dour face now beaming.

Weiss glanced at his latest electronic time-keeping apparatus. "We better get going. It's time for us both to come clean, don't you think?"

"You're not going to subject me to that again, are you?"

"I thought we agreed."

Weiss had persuaded Gerald that their weekly meetings should include time for personal confession and absolution. In a private location—usually inside Weiss's Porsche since they carpooled and Weiss refused to be seen in Gerald's Buick—they would alternately repent of their recent transgressions. Then by the authority vested in them by God they would pronounce each other forgiven. This was all to be done confidentially, in keeping with their ordination vow never to betray secrets.

"My roommate and I did this in seminary every week," Weiss had said the month before. "It's the most meaningful spiritual activity I've ever experienced. It will change your life."

"You want me to confess my sins to you?" asked Gerald. "That's a matter I'd rather keep between God and myself."

Yet before he knew it, Gerald was admitting that he had eaten too much chocolate cake and listening to Weiss's detailed description of his erotic fantasies about his 22-year-old youth director. Gerald dreaded what this month's confession might bring.

+++

"I'll go first," said Weiss, as he squealed out of the parking lot. "I'll start with the light stuff."

"Spare me the details."

"Well, it started out innocently enough. Last Saturday I was Googling for preaching material."

"Googling?"

"You know, on the Internet."

Gerald had heard plenty about the Internet and remained determined to avoid it for the rest of his life.

"Anyway," continued Weiss. "I had typed in 'se,' for 'sermon aids.' Suddenly out of nowhere this thought popped into my head—why not type in *sexy large-breasted horny virgin models*? So I did."

"That just popped into your mind?"

"Can you believe it? Then I clicked on 'search' and it was all down hill from there. I realize a bit of porn now and then is fine as long as your wife and parishioners don't know. But things got out of control. I couldn't stop myself. It was like some kind of power took over me. It started with images of bikini-clad women. A few more clicks and they were topless. Then it was on to full frontal nudity."

"Uh oh."

"Intercourse."

"Hmm."

"Lesbian scenes."

"Really?"

"Oral sex, anal sex, group sex … I even came across one site which showed a woman fellating a horse. I'm sorry I saw that. Once you get those images in your head it's hard to get rid of them."

Gerald winced. "You're telling me people look at that sordid material on their computers?"

"Don't be naïve, Gerald. It's a billion dollar business. If you can imagine it, you can find it on the Internet."

Gerald had never imagined a woman having sex with a horse, though he had once entertained a brief fantasy in which he envisioned himself a bucking bronco and Margaret a cowgirl out to tame him. Not that he ever shared his fantasy with Margaret. God forbid.

"This is most definitely more than I need to know," said Gerald.

"I charged 200 dollars on the credit card. Those porn sites aren't cheap."

"Don't you have a family to feed?"

"Oh no, it wasn't my personal card. I used the church's credit. I have a substantial discretionary fund."

"I don't want to hear any more."

Weiss appeared disappointed. "Aren't you going to chastise me?"

"Fine then. The next time you face such temptation remember nothing is hidden from the eyes of God."

"It's not God I'm worried about. If my wife catches me doing that, she'll smash my balls in a vise grip."

"Stop it now! No more of this, please."

Weiss looked like a child who had been informed that his playtime was over. "Tell me," he said, "when you hear my confessions, do you think I'm, well . . . despicable?"

"I think you have a few problems."

"When we talk like this it reminds me of something my old man used to say to me. Whenever he caught me doing something wrong, he'd say, 'Remember son, you're always an ass to someone.'"

"Your father sounds . . . interesting."

"He was a total shit. But what I'm saying is, I know there are people who don't like me. I just hope you're not one of them. You like me, don't you?"

Allan Weiss was an intriguing man. He was exasperatingly superficial yet more intelligent than most of Gerald's colleagues, professionally accomplished yet totally lacking in sensible judgment, alternately cocky like a schoolyard bully then as insecure as a motherless child.

They rode along in silence for a few miles. Gerald stared out the window at the passing countryside, trying to purge his mind of all he had unwittingly heard.

"I hate that place. It's like a cemetery for cars," Weiss said as they sped past Ray's Salvage lot. A large man with a crew cut and bushy goatee stood beside a recently wrecked Ford Taurus that sat alongside the entrance road, its front end so brutally mutilated that Gerald had to turn away.

"Well?" said Weiss, as they started up the mountain toward Dustin.

"What?"

"Since you don't want to hear any more from me, it's your turn."

"What?"

"Go on. Confess."

"I haven't thought about sex in months."

Gerald continued to stare out the passenger side window. Margaret had always been more open about sex than he was. Once, in the early years of their marriage, she suggested they might want to be more spontaneous while making love.

Gerald was a creature of habit. Lovemaking was like the Lutheran liturgy—a predictable, repetitive, weekly event devoid of excessive emotional expression—though it did allow for periodic moments of controlled internal euphoria. Certainly, he said, he would try something new as long as it did not disrupt their usual routine.

"I want you to go down on me," she said.

"I can do that," he said. "Next time."

Gerald was not certain what Margaret meant by "go down on me." Did he not already "go down on her" when he entered her from above? He had never heard the phrase before. Yet she said it so casually, she obviously assumed he understood.

Margaret gazed at him expectantly when they made love the following week, but she never mentioned it again—until a few days before the divorce became official. During a heated exchange over the telephone, they broached the subject of their long-term ineffectual sexual relationship. "You were a selfish lover. You wouldn't go down on me," Margaret shrieked into the phone before hanging up abruptly. Thus ended their final conversation.

"Come on," Weiss said. "There's got to be some transgression that's troubling you. It doesn't have to be about sex."

"I'm having trouble sleeping at night," mumbled Gerald.

"You can't sleep?"

"That's what I said."

Weiss was smirking. "That's the best you can do? Is there a commandment against insomnia?"

"Oh, forget it."

"Excuse me. My cell's vibrating." Weiss momentarily removed a hand from the steering wheel as he fumbled through his pants pockets searching for his phone. At the same time a bee, which had been resting on the dashboard, started circling Weiss's head.

"Help!" he shouted. "I'm being attacked."

As Weiss swatted at the bee, the Porsche crossed the centerline. The driver of a coal truck came barreling down the hill, laying on his horn.

Gerald's first thought was that Margaret would feel guilty when she learned a coal truck had mowed him down. He grabbed the wheel and steered the car back onto the right side of the road. The driver of the coal truck flashed his middle finger.

"I hate these mountain roads!" said Weiss, finally returning a hand to the steering wheel. The boyish grin returned to his face. "Thanks for saving my life. I guess you do like me."

"It wasn't your life I was trying to save. You need to slow down."

Weiss was not listening. "Hey there, honey," he said into his cell phone.

Four

Allan Weiss

Molly Rogers was one of the homeliest women Allan had ever seen. The first time he met her he decided immediately she would be the perfect personal assistant. Everyone else on the staff was decidedly attractive, from the chief custodian to the minister of music. But Allan had hired Molly following his fling with the former director of entertainment ministries, an affair that did not end pleasantly. He had sworn off adultery and hoped to avoid unnecessary temptation.

From her oversized nose and decaying teeth to her mottled skin and formless physique, nothing about Molly's appearance appealed to Allan. He simply made sure she worked in a private office removed from public view. Molly had a pleasant telephone personality, kept abreast of social trends, never betrayed Allan's secrets, and made a decent cup of herbal tea.

"Good morning, Pastor Al."

"God bless you, Molly. What pleasures await me today?" He hoped Molly would notice his new shoes.

"Twelve voice mail messages and two faxes from The Bishop's office. And some man with a crew cut and bushy goatee stopped in to inquire about joining the church. Wow! I love your new shoes, Pastor."

"Thank you, Molly." She always noticed.

"Your snailmail's on the counter. I haven't checked your e-mail yet."

"You can delete any messages from maryjolovesjesus478. She's a kind soul but I swear if she forwards me one more inspiring story about little Timmy the one-armed orphan boy with cancer, I'll fling my laptop out the window."

Molly faked a laugh. "BTW—we need to update the website. Jeffrey said there's a problem with the streaming video. Also people are having trouble accessing some of the archived pdf files and a couple of the FAQ links are broken. It's always something."

"The Lord's work is never done. Molly, do you know how much I appreciate you?" Allan winked. He found it liberating to flirt with a woman and not feel the least bit of sexual temptation. "Now which groups are meeting this morning?"

Molly glanced at a wall calendar advertising the services of the Pottersfield Christian Cosmetic Surgery Institute, a gift from one of NEW CREATION!!!'s prominent members. Allan's jealous colleagues referred to his congregation as "the pretty people church." He did not deny that he sought to attract attractive members.

Human beings are mostly shallow after all. The average person will inevitably choose image over substance. It is a basic marketing strategy. People drink a particular beverage because it's "cool," or wear clothes because they're fashionable, regardless of the product's quality. Certainly the same principle applies to places of worship. When the camera panned the congregation during Sunday morning telecasts viewers made judgments about the church on the basis of what they saw. And most of them would not consider joining NEW CREATION!!! if they saw a church full of ugly people.

Not that ugly people weren't welcome. All were welcome regardless of personality or status. The poor, the sick, the chronically vexatious—Allan never turned anyone away. However, he did make sure only good-looking people sat in the front rows.

"The Holy Rollerbladers meet in the southeast parking lot," said Molly. "And the You'll Never Wok Alone Christian Cooking Club is in the lower kitchen. They invited you to join them for stir fry."

"I hope they're making teriyaki."

"Also, the Paranoid Persons Anonymous group is meeting in an undisclosed location and The iPod Squad for God is in room 109. I can't figure those folks out. They sit around and listen to their own favorite Christian music with those earbuds."

"They do it in the company of other believers. Fellowship, Molly. We all need fellowship."

Allan stared out the window at the massive parking lot adjacent to his office. He relished standing in this very spot on Sunday mornings. He would crack the window open and breathe in exhaust fumes while he watched the traffic attendants wave their brightly colored flags. As they directed the 9:00 attendees out and the 10:30 crowd in, Allan would beam, sipping his triple mocha non-fat latte, pride rising in his well-toned chest.

Despite the congregation's booming success, Allan remained the sole ordained minister at NEW CREATION!!! In consultation with Molly, he controlled the hiring and firing of additional non-ordained staff, which now numbered eight persons.

"The communion buffet bread bakers will be in this afternoon. They wondered how the cranberry walnut went over."

"I thought it was delicious. That's what I love about this church, Molly! We have something for everyone."

"Speaking of communion, we got another one of those letters."

"I'm listening."

"Dear Allan, I will state this as respectfully as possible. I know we graduated from the same seminary and surely you studied the same subjects I did. So I ask you—what in God's name are you doing there in Pottersfield? I've heard from reliable sources that you are making a mockery of the sacrament of Holy Communion. Please tell me it isn't true. Your partner in the Lord's service, Robert Zimmerman."

"At least he's polite. Brad Kmocovich over in Bear Valley nearly tore my head off at our conference meeting last week."

"They don't appreciate what you're trying to do."

"I'd better whip off a response to Zimmerman. Nip this in the bud before he turns hostile on me."

"I've already crafted your reply."

"Molly, you are always one step ahead of me."

"The usual type of response—*Dear Robert, How pleasant to hear from you, my partner in the Lord's service. I pray this letter finds you in the best of health.*"

"Nice, Molly. You have a way with words."

Molly beamed. "Thanks, Pastor. *The rumors are indeed true. As of July 1, the members of NEW CREATION!!! have been gathering for a new and improved version of holy communion.*

"The All-U-Can-Eat Communion Brunch Buffet is not sacrilegious as you contend, but a contemporary American adaptation of a time-honored Christian ritual. Communion is, after all, a meal of bread and wine. You are no doubt aware of the current popularity of buffets and being a man of full stature I imagine you have enjoyed a few yourself. I can leave that part out, Pastor."

"No, I like that. It reinforces our point."

"The traditional ritual of holy communion involves only one kind of bread— often in the form of tasteless wafers—and wine—usually something cheap. This practice has become unattractive to contemporary American Christians who are accustomed to a great number of food selections. Therefore, we currently offer 25 different breads and 12 wine choices from 5 different countries as well as California. There's something for everyone! Breads are freshly baked each week by our preparation team. Wines are selected by connoisseurs.

"I assure you that while our celebration is an all-you-can eat affair we limit everyone to no more than 12 ounces of wine. I do not condone drunkenness. We provide a fine selection of non-alcoholic wines and grape juices for those under the age of 21. We are doing nothing illegal here."

"How can he argue with that?"

"Did not Jesus enjoy sitting down to a good meal? If he were around today, our Lord would no doubt pile his plate high at the buffet bar."

"Brilliant, Molly!"

This girl was sharp. She had taken a number of theology classes over the Internet.

"Just a bit more, Pastor. *Like many churches, we hold our communion service in the late morning. Is it breakfast? Is it lunch? We play it safe and call it brunch. God's blessings on your ministry. FYI—a festive and fruity Napa Valley Merlot and the frosted honey wheat loaf top our most popular selections.*"

"Wonderful! Where do I sign my name?"

"I've also started a draft of your next sermon."

"Thanks, Molly. BTW—the Spiritually Buff series received rave reviews."

"It's all in the delivery, Pastor."

"That reminds me—the teleprompter was too bright on Sunday."

"We'll take care of it. I was thinking this Sunday you could preach about abortion. We've had a number of requests for that."

"Abortion?"

"You're against it."

"That's what I thought."

"The latest polls show our members are 52 percent pro-life, 46 percent pro-choice. The other 2 percent say it depends who's making the choice."

"Do I want to tackle something controversial?"

"You could talk about world hunger. Ninety-four percent of the congregation is against it."

"Six percent are for world hunger?"

"These surveys aren't completely accurate."

"I wish it were Valentine's Day. I could preach about love. Everybody's in favor of love, aren't they?"

"Even us lonely souls, Pastor." Molly had a look of such profound sorrow on her face that Allan felt sorry for her. It must be hard to be homely.

"Choose whatever topic you think is most appropriate. I trust your judgment. Is that all?"

"Almost. Douglas Mundy will be in to see you shortly."

+++

As soon as Molly left to check on the teleprompter Allan turned on the radio and started to flip through his mail. On those rare occasions when Allan had to spend more than a few minutes alone he started to have troublesome thoughts. He worried that he might have a serious moral defect. Even after nearly 5 years in the ministry Allan found it difficult to be genuinely concerned about other people. He lacked that quality the pastoral care professor at seminary called "empathy." He could fake it, of course. He could shower others with compliments, but deep inside Allan hid the hideous truth—he cared about no one as much as himself.

When others told Allan he was an extraordinary pastor he felt like they were talking about someone else. It made him feel somewhat schizophrenic, as though his public persona and his secret self were mutually exclusive. He supposed that if people saw him as he actually was rather than the way they imagined him to be, they would dismiss him as a hypocrite. But it was more complicated than that.

+++

Allan rarely thought about the day he first decided to become a pastor. When he did, he always remembered the late afternoon sun warming the top of his head, the salty aftertaste of peanuts tingling on his tongue, the slightly euphoric feeling that results from too much soda.

They were together, the three of them. They were at the zoo—watching the seals or maybe it was the tigers. This day was special because Mom felt well enough to leave the house for once and Dad had quit drinking beer, hadn't had a drop in nearly three days. He told jokes and even Mom was laughing at them. That didn't happen often.

Al was nursing his can of grape soda, relishing every drop because his mother didn't often let him drink it. He'd been holding the can in the sun so long that the soda tasted warm and had lost its fizz. He couldn't bring himself to finish the last few drops because he knew it would be a long time before he would taste soda again.

"What's a ghost's favorite fruit?" asked Dad. Al knew the answer was "Boo-berries." He'd heard the joke at school. But he'd never heard Dad tell it. And when he said, "Boo-berries," they all laughed, the three of them, even Mom.

Then Mom said something strange. But it didn't seem strange at the time because Mom was a religious person and she frequently said religious things, even when they were talking about something that wasn't religious like ghosts eating boo-berries.

"After I'm gone, I hope you'll keep going to church," she said. "God has a plan for you, Al. One day you will do something truly amazing."

"What?" asked Dad. "How do you know?"

She smiled and said, "A Mother Always Knows."

Two days later she was dead.

+++

"Good morning, Pastor Weiss."

Douglas Mundy had recently joined NEW CREATION!!! and become an active leader on the youth committee. Lately, he had been preoccupied with his upcoming marriage to a Jewish doctor from Philadelphia who sat in the front row at worship and distracted Allan with her low-rise jeans. Allan figured Douglas was here to ask how his fianceé could join the church. She was, after all, the epitome of the NEW CREATION!!! member—intelligent, professional, and attractive. Plus she had great teeth.

"Good morning, Douglas! Please have a seat."

Douglas slumped into the Corsica armchair that graced Allan's plush office. Allan referred to it as his "crying chair." Distraught parishioners sat there while sharing their darkest secrets and receiving the pastor's counsel. Allan had strategically placed the chair in front of a large mirror. When he grew bored with his parishioners' ramblings he could admire his latest hairstyle while still feigning interest.

"Thanks, Pastor. How are Mrs. Weiss and the children?"

"Fine, fine. Have I told you how much I enjoy having you as a member of this church?"

"Thank you, Pastor. I heard Trinity celebrated a birthday."

"Indeed, she did. My little girl turned 6 on the first of August. They grow up fast."

"I thought your daughter was 8. Cathy told me they had a party for her in the PreTween Group."

"Cathy? Cathy Mickelson?" Allan's favorite youth director.

"Yeah, she and I are good friends."

Wait a minute. Kevin, his youngest, was 6. Could Trinity already be 8?

"You'd be surprised how hard it is to keep track of your children's ages. And everything else they're up to. Parenting is no easy task."

Douglas chuckled. "Hey, if you don't want your kids, I'll take them. Seriously, you must enjoy being a father."

Sometimes Allan regretted not spending more time with his children. Yet whenever he was with them for more than a few hours, they annoyed him. He hated to admit it, because it made him feel even more despicable than he already knew he was, but he did not much care for his children.

"How are your wedding plans going? I imagine it'll be a grand affair."

"That's what I'm here to talk about. We—we've called off the wedding." Suddenly Douglas' face was flushed and his mouth contorted like he was trying not to cry.

Woman Trouble. Allan should have seen this coming. The only time most men seek the counsel of a pastor is when they're having Woman Trouble. Usually after it's too late.

Allan leaned forward and assumed the "I feel for you," look he had learned in his pastoral counseling class. "Hey, it's okay."

"We broke up last week."

"Listen. This happens all the time."

"No. It's not like that. I'm gay. That's why we're not getting married."

Douglas peered up at Allan with inquiring eyes. Did he expect the pastor to be shocked?

"Hey, it's okay. Lots of people think they're gay. It's nothing to be embarrassed about." Allan had dealt with this situation on a number of occasions—mothers worried about their effeminate sons or wives who had caught their husbands in homosexual acts. These women were especially receptive to his counseling. They mostly needed to be reassured they were attractive. To Allan's delight, they usually were.

"I'm not embarrassed. I just don't know how to tell some people. Like my parents."

"It's like having a bad case of acne or the clap. It's totally curable."

"What do you mean?"

"Well, it's not like you can take a pill and make it go away. It's more of a psychological problem."

"What do you mean—curable? I was born this way." Douglas was assuming a combative demeanor. This was getting uncomfortable. The boy could be humping a goat for all Allan cared. Sex makes people behave in strange and irrational ways. Allan knew that.

"Listen, Douglas. I don't have anything against gay people. I like gay people. I like you. All I'm saying is, it's been proven people can change their sexual orientation with the right kind of therapy."

"Really? That's not what I learned in college."

It wasn't what Allan had learned either. But this had been a controversial issue at NEW CREATION!!! since they started marrying gays in Massachusetts. The latest poll revealed 71 percent of NEW CREATION!!!'s members considered homosexuality a sin. You could hardly argue with those numbers.

"Fortunately we have a group here that can help you. It's called the Abnormal Sexual Identity Transformation Team. It's mostly people struggling with homosexuality like you are. Also a few guys who dress in women's clothes. Be glad you don't have that problem!"

Douglas was not listening. "I took a human sexuality course in college. That's when I first realized I'm gay. Actually that's where I met Cathy."

"Cathy Mickelson?"

"Yeah. She knows. She's been a big help as I've been working through this."

"Cathy Mickelson took a sex class with you?"

"Yeah. So I've been part of an LGBT support group in Altoona for two years. I didn't have the courage to tell Allyson until now. I had planned to get married because I want to have kids. It seemed like it would be easier to just keep it a secret."

"Our Transformation Team has had much success. It's no secret that John Westbrook, our minister of fashion and interior design, is a recovered homosexual."

"I think my Aunt Marian knows I'm gay. And my cousin Danny. But I don't know how to tell my mother. She's going to freak out. And my dad. I can't begin to imagine how he'll react. They're good people, my parents. But kind of conservative."

"Your mother is Pastor Schwartz's personal assistant, isn't she?"

"His secretary. She's been working at Abiding Truth since before I was born."

"Good man, Pastor Schwartz. Good friend of mine."

"See the thing is—I feel like my whole life has been a lie so far."

Allan could relate. "Go on."

"I feel bad about stringing Allyson along. She's a good woman. But the attraction was never there for me."

"Hmm." Perhaps Allyson needed pastoral counseling.

"I feel I need to be honest now. Even if it upsets people."

Allan shook his head. "That's not always a good idea."

"What do you mean?"

"I don't advocate dishonesty. But sometimes the people we're close to aren't up to hearing the truth."

Like my wife.

The distinct aroma of tofu teriyaki had wafted into Allan's office.

"Listen, Douglas, I need to run."

"Thanks for your time, Pastor."

The boy shambled out of the office. He reminded Allan of a chastised puppy. Why was life so complicated? Why couldn't everything be as simple as Pastor Weiss made it sound in his sermons?

Five

Gerald Schwartz

"Sure is a beautiful day! You're looking hazy, Pastor. Trouble sleeping again?" Betty was peering into Gerald's study, smiling like she had won the lottery.

If I had any courage, thought Gerald, I would fire this woman.

"I swear you haven't had a good night's sleep since . . ." Betty's voice softened to a whisper and she said, "Since Margaret divorced you."

Gerald stared blankly at his secretary and choked down the dregs of his third cup of coffee.

"Honestly, Pastor, I wish you could get over it. There are other fish in the sea. I know there's a woman out there for you somewhere."

"I hate to fish."

"My mother always said when you have trouble sleeping you should close your eyes and go to your happy place."

"My happy place?"

"Just imagine you're doing something that makes you feel good all over. I always imagine I'm sitting with Dougie in my lap, watching a thunderstorm. He's only 5 years old and the rain's pouring down and the lightning's flashing but we're safe on our little porch. Before I know it I'm sound asleep."

Gerald knew he would never fire his secretary. Betty was faithful. She would always defend and respect him even if she disagreed with him simply because he bore the title of *pastor*. More importantly, since Margaret had left, Betty's optimistic disposition kept Gerald from falling into a pit of total despair.

There was a knock on the church office door.

"Is it Wednesday?" asked Gerald.

As soon as he said it the door burst open. Gerald peered over the top of his coffee mug, across the vast expanse of his desk, through the entrance to his study, out into the office where Betty stood. Gerald sensed Harriet's presence before he saw her. It felt as though all the oxygen had suddenly been sucked from the room.

"Well hello, Mrs. Redgrave! How are you on this fine day?" said Betty.

Harriet brushed past her. "I'm talking to Pastor. I don't have much time."

+++

"I don't suppose you've noticed the Reynolds family no longer attend church."

Harriet was scowling with her arms folded across her chest, a glare of vengeance in one eye and in the other an expression Gerald could only describe as pure sorrow. Harriet was of average height and weight yet as Gerald had frequently observed, she carried so much hostility that she walked like a hunchback.

"They're the ones with the children. Correct?" Gerald had securely wedged himself behind his desk like it was a suit of armor.

"Of course. He's an accountant. Works for the DOT. She's a nurse at Mountain View. They've got two kids."

"I know who they are. It's been refreshing to see children in church."

"Little girl's a brat. Boy could use some discipline, too." Harriet paced as she talked. "I raised three children. Soon as one of my kids made a peep in church I hauled his sorry butt out the door and let him have it."

According to the parish register Harriet had been married to a man named Harold, who died in 1990, though Harriet never mentioned him. Gerald had yet to meet any of her three grown children, who all had moved far from Dustin.

"I see," said Gerald, as his pastoral care professor had taught him to say when a parishioner lost his attention.

"We know what it says in the book of Proverbs—*He that spareth his rod hateth his son.*"

Harriet had a way of working scripture into every conversation, usually to justify her own behavior. Gerald was tempted to point out that the book of Leviticus instructs parents to stone their disobedient children to death. To the best of his knowledge, that was one biblical childrearing ordinance Harriet had yet to put into practice.

"I'd give Mrs. Reynolds a dirty look whenever those kids acted up. Even told her we still have a nursery. All she'd have to do is ask you for a key and move the Christmas decorations out of the way. But I guess she couldn't take a hint. Anyway, that's not the issue. Problem is, they've joined another church—that place in the valley with the good-looking preacher. Most Everyone thinks it's your fault the Reynoldses left."

Gerald knew "Most Everyone" meant Harriet and her favorite compatriots Edna Weinwright and Dorothy Moyers.

"Mr. Reynolds makes a good salary. And with what nurses are hauling in these days … I know what people give to the church is supposed to be secret but Joyce let it slip how much they were giving. This church can't afford to lose any more people. We can't meet our budget. Most Everyone thinks the first thing should be cut is your salary."

Harriet stopped pacing. She glared at Gerald with her vengeful eye, squinting with the other eye closed as though she were looking through a camera. Gerald knew she was waiting for his reply. He also knew that whatever he said would be used against him in the court of public opinion.

When Gerald failed to speak she prompted him, "I don't have much time. What do you have to say about it?"

Gerald could have asked Harriet to consider her own role in the Reynolds' departure. But he knew she was not capable of pondering the possibility she might have done anything wrong. He could have reprimanded her for peeking into the member contribution records. But he knew it would not stop her from doing it again. He could have complimented her like the genial spiritual leader he was supposed to be. But at the moment he could not think of anything kind to say.

He replied in his usual manner. "Thanks for your insights, Mrs. Redgrave. I'll take them into consideration."

Harriet slammed the door behind her. It took a few minutes for the oxygen to return to the room.

+++

"You all right, Pastor?" It was Betty again.

"Hmph."

"The mail came. You got a big envelope from the publishing company that does your brother's books. Did you order some copies?"

God forbid. Gerald's brother Nicholas had become well known in popular religious circles for his best-selling series of self-congratulatory books based on an inane concept he called *The Peleg Principle*. Peleg was an obscure biblical character mentioned in the genealogy of Shem. Nicholas Schwartz had transformed him into a hero for the ages.

Gerald opened the envelope and read the cover letter.

Dear Prospective Author,

Thank you for your submission to Light of the World Christian Publishing House. We have reviewed your manuscript entitled "A Comprehensive Epistemological Analysis of Neo-Seballianism Among Post-Patristic Gnostics." Unfortunately, it does not meet our publishing needs at this time.

Due to poor sales we have discontinued our academic line and are now producing books with a broader appeal to contemporary Christian readers. We have enclosed a list of our most popular titles to give you a sense of the types of books we are currently seeking.

Please note as of September 2004, Light of the World Christian Publishing House will be known as LiteWorld Press. For future reference—we prefer electronic submissions to hard copies.

Sincerely,

Rebekah Cortez, Acquisitions Editor

"I'm sure I've told you before, Pastor—your brother's books have changed my life."

Gerald had yet to venture beyond the second page of the first book, having dropped it into the parsonage's downstairs toilet shortly after reading the opening paragraph. He had not spoken to Nicholas for three years. Life was easier that way.

"What's the matter, Pastor? Is this about *your* book? They aren't going to publish it, are they?"

LITE-WORLD PRESS BEST-SELLERS

1. The Peleg Principle by Nicholas Schwartz
2. Smile! Jesus Loves You!: The Christian's Guide to Cosmetic Dentistry by Shelly Ray, "Miss Christian USA 2002"
3. The Peleg Principle Leather-bound Limited Edition by Nicholas Schwartz
4. The Peleg Principle Sing-a-Long Cookbook by Nicholas Schwartz
5. El Principio de Peleg en Español de Nicholas Schwartz

6. The Peleg Principle Large Print Daily Reflection Desk Calendar by Nicholas Schwartz
7. The Peleg Principle SupR DupR Xtra Special Coloring Book by Nicholas Schwartz
8. Miracle!: The True Life Story of Little Timmy the One-Armed Orphan Boy with Cancer by K. S. Church

"What's a hard copy?" asked Gerald.

"Don't be upset, Pastor. Remember—every time God closes a door, He opens a window."

"Could you leave me alone now? And shut the door behind you."

+++

There were no windows in Gerald's study, just four gray walls and a flickering overhead fluorescent light. Three walls contained rows of Gerald's books. The fourth was decorated with a collection of mementoes from Gerald's ministry in Dustin, including a framed copy of Irmalee Hackett's original composition, written on the occasion of his 25th ordination anniversary.

25 years in the ministry
Is enough to make your heart full of glee!
You spend all your life learning about God.
That is wonderful and not the least bit odd.
You give your life in service to the Lord.
You have lots of work to do—you must never get bored!
You teach us all a lot about religion.
Some of us learn much and others just a smidgeon.
You try to help people just like our Savior Jesus.
Even when we're not so kind you always try to please us.
One thing is for sure—you are very smart.
We don't understand you but we take your words to heart.

The fourth wall also held a row of portraits of all the pastors who had worked at Abiding Truth, arranged in chronological order. Next to Gerald's portrait hung a photograph of the irreproachable Joseph Franklin. His chin was tilted slightly upward and his lips pressed together in an expression Gerald could only describe as *smug*. Everywhere Gerald looked there were reminders of Franklin's enduring legacy, even in the parsonage where Franklin had left behind dozens of boxes of his personal possessions.

Why can't I have what Joseph Franklin had?

Gerald closed his eyes, hoping to gain a momentary respite, trying to recall details of the dream from which he had awoken several hours before. The night had started in typical fashion when Gerald woke from his semi-drunken slumber around 3:00 am. Then the cycle of unrelenting torturous thoughts began. *You're stuck and you're spinning your wheels. Is this where you hoped to end up after 30 years in the ministry?*

Gerald pictured the thoughts as demons sent by Whoever Was In Charge Of The Universe At The Moment to punish him. If the demons had names they would be Regret, Envy, and Doubt. Some nights Shame and Despair joined in the ridicule.

"It's your fault Margaret left," says Regret. "You chose the church over her. And what has the church done for you?"

"You've lost a third of your members in the past five years," says Envy. "Your brother's a best-selling millionaire author. And you are the pastor of a declining church in the godforsaken middle of nowhere."

Doubt delivers another blow. "Was it worth it? You're no longer sure there is a God, certainly not one who's benevolent."

Every night, the same routine. Gerald felt like a boxer who knew what was coming but could not get out of the way. Pummeled by the demons night after night, he crawled out of bed each morning emotionally bruised and battered, defeated before the day had even begun.

Except last night, recalled Gerald. That dream. Unlike the ones where he was presiding at the communion table completely naked, this dream had cheered him. Gerald could remember every detail.

He had fallen back to sleep around 5:00 am. Soon he was walking on a beach, holding hands with a woman whose face he could not see. The tide swept in gently against the shore. The ocean water trickled over their bare feet, sending a chill through Gerald's body as it washed the sand from the top of his toes.

Neither of them spoke. Gerald sensed a mutual attraction with the woman, yet their connection felt more spiritual than romantic, the warmth of his hand in hers an assurance that he was not alone in the world. He experienced an indescribable calmness. When Gerald turned to look at the woman he immediately recognized the shy smile from Miss Kirch's photograph. She had gleaming blue eyes, of such a remarkable hue they brought to mind the color of the horizon where the sky meets the ocean on a sunny summer day.

He awoke to a room filled with sunlight. Despite experiencing a slight nausea from the previous night's cake and bourbon, Gerald felt an overwhelming sense of relief, like a prisoner given a respite from his torture.

Now as he sat alone in his study Gerald remembered something peculiar about his dream. Though Miss Kirch's photo was black and white he had dreamt in color. And that reminded him of what Margaret had said.

+++

It must have been sometime in late spring, a few months before she left him. For several weeks the only sentences they had spoken to each other were, "Pass the salt," and "See you in the morning."

This day, however, Gerald has resolved to break the silence. They are seated in their usual spots at the dining room table. Gerald has finished his helping of Double Gloucester Chicken.

"I heard something amusing today," he says, his voice sounding a bit louder than he intends.

Margaret reaches for the broccoli, not acknowledging that she has heard him. Gerald resolves to carry on. "One of the Sunday school children asked her teacher a question."

Margaret lifts a forkful of broccoli to her mouth. He notices she still has paint on her fingers.

"This child asked the teacher if she remembered what it was like when everyone saw everything in black and white."

Margaret chews her broccoli then swallows with a gulp so loud Gerald can hear it sliding down her throat. Can't she acknowledge he is making an effort? She has accused him of keeping all his thoughts to himself.

Gerald explains. "The child wasn't referring to television programs or movies. She thought people saw the entire world in black and white. That's rather humorous, isn't it? Can you believe how much children are influenced by television?"

Margaret lifts an empty fork to her mouth. This is the most he has said to her in a week. This is an opportunity for genuine conversation.

"Margaret? Why aren't you responding?"

She rises from her chair and turns toward the kitchen. Then she stops and looks directly at him. "Gerald, you still see the world in black and white."

She flees into the kitchen. He can hear her sobbing. He wonders what she meant by her comment though he suspects he knows. This is her response to the argument they had a few weeks earlier after Abiding Truth's annual May Day potluck supper. Margaret had been upset because other than Betty and Sophie Oglesby no one touched her avocado mousse with sea trout tartare and caviar.

Gerald had merely suggested that in keeping with the insipid tastes of his parishioners she might consider bringing a tuna noodle casserole next time. And while he was passing on constructive criticism he hinted that perhaps her open-toed sandals and teal chiffon wrap were too colorful for a pastor's wife in rural Pennsylvania. He had overheard Edna Weinwright refer to Margaret as "a first class hussy."

He knows the rumors are flowing. Gerald's parishioners have been suspicious of Margaret since she attended her first women's guild meeting. She embarrassed Gerald by standing up and announcing that she was there of her own volition. She had her own mind and her own life and her own career as a professional artist. And maybe sometimes on Sunday she wouldn't come to church, not because she would be sick or want to sleep in, but simply because she would have other equally important tasks to attend to.

For an awkward second or two, all fourteen women in attendance sat in a rare state of total silence. Finally Margaret returned to her seat and Edna Weinwright asked, "What's volition?"

Despite the initial uproar she caused, Margaret attended both the women's meetings and Sunday services faithfully. Gerald grew accustomed to peering out from the pulpit and seeing her. Eventually he forgot she was there of her own volition.

Gerald can admit this to himself—he often took Margaret for granted. But he is not about to tell her that. Not after what she said to him. He reaches for a second helping of chicken.

+++

On the way to the ecumenical clergy gathering at the Methodist Church, Gerald found himself knocking on the partially opened door of Room 128. Miss Kirch was sitting on the bed, her hands folded in her lap. She glared at him as though he were an intruder.

"It's not time for our monthly appointment. But I was passing by and thought you could benefit from receiving communion," said Gerald.

The reason he was here had nothing to do with Miss Kirch's spiritual health. Gerald glanced at the bedside table where the mysterious photo rested. He felt his eyes drawn to it like he was a twelve-year-old schoolboy sneaking furtive glances at a pretty girl across the room.

What had she been like as a young woman? Men must have pursued her.

"How is Gracie?" Miss Kirch caressed the cross pendant she wore around her neck.

"Miss Kirch, I am Pastor Schwartz." Gerald had read that it is best not to correct persons with Alzheimer's but he was not about to let this woman continue to mistake him for the abominable Pastor Franklin.

"Come here, Pastor. Let me see you."

Gerald leaned toward her, so his face was a few inches from hers. "Yes, Miss Kirch?"

She jerked her head back like she was waking suddenly from a dream. "You're not Pastor Franklin. You're just pretending you're him."

"I'm not pretending," said Gerald.

"He's better looking than you. You're fat. You have bad breath."

Gerald knew not to take this personally. He had ministered to a number of persons with dementia over the years. He thought Miss Kirch might ask him to leave but a minute passed and it was as though he had just stepped in.

"I'm sorry I can't offer you cookies, Pastor."

"I've eaten plenty, thank you."

His life had come to this. Inane conversation with demented parishioners. Solitary evenings, holed up in the parsonage. Not a friend in the world. Not a friend like he used to have when he and Margaret sat by the living room picture window in the old house in Baltimore, nibbling on brie and crackers, sipping a mild chardonnay, rehashing the day's events. In those days, a couple glasses of wine sufficed.

In Baltimore he never lacked intellectual companionship. His parishioners were professors and professionals who engaged Gerald in theological conversations. Shortly after moving to Dustin, Gerald learned that few of his new parishioners shared his penchant for intellectual inquiry. One evening Gerald told Dick Weinwright he was "planning to break open some Bonhoeffer" before bed.

"I'm not much for those pansy-ass microbrews," said Dick. "Does Bonhoeffer make a light beer?"

Bonhoeffer? Light? Indeed!

"I saw your family in church, Pastor."

When they were first married Margaret had wanted to have children. But after years of failing to conceive they learned to avoid the topic. Margaret started bringing it up again years later—after it was too late, after menopause, after they had quit having sex. They always had the same argument.

"We should have adopted."

"Do you know how hard it is to be a pastor's child?"

He wondered what kind of father he would have been.

"I saw your family in church, Pastor. Gracie and you are a lovely couple."

No children. And now no wife.

"Gerald, I've changed. Can't you see that? I don't want to be a pastor's wife anymore."

"I could interview at one of those quaint country churches. In the mountains."

"I don't want to move. You're not listening to me."

"… lovely couple."

"There are several openings in western Pennsylvania."

"…a lovely couple."

"You're not hearing me, Gerald."

He was staring into her eyes now, sparkling like the ocean on the brightest day of summer.

"Long time ago."

Gerald blushed. He had been caught. "It's an attractive photograph," he said. "Are you ready to receive communion?"

Six

Betty Mundy

Betty was not surprised to discover the Dustin Public Library had no books on the topic of homosexuality. She had not planned to borrow any even if it did. Self-appointed town librarian Dorothy Moyers had never been to library school and therefore felt no obligation to honor the American Library Association's decree that all patrons be entitled to privacy. In fact, she considered it her God-given duty as librarian to keep her patrons abreast of what others were reading.

"Eleanor won't be bringing her butter cookies to pot luck," said Dorothy, as she sauntered toward Betty. "She checked out *The Healthy Eater's Guide to Low Fat Cooking*. Her cholesterol must be up again. Just so she doesn't make those macaroons that taste like sand."

"Uh huh," said Betty, who had slipped into the library while Dorothy was taking a mid-morning nap in her office.

"Can I help you? You know we have a computer now. It's much faster."

Betty preferred thumbing through the old card catalogs. She had heard computers track everything viewed on them. And if the library computer kept a log, so did Dorothy.

"Looking for something under 'H,' I see."

"Home repair," said Betty.

"I suppose so. I noticed your porch roof was leaking during that last rainstorm. Unfortunately, we only got one book about home repair and Leroy Zyszkiewicz's had it checked out for the past nine months. I asked Joyce if he ever intends on returning it. I mean he's not much of a reader."

"I know," said Betty. Leroy was a lector at Abiding Truth and every time he read you knew he was going to botch something. Last year during the Good Friday service he pronounced Annas, the high priest's name, so it sounded like the little hole everybody has in their rear end.

"Turns out Leroy's using the book to prop open a door that keeps slamming shut."

"Thank you anyway," said Betty. She slid the drawer shut and headed for the exit.

"Are you in a hurry?" Dorothy called after her. "I'm taking a poll and I'm wondering where you stand."

Betty stopped and spun around to face Dorothy, almost slipping on the recently waxed floor. As librarian, Dorothy considered it her duty to polish the floor and dust the shelves on a regular basis. She liked to joke that "you'll find no dust in Dustin's library and certainly no dirty books."

"Where I stand?"

"On the big debate at church."

"You mean about the new sign? I didn't realize that was a controversial issue."

Dorothy laughed. "When is anything at Abiding Truth not a controversial issue? You know how Eleanor likes to pick fights."

"So what's the problem this time?"

In the past ten years, sisters Eleanor and Edna had waged war over the length of the grass on the church lawn, the distance between pews in the sanctuary, and the best place to buy cheap toner for the copy machine. With the support of the council, Edna reigned victorious on virtually every decision. This only strengthened Eleanor's resolve to win the next battle.

"Most Everyone thinks the new sign should be like the old one."

"What do you mean?"

"White with black letters. But Eleanor's pushing for a black sign with white letters. What do you think?"

"I think it's going to be a long December." The annual congregational meeting was always held on the first Sunday in January. It was still October and already battle lines had been drawn.

"Seriously, where do you stand? I hear Eleanor's got lots of support on this one."

All conversations with Dorothy eventually led to her attempting to attain personal information, which she intended to freely distribute to other interested parties. Betty could not imagine what damage the woman would do if she learned Dougie's terrible secret.

"I'm undecided." Betty turned again toward the exit. "I'm sorry, Dorothy. I'd love to stay and talk but I'm in a hurry today."

Betty was almost to the door when Dorothy called out again. "We'll be presenting Pastor Schwartz with a list of complaints at the meeting too."

Betty stopped in her tracks, turning around slowly this time to avoid slipping.

"Why can't you leave the poor man alone?"

Dorothy was standing by a window, spraying Windex on a spot only she could see. "Come now, Betty. It's nothing personal. We're just looking out for the interests of our church. Abiding Truth has taken a beating in the last few years. Most Everyone thinks it's Pastor Schwartz's fault."

Betty was having trouble concentrating. This had been happening a lot lately. She would drift away in the middle of conversations, recalling that awful night. She wanted to return home, crawl into bed and pray for the horrors of the past week to disappear. She wanted her life to be the way it used to be when she and Clarence still talked to each other, before Dougie turned his back on God.

"Did you hear me?" Dorothy was saying.

"What?"

"I said Pastor's only been to see my brother twice since they put him in the hospice in Naptonville."

"That's right—I'm sorry. How is Johnny doing?" Betty felt like she had lost all her manners. She was so preoccupied with her own problems that she had failed to inquire about Dorothy's ailing brother.

"Not good. The cancer's spread everywhere."

"I'm so sorry."

"I've been planning the funeral. He's going to die, so we might as well be prepared."

"That sounds stressful." Betty tried to sound concerned and polite. "I suppose you've spent lots of time driving between here and Naptonville."

"What do you mean?"

"To see your brother."

"Oh no, I haven't seen him."

"Oh."

"Haven't seen that worthless bum since he borrowed $200 from me three years ago. Gambled it all away in five minutes. Looks like I'll never see that money now."

"I'm sorry."

"Pastor hasn't visited him since Wednesday. He's shirking his duties, I tell you. Excuse me a minute."

Dorothy reached for a feather duster that was lying on one of the bookshelves. She swished it along the windowsill and then peered down to examine her work. "You can't win the battle with dust."

"That's the truth," said Betty. She turned once more and headed to the exit. "I've got to run. Sorry about your brother."

"Tell Pastor we'll be wanting an open casket. So we can say a proper goodbye. I—"

Betty closed the door behind her while Dorothy was still speaking. She did not mean to be rude. She just needed to get home.

+++

In the borough's 174 years, only one homosexual had resided in Dustin. Les Cresco's brother, Charlie, had some problems as a teenager. Charlie's parents sent him to a counseling center where they reportedly attached electrodes to his privates and shocked him while showing him pictures of naked men. He returned home, totally cured. Charlie lived a perfectly normal life until he committed suicide in 1983.

Of course, Edna and Dorothy spread rumors about Mrs. Schwartz because she was an artist who liked to paint pictures of naked ladies, never wore dresses, read feminist books, kept her hair in a buzz cut, and moved to Harrisburg with her college roommate who also never wore dresses, had a buzz cut, owned a feminist bookstore, and posed naked for Mrs. Schwartz's pictures. But she had been married to Pastor Schwartz for 33 years. No lesbian could have done that.

Betty knew it was her fault Dougie was gay because it said so in the book she had purchased at the Narrow Road Christian Bookstore in Spooner's Grove. In chapter 2 of *Smothered by Mother: True Stories of Recovering Homosexuals*, K.A. Groettum, Professor of Moral Purity at Armageddon Bible College, had written: "Christian psychologists have isolated one factor above all others which leads a young man to choose a life of sexual perversity. An overbearing, controlling maternal figure who interferes excessively in his life decisions may cause him to rebel by developing an unnatural attraction toward other men."

The author told a heart-wrenching story about a domineering mother who constantly criticized her son's fianceé. Betty shivered when she read it. She had tried not to be critical of Allyson but Dougie must have sensed her disapproval.

Torturous thoughts kept her awake at night. She could not return to her happy place—imagining that she was rocking little Dougie in her lap. She ironed socks and swept the floor while racking her brains, trying to remember events from her son's childhood. Betty had never had a clue he thought he was gay.

Dougie had broken the news to Clarence and her while they were sitting at the supper table. They were talking about the chances of a snowfall before the first day of deer hunting season. The usual stuff.

Betty asked Dougie if he had put up his storm windows yet. She had taken a bite of her blueberry cobbler, and was waiting for his reply when Dougie blurted it out. "I have something important to tell you I'm gay it's true please don't be upset."

He ran his words together like he always did when he felt nervous. There was a pause, then one of those lulls that probably lasted a few seconds but felt like forever. She stared at the plastic fruit centerpiece that graced their kitchen table, unable to look her own son in the eye. She tasted the blueberry cobbler turning sour in her mouth. She kept wondering if he had actually said what she thought he had said, kept peeking over at Clarence, looking for a reaction.

Clarence stood up and walked into the living room. She could see from the way he had stiffened his back how much this troubled him, and conflict was bad for his heart. Still she resented him for abandoning her.

It was just she and Dougie in the kitchen then and finally she leaned over and hugged him. He asked if she still loved him and she said of course she did. He said he loved her too. Both of them started to cry. She held Dougie tight and kept peering over his shoulder at Clarence in the living room.

He was sitting on the sofa watching the Oprah Winfrey show. Everyone knows Clarence can't stand the Oprah Winfrey show. Usually at that time he would be watching *The Steelers Gridiron Report.* But there he sat, while Oprah's guest talked about the advantages of wearing open-toe pumps versus alligator slides. He stared at the screen as though he had never heard anything more fascinating than Oprah talking about women's shoes.

Dougie claimed he had "known" he was gay since he was 13. But because he grew up in "such a backward place" he had not been able to admit it until now. Betty had no idea what he meant. People in Dustin were not backward. Old-fashioned, yes. Dougie made it sound like that was wrong.

She should never have allowed him to attend Altoona State. Edna, whose cousin went there, had once warned her the campus was full of liberals, terrorist organizations, and sexual perverts.

Betty figured Edna was exaggerating. Now she learned that Dougie had taken a class she had never known about. The professor was gay and had started a group for students who were interested in becoming homosexuals. Unbeknownst to Betty, her son had been attending their meetings.

Betty had made Dougie promise not to tell anyone else in town, but when the two of them were alone he talked so lewdly that were he any younger she would wash his mouth out with soap.

"We are all sexual beings, Mother. I'm a sexual being. You're a sexual being. There's nothing wrong with that."

"I am your Mama. I am not," Betty lowered her voice to a whisper, "a sexual being."

She asked Dougie what made him think he was gay.

He said, "I never found Allyson arousing. I didn't desire her the way most men would."

"Allyson isn't the only fish in the sea. What about that sweet girl who works with the kids at your church?"

"Cathy Mickelson? We're good friends. That's all. You don't seem to understand. I can't change the way I am."

"What do you mean?"

"When I see an attractive man, I have feelings. You know, sexual feelings. I have fantasies of …"

"Stop it, Dougie! I am your Mama. Is there someone—I mean a boy … that you like?"

"Yes, there is. There's someone I think I love. I mean—I know I do."

"You're in love with another boy? Who is it? You didn't meet him in one of those gay pick-up bars, did you?"

"Listen Mother, if it makes you feel better. I haven't actually—well—I guess you could say I'm a gay virgin."

"You're a gay virgin? What does that mean?"

"You know, it means—I haven't had intercourse with—a man. I haven't—"

"Stop it, Dougie! I am your Mama. Don't talk to me like that." Betty tried to picture what it might look like if two men had sexual intercourse. She did not like what she saw.

"But you asked. I thought you wanted to know what I'm experiencing."

She wanted to know. She did not want to know. She did not know what she wanted to know.

"So you've never done one of those unnatural acts."

"I don't think they're unnatural. For you and Dad, they probably are. But not for me. I know that sounds confusing. You have to know I've struggled with this."

"So there's a chance you'll change your mind."

"No, Mother."

"You need to find the right woman."

"It doesn't work like that."

"Look, I understand Allyson is a bit uppity. Not that I object to her."

"Mother, that's the part you don't seem to understand. I am gay. I can't change my mind about it."

"Haven't you read the Bible? You could go to hell for this. You could lose your eternal salvation all because of some crazy feelings you're having."

Betty knew it was hypocritical to chastise her son. She had not prayed once since reading that book from the Narrow Road. Not even in church. She could no longer look at the picture of Jesus above the altar in the sanctuary. When she peered into His eyes—the same eyes that once brought her comfort in times of sorrow—all she felt was disappointment and accusation.

She should have made Clarence give Dougie a "birds and bees talk" when the boy was in junior high, but she could not blame Clarence for this. She was the one who told Dougie to stay away from girls. She was afraid he might get a girl pregnant like both of Sally Roessler's boys did. Why had she been so protective? Dougie could have impregnated every girl in his senior class and it would have been better than this.

Then there was the Julia Roberts episode when Dougie was a sophomore in high school. The three of them had planned a family outing for dinner and a movie in Naptonville. Clarence had suggested an Arnold Schwarzenegger film that was rated R and showed people's heads being blown off.

"I don't think Dougie should be exposed to that kind of violence," Betty said between trips to the all-you-can-eat salad bar at Ponderosa. She was proud of the fact that Dougie would still be seen with them in public. His voice had deepened and he was sprouting a moustache, but he would always be her little boy.

"Don't be so strict. There's nothin' wrong with a little blood and guts now and then," said Clarence.

"There's a new Julia Roberts film that *The Naptonville News* gave four stars. It's a family film. And we're a family."

"That's a woman's movie. Are ya trying to turn our boy into some sort of faggot?"

"Watch your tongue, Clarence Mundy." She knew her husband would defer to her wishes but not without indicating some displeasure.

Clarence chomped on popcorn and tapped his feet throughout the movie, unappreciative of Julia's acting genius. Near the end of the film when one of the important characters was dying both she and Dougie started to sniffle, and that set Clarence off. All the way home he complained about the movie and started laying into Dougie.

"What 15 year old boy cries at a movie? Hell, Dougie, you were actin' like a sissy. I didn't raise ya to be a fag."

Betty wondered if Clarence and Dougie remembered that episode. What had she been thinking—taking her son to a chick flick in the midst of his puberty? The Bible says, "Train a child in the way he should go, and when he is old he will not turn from it." The Bible cannot be wrong. All these years, she must have been training her son to become a homosexual.

Betty needed to talk to someone but she couldn't go to any of her friends. What would they think? She had tried talking to her sister Marian about Dougie's problem, an action she immediately regretted. Marian, who attended a liberal city church, seemed unconcerned that her nephew was a homosexual. She even had the gall to ask if he had a boyfriend, as if it were perfectly normal. Then she rambled on about how *her* son Danny was a real ladies man.

There was one person in Dustin Betty knew she could talk to. Maybe one of these days she would muster up the courage to tell Pastor Schwartz. He would never tell a soul. Still, she knew it was only a matter of time before word got out and her life would be ruined forever. There were no secrets in Dustin.

Seven

Gerald Schwartz

The church smelled mustier than usual. For some reason beyond human understanding none of the windows at Abiding Truth could be opened. Gerald had once raised the question of whether new windows or an air conditioning system should be installed, but Most Everyone said that would cost too much.

Today he momentarily wondered whether he might be the source of the odor since he had not showered for three days. Sophie Oglesby had yet to extend her biweekly offer to wash his laundry and Gerald had no clean towels. Besides laundering his clothes and bringing him meals, Sophie attended all of Gerald's Bible studies. Since his divorce, Gerald sensed Sophie's attention might be more than maternal. She had outlived three husbands, all of whom died from heart attacks. Gerald worried that she had unwittingly poisoned them with a steady diet of cholesterol and might be doing the same to him.

Gerald peeked up from his notes and surveyed the five Bible study participants who had gathered in the Franklin Memorial Meeting Room. Only Sophie appeared to be paying attention. Irmalee Hackett was flipping through her Bible. Dorothy Moyers was engaged in her favorite pastime, peering out the window, watching for passers-by. Joyce Zyszkiewicz was staring at a fly on the ceiling. Her husband, Leroy, a retired mine supervisor and one of the few men who participated in church activities not involving the use of screwdrivers or pocket knives, appeared to be asleep.

"In conclusion," said Gerald, trying not to rely on his notes. "Multiple theological motifs pervade today's pericope. Christology is central to John's narrative, and undoubtedly the disciples understood this miracle of transformation within an eschatological context. There are parallels with the Dionysian feast and possibly with some Hellenistic mythology, but that's a future topic. Any questions or commentary?"

"This is the story where Jesus changes water into wine, right? Is that in Revelations?"

"John, chapter 2." Gerald had spent 40 minutes explaining the text in detail and Irmalee had no clue which passage they were studying. Gerald knew what was coming next.

"Why aren't we studying Revelations? Didn't you see the last issue of *Weekly World Enquirer*?"

"I'm not an ardent reader of that particular publication."

"It says on the front page that Jesus is returning to earth October 12—just like the book of Revelations tells us."

"Well, that's certainly worth a headline." Might as well humor her.

"I'm not saying *Weekly World Enquirer* always gets it right. They were totally off with the story about Martians landing on the White House lawn. But if Jesus really is coming back in a few weeks, why the heck aren't we talking about it?"

"That's an excellent question," Gerald said, employing the method he had learned in the seminary refresher course, *Leading Effective Bible Study*.

"My sister's boyfriend is a minister and he preaches on Revelations every week."

Dorothy cleared her throat and looked Gerald in the eye. "What I noticed about today's story," she said, "is that even though Jesus turned water into wine, nowhere does it say he got drunk."

Bible study provided a forum for Gerald to learn the latest rumors Edna and Dorothy had been circulating about him.

"How come we never talk about the end of the world and how the Bible predicts everything that happened in the past 2000 years?" asked Irmalee. "My sister's boyfriend says it's all there in Revelations. Didn't you learn that in college, Pastor?"

"Your sister's boyfriend is undoubtedly well-intentioned," said Gerald, trying to prevent this conversation from spiraling beyond his control. "But not everyone who claims to be a minister is qualified to interpret scripture."

"Well, he makes sense to me. He went to school up in Dubois—Armageddon Bible College."

"I noticed something else about today's story. Nowhere does it mention Jesus taking naps when he should have been working," said Dorothy.

"Where did you go to college again, Pastor?" asked Irmalee.

Besides being Dustin's most prolific producer of poetry with hackneyed rhyme schemes, Irmalee was a self-trained organist who could not read music. Her repertoire consisted of a dozen hymns, none of which she ever played the same way twice. The previous Sunday she had became so absorbed in her syrupy rendition of *In the Garden* that she played three too many verses before Gerald caught her attention with the universal liturgical gesture for "Stop Immediately Before I Get *Really* Pissed."

Given free rein, Gerald would fire Irmalee without a second thought, but after thirty years in the ministry he had learned to choose his battles wisely. Gerald knew if he suggested replacing Irmalee his life would become difficult in ways he could not imagine. Irmalee's mother had been a Weinwright and there were Moyers on her father's side. With roots that deep, Irmalee's ass was firmly planted on the organist's bench and she would not be moved.

"I received my undergraduate degree at Johns Hopkins and my master of divinity from Princeton," said Gerald.

Irmalee said, "I don't know anything about those schools you went to, but it seems somewhere along the line you shoulda taken a class on Revelations."

"Revelation is a frequently misunderstood piece of literature," said Gerald, trying not to sound defensive.

"Well, my sister's boyfriend understands it. And it seems to me that if you're as smart as you're supposed to be, you'd understand it too."

"As I stated, Revelation is easily misinterpreted—which explains its appeal among eschatological sects such as the one your sister's boyfriend apparently belongs to. Joyce?"

"Why are you talking about sex?"

"Sex?"

"You said something about scat-o-logical sex. What is that? It sounds dirty."

"I don't recall—"

"You don't need to explain. Leroy just got a computer. I'll look it up on the Internet. And I have a granddaughter who started college. I'll ask her if she's learned anything about Revelations yet."

"Where does your granddaughter attend college?"

"Over in Spooner's Grove."

"Spooner's Grove?" Gerald was unaware of any institutions of higher learning in the area.

"She goes to SGCOB. It's on the corner of Church and Maple above the Suds 'n Duds."

"I regret to say I don't frequent the Laundromat. Though perhaps I'll be needing to soon." Gerald glanced at Sophie. Dorothy wasn't the only one skilled at the art of intimation. "What exactly is SGCOB?"

"Gee, Pastor, for someone who's been to college, there's lots you don't know. Spooner's Grove College of Beauty. She's getting a degree in hairstyling."

Good God. Did this woman think the "science" of hair cutting included the study of biblical apocalyptic literature? Why stop with a hairstyling degree? She could write her doctoral dissertation on manifestations of pattern baldness among 19th century dispensationalist theologians.

"This is the point I am attempting to articulate. A degree from Princeton is of a different caliber than one from that Bible camp in Dubois or a school whose campus is located above a Laundromat."

"I don't see why. School is school," said Joyce.

"Just because someone doesn't go to a school with a fancy name doesn't make them less smart than you," said Irmalee.

Gerald was irked. "I went to Princeton. They don't let any idiot off the street into Princeton."

Leroy, who had yet to speak, leapt from his chair and pounded his fist against the table. As he did so he knocked over a Styrofoam cup filled with coffee. "I've had enough of this shit!" he shouted.

He turned toward Gerald and wagged his finger. "I don't appreciate you insulting my granddaughter. There's more than one person in this church who thinks you're a stuck-up snob."

"I didn't mean anything derogatory." Gerald sounded more flippant than he intended.

"There you go using big words." Leroy kept wagging his finger. "Let me tell you somethin'. Just because you been to college don't make you smarter than the rest of us. There's lots of stuff you don't know."

Joyce tugged at her husband's shirtsleeve. "Calm down, Leroy."

"You didn't even know how to fix your own toilet. You didn't know how to turn off the water when it was pouring down the hallway. Never met a man didn't know how to fix a toilet 'cept my wife's brother and he's retarded."

"Oh, look at the time. We better wrap things up," said Sophie. She was standing now, absorbing the spilt coffee with a napkin and collecting Styrofoam cups.

"And you don't know a damn thing about huntin.' Don't even know the difference between a .22 and a .308."

"Heavens, Leroy, look at how you're sweating."

"Don't go thinkin' you're high and mighty just 'cause you wear that collar. I fixed your toilet and your shit smells same as the rest of ours."

Now they were all standing except for Gerald. Collecting their Bibles, pushing in chairs, and heading for the door.

"I should invite my sister's boyfriend to our next Bible study," said Irmalee as she left. "He could teach us a thing or two."

Gerald glanced at one of the Aschenbrenner Funeral Home calendars that hung prominently in every meeting room of the church. The next Bible study was scheduled for October 14, two days after the End Of The World. If the universe met its demise on schedule, at least he would not have to endure an encounter with a fly-by-night evangelist.

"I haven't forgotten you, Pastor. Just leave your laundry on my front porch." Sophie was still cleaning the table.

"I appreciate your help."

"I can't believe you never read *Weekly World Enquirer.* You should pick up a copy—just to see what people here are thinking about. And of course, *The Naptonville News*. But I suppose you already get that one."

"Regrettably, I do."

As a member of the clergy, Gerald received a complimentary subscription to the afternoon daily otherwise known as the area's second leading source of misinformation—Dorothy Moyers being the first. Gerald had been misquoted at least a half dozen times by *The Naptonville News.*

Most recently he had told the reporter responsible for the *Dustin the Wind* column that members of the Abiding Truth church council were "invaluable assets" to the congregation. Due to a poor phone connection—so claimed the reporter when Gerald called to complain—the quote read "unvaluable asses," which resulted in three days of anonymous phone calls from Dorothy to the parsonage until the newspaper printed a correction.

"Listen Pastor, not all of us think you're a snob. Leroy gets worked up sometimes. All he's saying is there's different kinds of smart and different kinds of dumb. And each of us is some of both. You know."

That afternoon on the way home from the hospital Gerald stopped at the EZStop in Colton. He headed to the rack in the back of the store where they kept the pornographic magazines and various publications of popular interest. After ensuring that none of his parishioners were present, he hastened to the checkout counter.

Gerald kept glancing over his shoulder as the pimple-faced cashier scanned his purchase—the latest issues of *Deer Hunting Monthly* and *Weekly World Enquirer*. God forbid that one of his parishioners should see him purchasing such banal material. Still, Sophie had a point. It would be prudent to gain a deeper understanding of Dustin's primary forms of entertainment—gossip and hunting. Gerald tucked the magazines under his jacket as he made his way to the door.

+++

It started at the top of Mount Kiersey and spread like fire down the mountain, a burst of dazzling yellow and orange. When the sun rose above the mountains, humble Dustin shone like a city on the hill, a vision so spectacular even Gerald Schwartz took notice. God was an unsupervised child with a paintbrush, determined to bring a smile to every cynic's face.

Gerald and Margaret had first visited the area at this time of year, these glorious vistas convincing them that the slow pace of mountain living would be the change their marriage needed. The people of Dustin were a refreshing change from the pretentious suburbanites in Gerald's previous parishes. Inarticulate perhaps, rough around the edges, yet grounded and unassuming—the salt of the earth. Gerald had yet to learn too much salt could be toxic.

The first week of November they moved into the parsonage, dumb-founded that the multi-colored landscape which had awed them three weeks earlier had transformed into a bleak and barren terrain. Rotting leaves crunched beneath their feet. Empty tree branches stretched out like skeletons against a gray sky. A week passed before Gerald saw the sun. It appeared momentarily one mid-afternoon, subdued, low on the horizon, before slipping behind the mountains. Not to worry, Betty told them. "The trees will be green again by May."

+++

October 12, the unofficial date for The End of The World, came and went. By the time of the next Bible study Irmalee's sister's boyfriend had abandoned his ministry for construction work because it paid better and Jesus, after all, was a carpenter.

Leroy had avoided Gerald since his outburst. Previous experience indicated that Leroy would silently stew for another week or two. Then one day he would approach Gerald about repairing something in the parsonage with no hint of bitterness, no indication that an altercation had taken place. It was Leroy's version of forgiveness—devoid of awkward apologies and conciliatory handshakes. Just pretend it never happened. If only Margaret could have forgiven like that.

Criticisms and challenges had been part of Gerald's ministry in Dustin for so long he would have been suspicious had they stopped. Still, in recent days Gerald had sensed an occasional rumbling beneath the surface of his life, as though the mountain on which he lived were a volcano about to erupt.

Edna, Harriet, and Dorothy huddled together at the rear of the sanctuary, whispering and glancing mysteriously at Gerald before Sunday services. One morning Gerald stepped into the alley behind the parsonage and found Dorothy tearing through his garbage. A few days later, while searching for his communion kit, he discovered most of the church council huddled around a table in the church library.

At first he thought he had forgotten a meeting. Gerald later attributed their furtive behavior to the fact that they must have been planning a celebration for the impending thirtieth anniversary of his ordination. He could not imagine any festivities would require much preparation. For his twenty-fifth anniversary he received Irmalee's poem, a plaque with the word *Lutheran* misspelled, and a $15 gift certificate to Dick's House of Movies—not valid for XXX selections.

+++

When Gerald stepped into the church office on Tuesday morning Betty was hunched over her desk, studying the names on the coffee hour host sign-up sheet.

"Mabel Hawthorne called," she said, without looking up.

"Oh joy."

"She asked you to pray for Andrea. She was raped and left for dead and now she has amnesia and can't remember her fiancé's name."

"How horrid! Is she one of Mrs. Hawthorne's relatives?"

"Oh, no. She's on Mabel's story."

"I shall pray for her expeditious demise."

"Whatever you think will help. By the way, is something wrong with Miss Kirch?"

"Why do you ask?"

"Mrs. Hawthorne's great-granddaughter who works at Valley View said you've been seeing her every day."

There were no secrets in Dustin.

"Miss Kirch has required spiritual assistance in recent weeks."

"So you know—Mrs. Hawthorne's raising a stink about you visiting Miss Kirch so much. She says you only come to visit her once a month and never stay long. She thinks you favor Miss Kirch because she's got money."

"What the—?"

"Between you and me, Pastor, I know why you don't visit Mrs. Hawthorne much." Betty leaned toward Gerald, and he noticed bags under her eyes. She whispered, "Her apartment smells like kitty poop."

Visits to room 128 at Valley View Manor had become a regular component of Gerald's daily routine. He had come to think of the photograph as an icon. The longer he stared at it, the more peaceful he felt. Even at 3:00 a.m., with the demons rising up from the darkness, he could close his eyes and envision the angel who would lead him back to sleep.

"Mrs. Warner had an episode," said Betty, continuing through her list of messages.

"What is it this time?"

"She's sure it's scurvy."

"I believe it's treatable with orange juice."

"She asked you to pray for sunshine. By the way, Pastor Weiss said he'd pick you up for lunch. He sure is a good-looking man. Clarence and I watch him on TV."

+++

Weiss was smiling like Miss America in the Rose Bowl parade. He had spent the past five minutes flirting with the hostess and was now trying to make eye contact with the waitress. "You're looking at my teeth," he said to Gerald, who was studying the menu.

"What?"

"I had them capped and whitened. You can never look too good."

"Huh?" Gerald stared down at a pile of ashes and a cigarette butt in a partially consumed cup of coffee left by a previous diner, which the busboy had yet to remove.

"Seriously, Gerald, have you considered working out?" Weiss peered across the table at Gerald's misshapen body like he was inspecting damaged produce at the grocery store. "There's a health club in Pottersfield. We could go there together for some bonding time."

Gerald momentarily recalled last winter's resolution to ride the stationary bicycle Margaret had left behind. Currently the handlebars served as a convenient place to hang his shirts, which saved the extra steps he would have to take had he hung them in the closet.

"I'll keep that in mind." *Bonding time?*

+++

After lunch and in the comfort of the Porsche, Weiss resumed his verbal assault on Gerald's physique.

"When people go to church they want to see a pastor who takes care of himself. They don't want to look at some frumpy guy."

Gerald felt his jaw grow tense. "I suppose you'll think me old-fashioned but I'm of the opinion that people attend church to worship God."

Weiss guffawed. "If people wanted to do that they'd be on the golf course or hiking up one of these mountains. People come to church for any number of reasons but few of them have to do with God."

How did this man pass his ordination exam? And why is his church thriving while mine flounders?

"People attend church to learn about God, to grow in faith. The sermon provides the ultimate theological pedagogical forum."

"Come on, Gerald. People don't go to church to learn anything new."

"Oh?"

"They just want the preacher to tell them what they already believe is true. Throw in a few of those tearjerker urban legends floating around the Internet and you've got all the material you need. Have you heard the one about little Timmy, the one-armed orphan boy with cancer?"

"I am pleased to say I haven't."

Weiss kept rolling, "People go to church to see people. We call it networking. They used to call it fellowship. But the person most people go to see is the pastor. And they want to see someone who looks good."

It all depends on the way you look—that was the essence of Weiss's theology in a nutshell.

Weiss slapped Gerald on the thigh and flashed a smile, revealing his newly capped incisors. "Ready for confession?"

Did he expect Gerald to share his darkest secrets after having spent the past hour insulting him? Or, as Gerald suspected, did Weiss approach these absolution sessions with the malicious pleasure of an exhibitionist who enjoyed shocking his colleague with his latest exploits.

"Do I have a choice?" asked Gerald.

"Things have started to warm up between Cathy and me. I know a little flirting is harmless, but I'm concerned I may have crossed the line."

"Which line?" Gerald felt both repulsed and curious, like an onlooker at a mountain road car crash.

"We've been playing around on our phones lately. Rather innocent stuff. Mostly IM."

"Who?"

"IM. Instant messaging. Cath and I started sending photos back and forth. All very innocent. Then this thought pops into my head—why not surprise her with a more revealing photo? She's always telling me I have a nice ass."

"Your youth director talks about your ass?" Gerald had once overheard a couple of his parishioners comment about the hair growing from his ears; he could not imagine them discussing his more intimate parts.

"Oh no," said Weiss. "Cathy's an upstanding Christian woman. She refers to it as my 'posterior.' She sits on the stage behind me when I speak. It makes me horny knowing I'm being watched."

"You get sexually aroused when you preach?"

"Hundreds of eyes fixed upon me, most of them female. And they're clinging to my every word. Surely you know that every heterosexual church-going woman fantasizes about having sex with a male pastor."

"Here I've spent all these years convinced that preaching was a holy act." Gerald felt like he was being vomited upon. The idea of Edna Weinwright or Harriet Redgrave entertaining a sexual fantasy was frightening enough, let alone one involving himself.

"You don't have to be sarcastic. This is an act of contrition."

"Is it?"

"You're acting like you find me repulsive."

"You're always an ass to someone."

"Hey, you remembered that." Weiss smiled. He reminded Gerald of a young boy, unable to contain his amusement. "I appreciate your listening to me. I know you like me. You said you do—"

Apparently, Weiss was waiting for a response. He glanced in the rear view mirror and exclaimed, "Oh shit!"

"Why are you pulling off the road?"

"A cop's pulling me over. Shit! I hate getting caught!" Weiss was spewing saliva across the dashboard. His tirade continued until the officer approached and tapped on the window.

"Good afternoon, sir," Weiss said as the window descended.

"May I see your driver's license and vehicle registration?"

Weiss flipped through his wallet then shuffled through a stack of papers in the glove compartment before finding the requested articles. Gerald saw his companion's face reflected in the officer's mirrored sunglasses. Now he looked like a boy who had been caught with his hand in the cookie jar. The officer studied the photo on the license.

"Hey, I know you! You're that TV preacher."

Weiss smiled and nodded. "Indeed I am. God bless you, sir."

The officer removed his sunglasses. "Your preaching has been a blessing to my family. My wife never misses your show. I can't believe I just stopped you for speeding."

"I am genuinely sorry about that, officer." Weiss procured a business card from his wallet and handed it to the officer. "Sir, I'd like to take this opportunity to ask you an important question. Do you currently have a church home?"

What was Weiss doing? This was hardly an opportune moment to spread the word of God.

The officer paused and looked up at the sky. "I'd rather not get into that. I'm a religious man, but I've had some bad church experiences."

"I'm sorry to hear that, officer. If you ever need to talk about it, I'll be glad to listen."

"Well, Reverend, if you've got time, I'll tell you the gist of it."

"I'm all ears, officer."

"My nephew has a little girl the pastor refused to baptize. Turned me off religion. Some ministers can be so stuck-up and narrow-minded."

Weiss chuckled. "We're not all that way."

"No, I'm not saying that. This was some ass—excuse me, Reverend. Got to clean up my language around you holy folks."

Weiss kept chuckling. "Oh, we're not perfect, officer. My colleague here can swear up a storm."

Gerald forced a weak smile.

"This guy—Reverend Schwartz or Schlitz, something like that. He's up in Dustin. Never met the guy. Maybe you've heard of him."

"Name's familiar," said Weiss, without a hint of duplicity.

"Anyway, he refused to do the baptism. He said he's got rules about who he baptizes. For cripes' sake, what would it hurt to do the family a favor?"

"Sir, I assure you we turn no one away at NEW CREATION!!! I'll baptize your nephew's daughter on Sunday, if you'd like. I'm doing another baptism and we could make it a double dipper."

The officer chuckled. "Ah, a little holy humor there. I might take you up on that. You're a hell of a—heck of a good preacher. I suppose you've got important church business to get to."

"The Lord's work is 24/7." Weiss reached into his wallet again and pulled out a slip of paper the size of a dollar bill. "Receive this with my compliments, officer. Should you decide to become a member of NEW CREATION!!! it's good for 20 percent off your first offering."

Gerald winced. A stern expression returned to the officer's face.

"Thank you, Reverend. Now I must inform you that you were driving 15 miles over the posted speed limit. I'll let this one go." He paused and looked up toward the sun. "Be on your way, Reverend. And please slow down."

The officer reached across Weiss's lap and extended his hand to Gerald. "Didn't mean to ignore you, Father. Got a name?"

There was an awkward pause and then Gerald said, "I'm Pastor— Pastor Joseph Franklin."

Eight

Allan Weiss

When Allan was tempted to doubt the existence of a benevolent deity he needed only to look at a woman like Cathy to have his faith restored. Who but God could have sculpted such a lovely figure? She was flawless from head to toe. Even her kneecaps and elbows were perfect.

His priggish colleagues might call it lust but Allan knew that when he gazed at Cathy, he was enjoying the bounty of God's good creation: the soft subtle curve of her shoulders, freckles like a thousand shining stars across her chest, and skin so perfectly smooth that he could not resist the urge to caress it.

"How pretty you are, how beautiful; how complete the delights of your love. You are as graceful as a palm tree, and your breasts are clusters of dates."

"Oh, Pastor Al," she giggled. Allan had been anticipating this moment for months. He sensed how much Cathy desired him. He saw it in her flirting eyes. He heard it in her eager voice.

"Shh, I'm quoting scripture. 'I will climb the palm tree and pick its fruit. To me your breasts are like bunches of grapes, your breath like the fragrance of apples, and your mouth like the finest wine.'"

"That's not scripture, you naughty boy." Coyness masking desire. He passed his hand along her breast. He felt the nipple erect against the cotton fabric of her top. Beneath the tentativeness, pure lust.

"Song of Solomon. Today's English Version. Wouldst thou preferest King James?"

"King James has nothing on you, Pastor Al." Her eyes sparkled. A sly smile revealed her sensuous tongue darting beneath her perfect teeth. Even the air in Allan's bedroom smelled sweet and fresh. Cathy was a flower in full bloom and Allan a bee drunk with nectar.

"'Behold, thou art fair, my love; thou hast doves' eyes within thy locks: thy hair is as a flock of goats, that appear from Mount Gilead."

"A flock of goats? You know how to make a girl feel good," She tossed back her golden curls in transparently feigned displeasure, her bright eyes still sparkling. In a few minutes he would finally be deep inside her.

"Dost thou mocketh God's holy word?" Allan had committed three versions of the entire Song of Solomon to memory.

"Oh no, I'd never do that." Cathy's smile dissipated. This girl could be too serious sometimes.

"I was joking, Cath."

"It's not that I don't enjoy it." She pulled his hand away. "Do you really think we should be doing this?"

"What do you mean?" It intensified his excitement when a woman held back like this.

"This is where you live."

The members of NEW CREATION!!! paid Allan a tax-exempt housing allowance, which enabled him to buy a home in the most affluent neighborhood in Pottersfield. The Olympic-sized pool and tennis courts, landscaped Zen rock garden, and a deck with a view of the mountains impressed even the wealthiest of Allan's parishioners.

"It's okay. Nobody knows you're here."

"But this is where your wife and children live. Their pictures are on the dresser. It's like they're looking at us."

Virginia was out of town for the week, visiting her mother in Ohio. The children were staying at a neighbor's house. Allan had to work every night this week and couldn't possibly be around to make sure they were properly fed and tucked into bed by eight.

"They're just pictures."

"That one over there on the dresser looks creepy. It's like she's frowning at us."

"What? Oh, that's Virginia's Aunt Vera. Lived to be 104. Never smiled once. You have to ignore her."

Before she died, Vera had warned Virginia not to marry Allan. She called him a philanderer. Returning one hand to Cathy's breast Allan reached around her back with the other hand and placed Vera's photo face down on the dresser. *Philanderer? Ha! What did that centenarian prude know about men anyway?*

Cathy continued to balk. Allan pulled her closer and softly caressed her back. He had completely lost his erection. "Cath, what's the matter?"

"I know people say it's just sex but it's my first time . . ."

"Your first time?" *Shit.* It's never just sex when it's the first time. This event would take on emotional significance of mythic proportions if it were anything like *his* first time. Whatever happened to Mrs. Harrison, anyway?

+++

It had been the most incredible experience a hormonally overwhelmed 14 year old boy could hope for. That morning he had preached his first sermon—on Youth Day, the Sunday after Christmas when the pastor always went on vacation. He did it because it would have made his mother proud. It had been nearly eight years since she had died and five years since his father's death, and he was living in Bethesda with his aunt then.

It had surprised him how important he felt standing in front of the congregation. For fifteen minutes, everyone listened to him, and that didn't happen often.

Three hours later he finished making love to his former Fourth Grade Sunday school teacher in the damp basement room where they kept the arts and craft supplies. He was amazed at how facile the act of intercourse had been. With the ease of an expert she had leaned back against a stack of Noah's Ark paper cutouts and guided him inside her while his pastel cotton trousers still clung to his ankles.

"You really liked my sermon?" he asked as Mrs. Harrison fastened the buttons on the front of her blouse.

"Oh my! *You* certainly have no trouble getting it up," she said. She sounded short of breath.

"You liked what I said? About us being spirits in the material world?"

"You're a natural. You looked good up there."

"And the connecting principle linked to the invisible. I borrowed that from Sting. He's, like, my favorite spiritual thinker."

"Sting?"

"You know, from The Police."

"Police? Sting? Listen, Al, nobody should know about this."

She had taught him about the ten commandments and the twelve disciples. She always sat in the third pew from the front and sang in the choir and made blueberry muffins for coffee hour. She wore the same Avon body lotion his mother had worn. When he was 9, and the memories of his parents' deaths were still fresh, he would sit in Mrs. Harrison's class and pretend that she was his mother now. She had two sons who were younger than him.

If she adopted him, he could be their older brother and teach them how to make model airplanes and play Whiffleball. Every evening they would sit together at the supper table eating fried chicken and mashed potatoes with gravy and the green bean casserole dish with French fried onions on top that Mrs. Harrison brought to potlucks. Mr. Harrison would be there, too, but he wouldn't say much. He would eat and smile because he was happily married and loved his children, even the adopted one.

Later that night when Al was alone in his bedroom, he thought about what he had done with Mrs. Harrison and started to cry. He had lost his virginity with a 40 year old who looked hotter than any girl in the Eighth Grade. But he felt empty inside because now that they had made love, Mrs. Harrison could never be his mother, not even in his imagination.

A week later, they made love again in the back seat of the Harrison's station wagon. Al never cried about it after that.

+++

Allan glanced at his watch. He had planned for a quick romp before returning to church for the "Come as Your Favorite Saint" Christian Pre-Halloween Rave planning meeting.

"Listen, Cath, your first time should be special. I hadn't realized you're a virgin."

"A virgin? Oh, no, Pastor Al," Cathy giggled nervously. "Is that what you thought? I meant this is my first time with a married man."

Phew! Time to seize the moment.

"Cath, there's no need to feel guilty. You know that scripture I quoted?"

"About my hair looking like a flock of goats?"

"King Solomon wrote that. Do you know anything about him?"

"He was really smart, wasn't he?"

"He also had thousands of wives. And concubines."

"What are concubines? Are you saying that's what I am?"

Time to bring this belabored conversation to an end.

"Cathy, my dear, a concubine is a woman so stunningly beautiful that a man who stands in her presence is so overwhelmed by desire he will do anything and go anywhere, anyway he has to, in order to be with her always." Allan wrapped both arms around her back and drew her closer, gazing into her eyes all the while. "Since that is how I feel about you, then yes—you could say you're my concubine."

Man, that was good. Words seduce. Preachers know that.

The hyperbole appeared to be having its desired effect. Now she was melting into his arms, her tongue searching for his, her hips swaying like this was the last slow dance of the evening. Now he could taste the sweetness of her breath again. Now he felt his erection returning.

Cathy had pulled off her top and unfastened her bra and Allan had one leg out of his pants. Tongues touching, his fingers caressing the back of her neck, her hand firmly resting on his well-sculpted posterior, they shuffled across the room like contestants in a three-legged sack race, and rolled onto Allan and Virginia's king-size mahogany four-poster bed.

Cathy's breathing quickened, and Allan knew she wanted him now. The innocent schoolgirl overcome by lust, no longer able to rein in her desires. Now he was Solomon, now he was King, the man no woman could resist.

He loved the way her eyelids fluttered and her soft curls fell against the pillow, the way she pressed her tongue against the inside of her cheek and shuddered when she drew in her breath, the way she tightened her arms around him as their healthy bodies glowed, slick and muscular. He heard his own breathing quicken and felt his body grow taut. Her body quivered as he slid inside her and all he wanted was to pull her closer, to fall into the abyss where time and trouble melted away and nothing mattered but this moment now. If only it could always be This Moment Now. Forever and ever. Amen.

He buried his face in the small of her neck as he came inside her, each spasm more pleasurable than the last. He pressed his ear against her cheek and felt her body shift beneath his. She lifted her head from the pillow and screamed.

At first he thought she had climaxed too, her orgasm so intense that this was her only release. But then she cried out again with a shriek that would continue to ring in his ears long after the moment was over. This was no shout of ecstasy but pure, unbridled fear.

She was looking toward the door and when he looked there, too, he saw the source of her terror. In the doorway, there lurked a human skull the color of chalk covered by a dark and shadowy hood. At first it appeared to be floating in midair. Then Allan noticed a complete skeleton beneath the skull. One hand clutched a sickle. The Grim Reaper was standing at the door, a grisly visage in black and white. Allan felt his heart skip a beat, and for a fraction of a second he was primeval Adam stared down by death, caught in a trespass of his own selfish doing.

Then he saw that this Reaper was but four feet tall and wore black and white Nike tennis shoes like those he had recently purchased for his daughter. As he returned to his senses, Allan experienced an intense momentary relief. It was only his daughter, decked out in her Halloween costume. In the next moment relief gave way to dread, as he realized the fate awaiting him would be harsher than any punishment death could dole out.

He was naked, with nary a fig leaf to hide behind, having just copulated with his 22-year-old youth director, in his own home, on the bed he shared with his wife, in the presence of his 8-year-old daughter. He had a hell of a lot of explaining to do.

In an instant, the girl turned and fled from the room. "Trinity!" he called, but his daughter did not answer. Allan leapt from the bed, remembered he was naked, and pulled on his pants as fast as he could. He did not know how much his daughter had seen, or how much she understood. She must have sensed that something was not right, that Ms. Mickelson, the woman who organized cookouts and parties at the church, did not belong in her parents' bed.

What was Trinity doing here anyway? And why was she wearing that gruesome costume? Last year Trinity had dressed as a bunny rabbit. Wasn't she supposed to be a clown this year?

After Allan had slipped back into his shirt and straightened his pants, he headed to the kitchen. Trinity was sitting on a barstool at the counter where they usually ate breakfast. She had removed her mask and placed it on the counter beside an open cereal box and a dried piece of egg. It did not appear so menacing sitting there next to Tony the Tiger.

She still wore the one-piece skeleton costume, though she had started to unzip it in the back. Trinity appeared neither frightened nor angry. The girl had never been easy to read, prone to melancholy moods.

"Trinity, dear." Allan sat on a stool beside his daughter and reached for her hand. She turned away. "Trinity, what you saw in the bedroom—it was, well, Ms. Mickelson and I were practicing for a skit."

No, that wouldn't work. Why would they be rehearsing a church skit without clothes? "I mean, we were praying and—"

Praying? That made no sense at all. He never did well without a script. He certainly could use a teleprompter now.

"It's hard to explain, dear. You probably wonder why we didn't have any clothes on. That's because..." The girl was as stoic as a statue.

"Listen, dear, this is something your mother might not understand. That is, she might take it the wrong way. I mean, you can't say anything about this to her. All right? It wasn't like... Look, someday you will... I mean, I don't even understand it myself. No, I mean ... Hey Trinity, how would you like to go to Disneyland?"

Nine

Gerald Schwartz

On the nights when Calm prevails he sees her shortly after he closes his eyes. He wakes as usual around 3:00 a.m., staggers to the bathroom, and relieves his bloated bladder. After soothing his parched throat with a glass of water, he fumbles through the dark hallway and back to his bedroom. He lies down and stares across the room while the shadows come into focus, as Envy raises its mocking voice and Doubt starts cackling in the darkness.

He closes his eyes and wills her to take form before him. First he sees the gentle curve of her cheek, then her lips, and that mysteriously comforting smile. Soon he feels the warmth of her hand in his own. He hears the steady rhythm of the waves and times his breathing so that, as his chest falls, the water comes rushing toward them.

The demonic voices gasp for air, fading now, drowning in the rush of the soporific waves. He stares into her eyes—those perfect blue eyes—the color of the place where sky meets water. He peers over her shoulder and there is the ocean, an eternal blanket of blue. He wakes to sunlight.

That is how it happens on the nights when Calm prevails. But not every night is like that. Some nights he closes his eyes and tries to focus but the only image that comes to mind is the unsightly countenance of Harriet Redgrave. The only sound he hears is the insufferable chatter of Edna Weinwright and Dorothy Moyers, raising their voices to join with the demons in a torturous cacophony.

He cannot bear more nights like those. He cannot battle the demons alone.

+++

Gerald could generally hold his alcohol, but for some reason the three beers he had consumed at Ed Jacobson's house were not settling well. Mrs. Hawthorne's nearly hysterical babble was giving him a headache. He had never seen her so excited.

"It's incredible, Pastor! Can you believe it? A miracle here in Dustin!" Her arms were shaking as she lifted a plate containing a single chocolate gob.

"Look at it, Pastor. You have to see it from the right angle."

She had already poured him a cup of coffee and placed a plateful of chocolate gobs in front of him. Thinking some food might settle his stomach, he had quickly consumed two of them and started on his third.

Gerald was not in the habit of sharing alcoholic beverages with his parishioners, preferring to drink alone. But after receiving what Ed called "his monthly dose of communion," the widower had asked the pastor to stay for a few beers. He sounded so desperate for companionship that Gerald could not refuse.

Mrs. Hawthorne kept shoving the plate in his face. "Can you see it? Plain as day."

Gerald shook his head and squinted. "I'm sorry to disappoint you but all I see is chocolate cake."

"See, there's the beard. It's a miracle! I can't believe I actually baked this!"

Gerald kept straining his eyes and turning his head. No matter how he looked at it, he could not detect the image of Jesus Christ that Mrs. Hawthorne claimed to see in her sacred gob. He could sense her mounting irritation.

"I don't know why you can't see it, Pastor. My daughter noticed it right away. First she thought it looked like Elvis. Till she saw the beard."

"Well, I am a bit far-sighted."

"My daughter said it's like that miracle in Scranton a few years ago. You know, the one where our Lord revealed Himself to four teenage girls in the shell of a chicken burrito."

"I did not hear about that."

"Good heavens, Pastor. Don't you read the papers?"

"Apparently it didn't make *The New York Times*." Another reason to read *Weekly World Enquirer.*

After thirty years in the ministry, Gerald figured he had witnessed every kind of bizarre religious experience imaginable. In his last congregation, a woman claimed if she sat in the northwest corner of her living room and hummed softly, God would speak through her dog and give her the next day's weather forecast. Ironically, God's predictions were only 50 percent accurate.

"My daughter says I should call Channel 7 and get them over here. It's been a long time since Dustin made it on the six o'clock news. Come on, Pastor, look harder."

"Well, perhaps I do detect a few indistinct facial features," said Gerald, hoping to appease Mrs. Hawthorne.

Gerald was feeling queasy. He had intended to drink only two beers. But Ed would not let Gerald leave until he gave a professional second opinion about whether the alpha-blocker Ed was taking for hypertension would interact with Viagra.

Gerald did not dare to ask why Ed, a recently widowed 80-something homebound man, might be taking Viagra. He had noticed that Ed's disposition had improved since his last visit. Today he mentioned the dearly departed Annie only once. When Ed opened his third Rolling Rock, Gerald figured it would be polite to help him finish off the six-pack. Besides, if he did not drink the last beer he knew Ed would. While he was not a physician, Gerald felt certain that the combination of an alpha-blocker, Viagra, and four Rolling Rocks would be lethal.

Mrs. Hawthorne placed the plate containing the sacred gob on the coffee table, which Gerald used as a makeshift altar for communion. "Say a blessing over it," she said, as she settled into her armchair.

Gerald busied himself by reaching for his communion kit and setting the paten and miniature chalice of wine next to the gob. "Religious experience is a subjective matter. I prefer to place my faith in the tried and true," he said. Gerald held up his Bible.

"I hope you don't think I'm making this up, Pastor. When I look at this gob, when I hold it in my hands, I feel the Lord's presence. It gives me the shivers."

Mrs. Hawthorne raised her shoulders and started to tremble for added effect.

"God is everywhere, Mrs. Hawthorne."

"Besides my daughter, I have five other witnesses who will testify that they can see the face of Jesus. Even Vera here can see it. Can't you, sweetie?" Mrs. Hawthorne scratched the head of the fattest of her three cats, which was eyeing Gerald suspiciously.

"I am not quibbling about whether the face is present or not. I'm simply saying that we cannot reliably base our faith on signs and superstitions."

"My daughter says I should auction it off on eBay. She says I could make a crapload of money."

"Let us pr—aay," said Gerald, suppressing a belch. The rumbling in his stomach reminded him that Rolling Rock was aptly named.

Mrs. Hawthorne bowed her head, folded her hands together on her lap and waited for the pastor to begin. She reminded Gerald of a sleeping child—incessantly annoying when awake, angelic in repose.

After Gerald pronounced the post-communion prayer Mrs. Hawthorne rose from her chair and headed to the kitchen. "Excuse me Pastor, while I write a check for my offering."

While he waited, Gerald noticed a copy of *The Peleg Principle for the Homebound* beneath Mrs. Hawthorne's coffee table.

"You're heading off to see Kristina Kirch again, I suppose," Mrs. Hawthorne called from the kitchen. He could hear her rustling through a drawer.

"She's not been well," said Gerald. He reached for one last gob to tide him over.

It wasn't until he took a fourth bite of the gob that Gerald realized he was in the process of desecrating Mrs. Hawthorne's sacred object. *Holy shit.*

Carefully, Gerald removed the uneaten portion from his mouth and looked down at the semi-circular remains. The fattest of Mrs. Hawthorne's three cats glared at him accusingly.

With the evidence of his crime still in his hand Gerald bolted for the front door, bumping into a lamp stand on the way. A table lamp crashed to the floor along with a vase of flowers, sending the cat scurrying.

"What's that, Pastor?" Mrs. Hawthorne called from the kitchen.

Gerald shoved the remains of the sacred gob into his mouth as the door slammed behind him. Like Lot fleeing Gomorrah, he did not look back.

+++

Miss Kirch appeared more alert than usual. She was sitting in the wheelchair with a pillow propped behind her back. An LED clock radio resting on a shelf near the television showed the time in large red numbers: *4:37*. It was tuned to a local rock station, probably not Miss Kirch's music of choice.

"Hello, Pastor," she said, more enthusiastically than usual.

"I've brought you communion."

"Thank you. How are Gracie and the children?"

"The children are fine."

"I saw them in church last Sunday. They're growing fast."

"You know how kids are." Gerald could engage in inane conversation when he needed to.

"You and Gracie are a lovely couple."

"I'm blessed to have her in my life."

Gerald felt awkward impersonating his predecessor. Miss Kirch was staring at him in a way that set him on edge. Gerald set his communion kit on the nightstand and opened it. He placed a wafer on the miniature paten. Out of the corner of his eye he could still see the photograph, beckoning to him.

"Take and eat; the body of Christ."

She continued to stare, her eyes glazed over, her mouth gaping as he placed the wafer on her tongue.

Gerald glanced at the photo. He felt like some sort of criminal furtively plotting his strategy.

From the hallway there came the sound of dishes crashing against the floor. Startled, Miss Kirch turned her head and looked toward the door. Gerald could not have planned it better. He snatched the photo from the bed stand and slipped it inside his brief case.

When she looked his way again Miss Kirch jerked her head back, surprised to discover someone sitting so close to her. She leaned toward him and blinked a few times like someone adjusting to a burst of bright light.

Miss Kirch's mouth opened wide in a crooked smile such as Gerald had never before seen on her face. It was not like the shy smile in the photograph, though she did look younger somehow. Miss Kirch continued to hold her mouth open and Gerald noticed she still hadn't swallowed the communion wafer.

"Joe, is that you?" she asked, looking at Gerald's clerical collar.

"Excuse me?"

"You're looking handsome today, Joe."

Joe? Joseph Franklin? Were they on a first name basis?

Miss Kirch leaned closer so that her face was a few inches from Gerald's. She raised her hands and stretched her bony fingers toward his head. "I'm the one you want. Say you love me more than Gracie."

Gerald noticed how her eyes were cloudy, like she was dazed or dreaming. He sensed what was about to happen yet felt unable to prevent it, as though he, too, were in a trance.

Miss Kirch grasped the back of Gerald's head and with uncharacteristic force, pulled him toward her. By the time Gerald realized what she had done, her parched tongue was slithering inside his mouth. She wrapped her lips around his and emitted a sound that was something between a groan and a whistle. Gerald could taste the pea soup she had eaten for lunch. He pulled back and she fell forward, her head landing in his lap.

A suffocating stench was filling the room, the unmistakable reek of bowels unloosed. For a moment Gerald worried he might be the source of it. He noticed Miss Kirch's fingers creeping across his lap. Her touch was so light it felt as though some sort of insect had landed on his pants.

Gerald slapped at Miss Kirch's hand. Obstinately determined, it continued its descent, advancing upon the desolate nether regions of Gerald's groin. This effected a sensation he had not felt in awhile—a rising again to new life. Horrified, he pushed her hand away and grabbed her by the arms, forgetting for a moment that this was no insuperable demon he was battling but a frail, elderly woman. As he shoved her back into the wheelchair, he felt her body go limp.

Gerald shouted then, so loud they must have heard him down the hall, "I am Pastor Schwartz, goddamnit!"

He leapt from his chair and dashed toward the bathroom, acrid liquid rising in his throat. He flung himself forward like a runner diving for the finish line, stumbled across the floor and landed against the sink, into which he immediately began to vomit. He heaved three times and then turned on the water in a futile effort to wash chunks of partially digested chocolate cake down the drain.

As Gerald attempted to regain his composure he peered into the mirror above the sink. In the reflection above his shoulder he saw that an aide had come into the room. She was repositioning Miss Kirch in her wheelchair.

"Whew-hew! Looks like someone needs a change," she said. "Reverend Schwartz, are you all right?"

Gerald recognized the aide as Mrs. Hawthorne's great-granddaughter. He turned and stared at her across the room. "I'll be fine," he said.

"Poor woman," she said. "My mama says Miss Kirch used to be a beauty. It's hell to get old."

Miss Kirch's eyes were half-closed now and her head was tilted to the side. Her mouth remained open wide. Far-sighted man that he was, Gerald noticed that, in spite of what had transpired, Miss Kirch had yet to swallow the partially dissolved wafer. It still clung to the roof of her mouth like a scab that would not heal.

Part Two

Fall into Winter

Ten

Gerald Schwartz

November 17, 1970

My Dearest Joe,

If I am able to resist temptation, this shall be my last correspondence with you. It has been a privilege to work for you and your lovely family.

I understand our relationship over the past month has been, as you say, "inappropriate," and would be detrimental to your ministry should others find out about it. Still my feelings about this matter are mixed. Perhaps I am not completely repentant, for I hope to find a way to continue our relationship. Certainly, divorce would be disruptive to your family and I do not want to hurt the dear children. Still I cannot stop loving you. I will always cherish our time together.

As you suggested, I am moving to Somerset. Mother is not well, and she will appreciate my presence. I hope someday to return to Dustin, perhaps after Mother is gone and you and your family have moved on. Are you still planning to interview at that church in Erie?

May God bless us, dearest Joe. I will always love you, Kristina

+++

Somerset, PA

December 12, 1970

Dearest Joe, My one and only love,

I can barely stand to be alive. I feel so abandoned, so alone. Not a night goes by that I do not toss and turn, unable to sleep, tormented by the grief of letting you go.

Please tell me again that you love me. I would make such a wonderful wife for you. Am I such a sinner that I must be punished like this? Please tell me you miss me, too. Tell me you love me most of all.

I cannot stop crying and I will always be in love with you.

Love, the future—I hope and pray—Mrs. Kristina Kirch Franklin

+++

January 12, 1971

Dear Joe,

Northfield Public Library
210 Washington Street
Northfield, MN 55057

Do you think she's more attractive than me? Does she love you more than I do? Is she better in bed? Is she a better housekeeper? When I cleaned the parsonage, not a speck of dust remained. Does she do better than that? Has she removed all the dust from your dirty little life? Do you think about me at all? Do you ever look at that photo of me or have you tossed it away just like you've tossed me away?

I could tell her all about us. What do you suppose would happen then? She'll leave you. And then you'll have no one. You'll be alone. All Alone. Please tell me you want me. Because if you don't want me I can make sure you don't have her.

+++

January 24, 1971

To: "Reverend" Joseph A. Franklin

From: Someone You've Hurt Deeply

I know you love me more than her. You just won't admit it, you bastard. So you've told her and she's forgiven you. I DON'T KNOW WHY, you rotten slimeball!

I could destroy your career! I could tell everyone at Abiding Truth about us! I don't think they'd be quite so gracious as your sweet little wife has been! Do you?! I don't know how you call yourself a man of God after the way you've cast me away and brushed me off like dirt. I hope you rot in hell.

Signed, You Know Who

+++

December 3, 1971

Dear Reverend Franklin,

Please accept my apologies for any unnecessary distress my unChristian behavior may have caused you during the past year. I am doing much better now thanks to the excellent care of Dr. Nicholas Fisher at the Psychiatric Center. He suggested I write this letter to bring closure to our relationship. I am embarrassed by my actions and promise I shall never again interfere with your life. Send my greetings to Gracie and the dear children. May you all have a blessed Christmas.

Sincerely,

Miss Kristina Kirch

Somerset, PA

+++

Gerald was not a curious person by nature. For seven years, boxes of Joseph Franklin's personal possessions sat untouched in the parsonage attic. Not once had Gerald considered opening them.

When Gerald and Margaret moved into the parsonage they found a note from Franklin indicating he would return to claim the boxes. He and his wife had moved to Greensburg, a couple hours away. After Franklin died, his wife never returned to Dustin. The items in the attic were forgotten. Until now.

Gerald had not expected to discover any evidence Franklin had carried on an affair with Miss Kirch. Why would a revered man of God leave behind incriminating material? Did he continue to love her? Perhaps he never overcame his guilt. Or maybe he simply concealed the letters in a place he assumed no one, not even Dorothy Moyers, would consider looking.

The reason Gerald thought to search in the dusty passageway under the eaves was because he remembered Margaret's comment years before that such a spot would be the perfect place to conceal evidence of a crime. The space was so narrow that Gerald feared he might become wedged between the walls and no one would find him until his oversized frame had been reduced to dust and ashes. But Gerald could see from the glow of his flashlight that there was a box back there. And someone would not have placed a box in such an inaccessible location had he intended for any one else to find it.

The box contained a number of items that a pastor might not want his parishioners or wife to discover, including a couple dozen issues of *Playboy*, a carton of cigarettes, an unmarked bottle of pills, a handful of lottery tickets and a box of Hostess Twinkies Gerald was tempted to eat despite their indeterminate age. When Gerald found the sealed envelope with a handwritten label: *Confidential. Property of Rev. Joseph Franklin* he tore it open before he could give the matter much thought. As the current pastor of Abiding Truth, was he not entitled to his deceased predecessor's confidential material? Probably not, he now concluded. Franklin's affair would become one more burden for Gerald to bear, an oppressive secret he could never share.

+++

Quarter to eight. Another two hours to go. For the fourth time in ten minutes Gerald glanced at the grandfather clock that graced the northwest corner of the main viewing parlor. Tonight, like many nights, the Aschenbrenner Funeral Home was the liveliest place in town. A stately structure, the funeral home was built in the 1870s as a residence for the owner of the now-defunct coal mine. The home had maintained its dignity, even as the surrounding neighborhood endured an insidious decline. When Gerald admired the mahogany woodwork and hand-gilded brass sconces he sometimes felt as though he were back in Baltimore.

Yet despite its majesty, the Aschenbrenner Funeral Home was located in Dustin. A mere glance at the black velvet painting of Jesus with luminescent eyes or the flashing multi-colored line of Christmas lights strung along the wall behind the casket reminded Gerald of that.

If given a choice, Gerald would avoid funerals, weddings, roast beef suppers, and other events where people were prone to erratic emotional outbursts. He never knew how to respond when someone started wailing inconsolably. Which is exactly what Dorothy Moyers did when she peered down at her brother's lifeless remains for the fifth time this evening.

The first four times she had stared at the body like she was in a trance and walked away, expressionless. Now she was leaning over the casket, her eyes a few inches from the body. "Oh Johnny!" she screeched. "My poor brother!"

Dorothy had just chastised her pastor for failing to visit John on the day he died. Gerald reminded her that he had brought him communion on three separate occasions, which was more than sufficient considering John was an avowed atheist.

"He deserved better treatment from his pastor," she said, standing so close Gerald could smell the gin on her breath.

Gerald was not certain how John had managed to remain on the church rolls. He assumed it had something to do with being Dorothy's brother and Dorothy being Edna's best friend. Theoretically, one had to attend worship at least once a year and contribute an annual minimum of one dollar to be a church member.

Two years ago at Easter, the first and final time Gerald had seen John inside the church, he slipped Gerald an envelope containing a check in the amount of $1.25. In the accompanying note, he indicated he was contributing a little extra because he liked the pastor and understood the contribution was tax deductible.

Betty was standing next to Dorothy with her hand on the grieving woman's shoulder. "It's okay," she said, "Let it out."

"I can't believe he's gone! My dear brother!" shrieked Dorothy. The makeup on her cheeks was streaked with tears and her dress was rumpled from leaning against the casket.

"This must be hard," said Betty.

"He's gone! Gone! Gone! I'll never see him again." Dorothy shrieked in a tone so high-pitched Gerald's ears were ringing. He hoped she would not carry on like this at the funeral.

"You'll see him again in heaven." said Betty. Gerald was not sure he would have said that. Betty gave everyone the benefit of the doubt.

"You've got to be kidding!" Dorothy shouted. She turned toward the casket and poked her finger into the corpse's chest. "If this bastard doesn't rot in hell, I don't know who will."

Betty stood at her side, unflinching. Gerald half expected John Moyers to sit up and slap his sister across the face, as he reportedly had done on a number of occasions. But the moment passed and Dorothy moved on to direct her rage at the living. "There's dust on the flower stand. This place is filthy. Where is Mr. Aschenbrenner?"

"You can't win the battle with dust," said Betty.

Dorothy stormed out of the viewing area in search of the missing funeral director and nearly collided with Harriet, who was making a beeline for the door. "Dorothy, you have my sympathy," Gerald heard her say brusquely, before adding, "I don't have much time. Got a turkey in the oven."

A man Gerald had never met before staggered toward him with his hand outstretched. He had a cigarette in his mouth with nearly an inch of ash on its tip. He shook Gerald's hand so vigorously that the ash tumbled onto the pastor's trousers.

"Happy Thanksgivin', Reverend. I'm Charlie Moyers. I'm the oldest brother of the guy who croaked. You know—Dorothy's my sister."

Gerald said, "You have my condolences." Uncertain how this statement might be construed, he added, "I'm sorry about your brother."

"I'm not. But I would like to 'pologize for my sister's behavior. I know you did a lot for Johnny. Dorothy, well, she …"

"I understand," said Gerald. "It's a common defense mechanism."

"What's that?"

"Your sister. She's seeking to absolve herself by projecting her own abandonment of familial responsibility upon a vicariously culpable representative. Happens all the time."

Charlie wrinkled his forehead. "Yeah, I was gonna say she's got a stick up her ass. But what you said makes sense too." He stumbled toward Gerald and slapped his hand against the pastor's back. "I understand you're a drinking man, Reverend. Didn't think you guys was allowed to do that. Next thing the Pope'll be letting you screw chicks and eat T-bones on Friday. Or is that bacon you ain't allowed to eat? I get my religions mixed up."

"Oh no, we Lutherans can do anything we want. As long as we don't get caught." Might as well play along.

"No shit! Hey, why don't you join us in the back room for a couple shots? Don't know 'bout you but I ain't gonna make it through this 'less I'm totally wasted."

Gerald declined the invitation, remembering his vow to refrain from drinking anything stronger than beer in public after the incident at the Wilmore/Sidman wedding reception. Gerald prayed in public. He drank in private. He knew from experience that prayer and alcohol are a potentially dangerous combination.

+++

Edna's voice carried like that of a drill sergeant with a blow horn. "Nobody could do a funeral like Pastor Franklin did," she bellowed to a group of women that included Irmalee, Betty, and Sophie. "When he got done preaching you felt like the dead person was your best friend—even if you'd hated him all your life."

"That's right," said Irmalee, "Pastor Franklin knew how to make you feel bad—in a good sort of way."

"God rest his soul," said Betty.

If only they knew. Gerald longed to blurt out the damning truth. How had Joseph Franklin managed to conceal his act of adultery from the prying eyes of his parishioners? Gerald felt like he could not have a bowel movement without someone commenting about how much toilet paper he used.

But Gerald was no snitch. A revelation of his predecessor's indiscretion would also implicate Miss Kirch, which he was not about to do.

"You could always understand what Pastor Franklin was saying. He spelled it out in plain English, just like Jesus," said Irmalee.

Gerald fancied that, had he been Joseph Franklin, he would have resisted the temptation to commit adultery. Yet when he gazed at the entrancing face in the photo he now kept by his bedside, Gerald felt an indescribable peace. Meditating on Miss Kirch's photograph was a religious experience. And after thirty years in the ministry, Gerald knew that religion, like sex, makes people behave in strange and irrational ways.

Edna pointed across the room at Charlie, who was emerging from the men's restroom. "That's Dorothy's other brother. Lives in Bedford."

All four women turned and stared at Charlie, who was staggering toward the casket.

"Dorothy says he's got problems at home. His wife's son by her fourth husband is giving them a hard time. Turns out the boy uses marijuana and he's also a homosexual."

"One thing leads to another," Irmalee said. "Before you know it, he'll be smoking crack and getting a sex change operation."

"Oh, those homos are disgusting," said Edna.

Gerald noticed that Betty's face had flushed bright red. She glanced at him and pressed her lips together.

"I hear they're taking over the Internet," said Irmalee. "Prudence Weidenbach told me she heard it on Reverend Maxwell's radio show. They flash those sublimal messages across the computer screen and next thing you know, you're starting to have strange ideas."

"What kind of ideas?" asked Edna.

"If I told you, it would make you sick."

Out of the corner of his eye, Gerald noticed that Charlie Moyers appeared to be sick. If he was not mistaken, John's older brother had vomited into the casket. In his 30 years in the ministry, Gerald had witnessed stranger things. He once watched a deceased man's estranged wife point a shotgun at the corpse's head and threaten to blow it off if he dared come back to haunt her.

Still, this was shaping up to be one of the more dysfunctional funerals Gerald had attended.

"Pastor, doesn't it say in the Bible that homos can't go to heaven?" asked Edna, finally acknowledging Gerald's presence.

Gerald cleared his throat. "Well," he said. Unlike some of his liberal colleagues, Gerald could not in good conscience condone homosexual acts. Still, he despised oversimplified assertions made by self-righteous religious watchdogs such as Edna Weinwright. "The apostle Paul uses a word of indeterminate etymological origin— *arsenokoitai*—to condemn activity which bears some resemblance to homo-erotic behavior."

"Huh?" said Edna.

"The word is conspicuously absent in the extant Greek literature prior to Paul's usage. Of course, it may be a Pauline adaptation of words appearing in the Septuagint translation of Leviticus 20:13."

"Shoot, Pastor, don't give us one of your half hour lectures. Just tell us yes or no—can homos get into heaven?"

"Well—"

"Yes or no?"

Gerald had never felt comfortable around homosexuals. He did not like women touching him, let alone men. But this he could say with absolute certainty—he would rather spend eternity with Michelangelo than with Edna Weinwright.

Gerald glanced at Betty, who was still biting her lip. He noticed how her eyes were flittering and he felt a pang of emotion he recognized as pity.

"Well," he said, "If I read the scriptures correctly, homosexuals will likely end up in the same place as those who eat BLTs and read *Weekly World Enquirer*."

Betty's grimace momentarily transformed into a slight smile. Edna shook her head. "What the heck do sandwiches and newspapers have to do with homos, Pastor? Can't you just lay things out for us in black and white the way the Bible does?"

"I get it," said Sophie, speaking for the first time in ten minutes. "The Bible says to stay away from pork and gossipers. You know. Let the one without sin cast the first stone." Sophie winked at Gerald.

"What?" said Edna.

"You look hungry, Pastor," said Sophie. "I brought some ham sandwiches."

"Sounds delicious," said Gerald. He snuck a peak at Ashenbrenner's grandfather clock. Quarter to eight. Another two hours to go.

Satisfied that he had mingled sufficiently, Gerald followed Sophie through the crowded visiting area. Milly Vogel and Jane Herberger smiled at him as he eavesdropped on their conversation.

"I love these holiday funerals," said Jane. "The blinking lights give the deceased a special rosy glow."

"I hope I go at this time of year," said Milly.

"Johnny looks real handsome," said Jane. "But I'm wondering if Mr. Aschenbrenner should have used more formaldehyde. You go up to that casket and take a whiff—it doesn't smell so good."

As they weaved through the crowd, Gerald noticed Lois Warner making her way toward him. She walked with a pronounced limp.

"Good evening, Mrs. Warner."

"How are you, Pastor?"

"I'm fine. Thank you." Gerald knew that if he wanted time to enjoy his sandwich he should not inquire about Mrs. Warner's current state of health.

"Don't you want to know how I am?" she asked.

"How are you, Mrs. Warner?"

"Do you really want to know?"

"Certainly."

"Because lots of times when people ask me, they don't really want to know."

"How are you, Mrs. Warner?'

"Then when I tell them they don't listen to me. I could be dying and they wouldn't even care."

"How are you, Mrs. Warner?"

"If you're asking just to be polite, say so. I don't want to bother you if you have more important things to do."

"How are you, Mrs. Warner?"

"Dreadful, Pastor. Simply dreadful." This was one of her standard replies. Others included, "It's a good thing I signed my will," and "I'm praying for the Lord to put me out of my misery."

"I'm sorry you're not feeling well."

"I know you are. But I'm not asking for anybody's sympathy. Please, will you pray for me? I've severely damaged my leg. Doctor said it's only a sprained ankle, but I'm sure they'll have to amputate."

Gerald carried his *Minister's Prayers for Every Imaginable Occasion* with him for moments such as these. During his thirty years of ministry, Gerald had recited nearly every prayer in his well-worn book with the exception of a few he hoped he would never need, including 'In the Event of Nuclear War.' As he reached toward his inside jacket pocket, Lois grabbed his arm.

"Not one of those canned prayers. That Methodist lady pastor came to visit me last week and she said a nice personal prayer."

"She did?" Gerald despised personal prayers, prone as they were to sentiment and banality.

"I hope you don't mind I called her. When you're sick like me you need all the prayers you can get. I got Catholics praying for me, and Baptists, and about ten different TV evangelists."

"I see."

"That lady pastor laid her hands on me after I slipped on the ice and severely damaged my you-know-what. She said a personal prayer and it healed right up."

Gerald bowed his head. "Let us pray."

"Something personal, Pastor."

"Gracious heavenly Father, we offer this supplication for your servant Lois. Grant that—"

"Warner. Tell Him it's Lois Warner. There's four different people in town named Lois. I don't want Him to get confused."

"For your servant, Lois Warner. Grant healing to her body and peace to her soul—"

"My ankle, Pastor. Pray for my ankle."

"Grant healing to her ankle—"

"My left ankle."

"Grant healing to her left ankle—"

"Lay your hands on it, please. Use your special powers. Please pray they won't have to amputate."

Gerald placed his hand on Lois' shoulder. He was not about to bend over and touch her ankle. Thank God the Methodist pastor had already healed her you-know-what.

"Oh no! I'm starting to panic, Pastor." Gerald feared this would happen. "My heart's beating funny. I'm having an episode! Call 9-1-1. I'm having a heart attack!"

Gerald was uncertain how to proceed. Fortunately one of Mr. Aschenbrenner's assistants seized the opportunity to play hero.

"Woman's having a heart attack over here! Sit down, ma'am. We've got an ambulance on the way."

Mrs. Warner headed for the nearest chair, forgetting to limp. Sophie, who had been waiting with Gerald's sandwich, whispered, "That Methodist pastor has nothing on you."

"What's that?"

"You made Mrs. Warner's ankle good as new. You know."

The string of multi-colored lights kept flashing above the vomit-stained casket. Sometimes on nights such as this one it seemed that Gerald's life had become frozen in time. He glanced at Aschenbrenner's grandfather clock. Quarter to eight. Another two hours to go.

Eleven

Betty Mundy

It had been 10 years since Betty had climbed to the top of the bell tower. Despite the draft flowing through the slats on the north side, she thought of this as a warm and comfortable place—a good place to think about her life. This had been one of Betty's favorite spots to play as a child. Because the bell tower could be accessed from outside the church she, Milly, and Cindy Haverford spent countless hours at the top of Dustin's tallest structure.

The Abiding Truth bell tower never actually housed a bell. According to the congregational archives, a controversy arose as the church was being built about whether to install a fixed bell with its clapper controlled by a rope, or a swinging bell with a freely hanging clapper.

Those in favor of the fixed bell started sitting on the pulpit side of the sanctuary, leaving the swinging bell supporters the lectern side. Naturally, the Moyers and the Lorettos lined up on opposite sides of the issue, as did the Weinwrights and the Vogels. Even now, 118 years later, where members of Abiding Truth sat in church depended on their lineage.

The only exception was Eleanor Moyers Rigby, who chose to switch sides because of her ongoing feud with Edna. She once declared at a congregational meeting, "I'd rather sit with a bunch of Lorettos and Vogels than anywhere near that rotten ex-sister of mine." This did not endear her to the Lorettos and Vogels.

Unlike subsequent conflicts at the church, the bell controversy was resolved with a compromise. The congregation decided a bell was unnecessary since its purpose was to summon people to worship and everybody already knew when worship started. Only Betty and a few others knew about the original controversy that divided Abiding Truth. However, everyone above the age of two knew where not to sit.

Today Betty was thinking about none of this. She was remembering the day when she, Milly, and Cindy smoked cigarettes here in the bell tower. Betty, who had just turned twelve, had been worrying that they might set the church on fire or leave behind ashes. "What if Pastor Franklin finds out?"

"You worry too much," said Cindy, who had turned twelve six months earlier. "Smoking isn't a sin. Both my parents smoke."

"Yeah, but they're grown-ups. And they're married," said Betty. She inhaled too deeply and started to cough.

Cindy and Milly started laughing. "Smoking isn't like sex. You don't have to be married to do it," said Milly, who had once witnessed her parents engaged in the act of intercourse.

"You don't have to be married to have sex, either," said Cindy. "My brother and his girlfriend do it three times a day."

"My mother says all boys want is to get you into bed," said Milly.

"That's true. When a boy sees a girl's breasts, he gets a stiffy," said Cindy. Unlike the other two girls, Cindy already had breasts.

"A stiffy?" asked Betty.

"A hard-on. His cock gets really big and it starts bursting out of his pants."

"Shh," said Betty, "We're in church. You can't talk like that here."

"Charlie Cresco got a stiffy in the boy's shower after gym class. Roger Weinwright told me," said Cindy.

"Charlie Cresco's a homo," said Milly.

"Roger said it looked like a giant banana," said Cindy. She tapped on her cigarette and watched the ashes fall to the floor.

"Stop talking like that," said Betty. "Charlie's a nice guy."

"He's a faggot. Looking at all those naked boys turned him on."

"Don't say that!"

"It's true. Everybody knows it."

Today as Betty shivered on the dusty steps of the bell tower, she felt overwhelmed with loneliness. This place reminded her of Cindy, who died from complications following an illegal abortion the summer after their junior year. That was 1969. Things were different then. Later that same summer, Charlie Cresco was discovered in this very bell tower engaging in lewd activity with a boy he had met at church camp.

Maybe that was why she felt drawn here. She had always liked Charlie. A few years after he got cured from his problem, he married a girl from Colton and they moved to Ebensburg.

Sometimes Betty wondered what it would have been like to be married to Charlie. He was kind and sensitive, and a good listener. She had even kissed him once—in the school play, when they were sophomores. Maybe if she had married Charlie he would not have hung himself. Not that there was anything wrong with Clarence. A woman could not do much better than Clarence. Still, sometimes Betty wondered.

Betty kept wondering about the boy Dougie said he loved. What kind of man would her son find attractive? Obviously there were homosexuals in Altoona. There might even be a few in Pottersfield. One thing was certain—Dougie did not meet this man in Dustin. And another thing, too—had he stayed in Dustin this never would have happened.

+++

Their house never felt small or shabby until her sister came to visit. Marian lived in a prosperous suburb of Pittsburgh now that her husband had started raking in big bucks from his cosmetic dentistry business. Marian never flaunted her wealth. Still, it was hard for Betty not to feel inferior when her sister lived in a six-bedroom Victorian with an in-ground pool in her backyard. Her upstairs bathroom was nearly the size of Betty's kitchen.

Betty had been to Marian's house only twice, since neither she nor Clarence would drive anywhere near Pittsburgh. The last time, Betty took a bus, which she vowed never to do again after sitting beside a man who kept sticking his hand down his pants. But Marian frequently returned to Dustin for visits. She said she enjoyed catching up on gossip and seeing friends from high school. Still, sometimes she said things that sounded snobby, like she was more cultured now that she lived off the mountain.

When Danny was in high school, Marian bragged about his extracurricular activities. He was on the debate team and was captain of the orienteering team. Betty had no idea what orienteering was. She was too embarrassed to ask Marian, who raved about it like it was an Olympic sport.

Betty had Dorothy look it up at the library and found out it was an activity where people get lost in the woods on purpose and try to find their way out using maps and compasses. Betty was tempted to tell Marian that, had she raised her son on the mountain, he would not need maps to find his way out of the woods. And debate? Attend a few meetings at Abiding Truth and you'd learn all about that. Though Betty supposed you weren't allowed to address your opponent with four-letter words in actual debate tournaments.

But Betty kept her mouth closed. Besides, she would never trade lives with her sister. Even with Clarence's disability. And Dougie's problems.

"Are they still giving these out?" Marian was pointing at the new Aschenbrenner Funeral Home calendar for 2005, which Betty had posted on the kitchen wall near the telephone.

Marian had come to Dustin for an early family Christmas celebration. Danny had dropped in fresh from his latest job interview at a major brokerage firm in Boston. Dougie had come by for the first time in a week, before he and his cousin headed down to the Korner Tap to watch the Panthers game. Clarence was at the Buckshot Club, where he had been all day since he was not talking to Dougie. Clifton stayed home as usual. So it was not much of a celebration.

Marian laughed. "Those calendars haven't changed for 35 years."

"There's nothing wrong with that. If it isn't broke, don't fix it." Since Betty had told Marian about Dougie, everything her sister said sounded like a criticism.

"They still have those grainy black and white photos that old man Aschenbrenner took in the 70s. The only thing different is the year."

"That's not true. Last year they took out the photo of the old fire station."

"It's about time. That place burned down in 1987. Hey, do they still have that same slogan? Oh yeah, there it is. 'Aschenbrenner— Because Everyone's Got to Go Sometime.' Sounds like they're selling toilets."

This must have been the 300th time Marian had told that joke. Betty had an uneasy feeling about the day. She had a sense that she was about to do something God would disapprove of. Worst of all, she was starting not to care what God wanted her to do. Except for the Lord's Prayer—and she only said that in church—she never talked to Him anymore.

+++

The sisters moved into the living room for their annual gift exchange. Betty leaned back into the sofa and felt her eyes drawn to the water spot on the ceiling directly above her. The wallpaper was peeling on the west wall above Clarence's gun rack. The carpet was frayed in front of the sofa where

Spot slept. Why did she notice these problems only when Marian came to visit?

"Your tree looks nice," said Marian. At least Betty had that going for her.

Though Clarence was not supposed to lug felled trees through the forest on account of his heart, he had done so for each of the past fifteen years. As a city dweller, Marian had switched to artificial trees, another one of those differences that revealed how much the sisters had grown apart.

Marian said, "The sweet smell of a Douglas makes me think of Grand-pappy's place. Remember how we used to play hide n' seek up there?"

"Sure do."

"And I used to pull the flowers out of Grandma's garden," said Marian.

"I'd get punished for it."

"She said it was your job to keep me out of trouble. Since you were old-er."

"She'd make me peel potatoes as punishment."

"While I got to eat ice cream."

"Vanilla ice cream."

"With chocolate sauce."

"You'd sit there smirking at me, with chocolate all over your face, like you were totally innocent."

"I always could outsmart you."

"You didn't outsmart me. Grandma favored you. She ignored all the bad things you did."

"Maybe I never did anything bad."

"Ha!"

Marian handed Betty her gift. "I got you a book. You're going to love it."

Betty gasped when she pulled back the wrapping paper and saw the book's title. She tried to avert her eyes from the cover, which was adorned with a brightly colored abstract pornographic drawing.

"Take a look at the table of contents," said Marian. Betty could scarcely believe the title—*The Christian's Guide to Great Sex*. She opened the book and gazed down at the first page with a mixture of curiosity and dread. She felt like a child peering into a casket.

"I can't believe you gave me this."

Betty closed the book and tried to distract herself by admiring the papier-mache snowman that Dougie had made in art class when he was a Fourth Grader. Every Christmas Betty placed it on the coffee table and kept it up longer than any of the other decorations.

"I imagine that as long as you and Clarence have been married, sometimes the sex gets a little dull."

"Clarence and I are doing fine."

"Be honest, sis. It happens to everyone. For a while there, with Cliff and I, it was wham, bang, and over in five minutes."

"Marian! I don't care to hear about your personal life."

"Men get in a rut. They aren't imaginative when it comes to a woman's sensual needs. I promise you—this book will bring more pleasure into your sex life."

Betty could not believe she was having this conversation. Since when was sex about pleasure? Sure, it felt good sometimes. And there were times when Betty suspected it could feel even better. Still she knew from her Eighth Grade confirmation instruction that the primary purpose of s-e-x was for married women to show their husbands that they love them, even when they don't.

Betty flipped through the book, which contained illustrations of people engaged in activities best done with the lights out and certainly not for the benefit of others. She read the back cover jacket, which noted that the enclosed biblically sanctioned activities were intended for married couples only.

"Thanks for the gift," said Betty. "But I'd rather not talk about this sort of stuff."

"Why not?"

"Because, you know—"

"Because you're embarrassed. My friends and I talk about these things all the time. We discussed this book at my church women's circle."

"Well, I'd rather not." Betty kept flipping through the book. She could not imagine a group of mature women gathered in the house of the Lord, sipping coffee, and talking about topics such as . . . "Creative Cunnilingus for Christians." For goodness' sake! That's what it said on the top of page 87!

Marian peered down at the page Betty was pretending not to read. "You've got to show Clarence that chapter!"

Betty had wondered what "cunnilingus" was since she heard it mentioned on one of the late night cable shows Clarence watched. She had been too embarrassed to ask anyone. People in Dustin did not use the word often, certainly not in public.

"Clarence and I don't talk about things like that."

"See, that's your problem! No wonder it took Dougie all these years to come out. How could your son explore his sexual identity in a sexually repressed environment where no one talks openly about sexual matters?"

Betty could not believe Marian had used the word "sexual" three times in one sentence. "So you're saying I'm a bad parent?"

"Of course not. It's not your fault you failed to see that Dougie's gay. I suppose I should have told you when I started to see signs."

"Which signs?"

"Oh, I don't know. I could just tell. Call it an aunt's intuition."

"Why didn't I see signs?"

"Listen, sis. It doesn't matter. Just accept the fact now that you know about it. He needs your love and support."

"He has my love and support."

"You need to loosen up. Sex is perfectly natural. You act like even talking about it is a sin. Like you're ashamed to be a sexual person."

"Shame's not a bad thing."

"Really?"

"When Adam and Eve disobeyed God they felt ashamed. Which is exactly how they should have felt."

"Come on, sis. You don't believe that story's true do you?"

"It's in the Bible. Of course, it's true. 'The word of our God will stand forever.' Isaiah 40, verse 8." How could Marian claim to be a Christian when she did not believe half the things in the Bible?

"The Bible was written by people who thought the world was flat."

"The Bible was written by God."

"So God thinks the world is flat?"

"If God says the world is flat, then it's flat." And when Marian moved to Pittsburgh, she must have fallen over the edge of it.

"I can't believe you're so naïve."

Why were people always calling her naïve? Like they all knew something she didn't.

"I am not naïve. You're the one who's …"

"Who's what?"

Marian was smirking. Four-year-old Marian, sitting at the table in Grandma's kitchen, chocolate sauce all over her face, while Betty peeled potatoes.

Fourteen-year-old Marian, eyes glazed over, snickering obnoxiously at her own private joke. *Can't believe you never smoked pot, Betty. You should get out more.*

Forty-something Marian, wise to the ways of the world, married to a dentist, living in a mansion, sipping margaritas at the edge of her pool. She could tell her nephew was gay. She could tell just by looking. Chocolate sauce all over her face. Smirking. Snickering. Sticking out her tongue when Grandma wasn't looking. Snickering obnoxiously at her own private joke.

"Well?"

Betty slammed the book down on the coffee table. Dougie's papier-mache snowman tumbled to the floor and its head popped off.

"Goddamnit it all to hell!" shouted Betty.

Marian gasped. It took Betty a few seconds to realize what she had said.

Twelve

Betty Mundy

They made up. They always did. The differences between them were becoming wider yet they always managed to make up. Still, Betty was having a hard time forgiving herself. In the past twelve years she had not said anything more disrespectful than "darn." Yet it wasn't her vulgar language that most bothered her but the willful disobedience in her heart. Her gutter mouth was the symptom of a deeper problem. She was turning from God.

+++

It was warm enough to walk across town to the cemetery. The sisters' annual holiday celebration always included a visit to the family plot. Danny and Dougie agreed to meet them there before supper so they could pay their respects to the dead like a good family is supposed to do. Since Clarence couldn't be bothered to show up, Betty figured they would stick to visiting Lorettos. Most of the Mundys were buried in the northeast corner where the snow was deeper. Betty was in no mood to stomp through snowdrifts to visit dead people who weren't nice to her when they were alive.

Danny and Dougie met them at the entrance to the cemetery. Betty could tell they had been drinking. Danny said the game had gone into overtime and you can't cheer for the Panthers without a beer in your hand.

It was good to see the cousins together. Sometimes when Betty looked at them she pictured them as they used to be: playing street hockey in the driveway, taking aim at tin cans with their BB guns, covering for one another when they got into trouble, usually for breaking a garage window with BBs or an errant hockey puck.

On their way toward the Loretto lots they passed Cindy Haverford's gravesite. Betty paused for a moment at this spot as she always did and Marian stopped beside her. Betty wasn't sure if Cindy was still in the ground or in heaven or—God forbid—in that other place on account of her sin. Nobody in town talked about what had happened.

Marian grasped Betty's hand. Over the years, the sisters had several heated conversations about abortion. Marian once remarked that had abortion been legal in 1969, Cindy would be alive. Betty acknowledged that was true. She also knew what Cindy did would have been wrong even if it were legal. Still, some days, even after all these years, Betty missed her childhood friend so badly she didn't know what to think.

"If she'd had that child he'd be thirty-five years old," said Betty.

"Let's not think about that," said Marian.

"Cindy would probably be a grandmother."

Something I'll never be.

They trudged on. When they passed little Vera Weinwright's grave, Betty momentarily felt sorry for Edna.

Several granite headstones graced the Loretto corner, the oldest and largest of which marked the burial spot of Betty and Marian's great-great-grandparents. As Betty brushed snow and ice from her parents' headstone she noticed how quiet the cemetery was. Neither Danny nor Dougie had spoken a word for the past ten minutes. "Hey boys," she said, "Cat got your tongues?"

Danny nodded at Dougie. Betty smiled but the boys continued to look at each other with serious expressions on their faces like one of them had just busted a garage window.

Danny said, "Doug and I want to tell you something. But I guess we've got cold feet."

Now that the sun had set and the northwest wind had picked up, the temperature had dropped a few degrees. Betty's feet were cold too.

Danny pressed his lips together and cleared his throat. Betty noticed how much he looked like his father. "So what we want to tell you," he said while looking at his cousin, "… is that Doug and I got married last week."

He paused then glanced at his mother. Dougie was staring at the ground and kicking at the snow with his foot.

"What are you saying?" asked Marian. She pressed a finger against her glasses and slid them up the bridge of her nose.

Nobody answered. The wind was blowing quite hard now. Dougie wasn't wearing a hat and the top of his jacket was unbuttoned. He was shivering.

"You both got married last week," said Marian. "You mean?"

"Umm," said Danny.

Marian looked genuinely confused, which was exactly how Betty felt.

"You aren't even seeing anybody right now, are you, Danny?" asked Marian. It sounded more like a statement than a question. "And Dougie broke up with Allyson. Because he's gay. Right?"

Dougie's nose was starting to run. He sniffled and wiped his nose with his jacket sleeve. Betty pulled a tissue from her pocket and handed it to him.

"That's it," said Danny. His voice sounded flatter and less emotional than usual. "Doug and I got married last week. To each other."

"I don't understand," said Betty.

"What do you mean?" asked Marian.

"We drove to Boston together for my job interview," said Danny. "You know it's legal there."

"What's legal there?" asked Marian.

"I don't understand," said Betty.

"You know, marriage. Gays can marry there," said Danny.

"But you're not gay," said Marian. "I mean, Doug is. Right? What are you saying?"

"I'm saying we're legally married. Well, not here in Pennsylvania. They won't recognize it, of course. But in Massachusetts we're married."

"But you're cousins."

"In Massachusetts cousins can marry," said Danny.

"I don't understand," said Betty. She wished Dougie would say something.

"But Danny—you're not gay," said Marian.

"I'm gay, mom," said Danny.

"No, you're not."

"Yes, I am. I ought to know." Danny sounded sarcastic. Then he said, "I kind of thought you knew."

"We know this is a shock," said Dougie. He was still kicking at the snow with his foot.

"We acted kind of rashly," said Danny.

"That's why we wanted to tell you," said Dougie.

Danny said, "It was rash. But we don't regret it. We just felt we had to do it before we told you. In case you tried to talk us out of it."

"I don't understand," said Betty.

Marian turned toward her. Her face had become so pale Betty worried she might pass out, like she did after their father died. "Our sons have gotten married to each other," she said. "It's not legal, but for some reason—"

"It's legal," interrupted Danny. "We have the document to prove it."

"But how? Why? I don't understand," said Betty.

"I don't know why," Marian snapped. "Apparently to make our lives miserable. As some kind of joke, I guess."

"It's not a joke," said Danny. "Doug and I love each other. We've loved each other for as long as we both can remember. And we want to continue to share our love for the rest of our lives. I told Doug we didn't need to get married to do that. But he—"

Marian turned away. "No! I don't want to hear this!" she shouted. Her voice was partially muffled by the wind.

Dougie looked at Betty. He had a long strand of snot hanging from his right nostril. "I just wanted to make it legal before we—before we, you know—"

Danny encouraged his cousin, "It's all right, Doug. Just say it."

"You know, Mother. I believe sex belongs in marriage. Because that's what you taught me and that's the way I believe God wants it to be."

Betty nodded.

Dougie had found his voice but you could tell he was nervous. He was running some of his sentences together. "But this isn't about sex it's about love Mother I don't expect you to understand. But you know how much Dan and I love each other and how since we were little we've done everything together we've shared our secrets we're best friends we're soul mates. The fact we're cousins— well, maybe that was God's way of bringing us together most people have to go looking for their soul mates."

Betty had no idea what Dougie meant by "soul mates." Was this one of those phrases gay people used?

"We had a civil service. A JP in Provincetown did it for us but I'd still like us to have a religious service so we can have our relationship blessed I mean I know God already blesses our love but I want— we want your blessing too and Aunt Marian's and we can talk about this later. We know it must be a shock."

Danny said, "We just wanted you to know."

Marian glowered at Danny like he was five years old and had just run into the street. "Why on earth did you do this? Did Doug talk you into this?"

"I did it because Doug and I are in love and we want to spend the rest of our lives together. As a couple."

"But you're cousins. You're friends. This doesn't make any sense. Don't you see what you're doing? You're fucking up your lives! You're fucking up my life!"

"I'm gay, mom. I've been gay since the day I was born. I can't believe you didn't know this. I thought you had an open mind."

Marian grabbed her son by the arm. "My mind is open! How dare you insinuate that I don't have an open mind! Fuck you, Danny! Fuck you!" Marian pushed him away, and though Danny was much stronger than she, he did not resist. He fell into Dougie who caught him in his arms.

Marian stormed away, heading back toward the cemetery entrance. When she was out of hearing range, Danny said, "That didn't go so well."

Dougie said, "I thought Aunt Marian would understand."

"Yeah," said Danny. "She and Dad eloped. People tried to stop them from getting married. Because of prejudice. How are we any different than they were?"

"Of all people in this family, I thought she'd be the most supportive," said Dougie. Then he looked up at Betty, suddenly, like he had just remembered she was still standing there.

Danny turned toward Betty and said, "I assumed Mom knew. She and I don't talk much anymore. We're not as close as you and Doug are."

"Will you move to Boston?" Betty had so many questions she didn't know where to start. Most of the questions she didn't dare to ask.

"Well, that's the second part of this," said Dougie. "Since we're not residents of Massachusetts and because of some stupid law the governor's enforcing, we needed to state our intent to move there. Fortunately, Dan got the job."

"So you're moving?"

"Yeah. We're looking at apartments."

Betty knew this day would come. She just hadn't expected it to happen quite like this. "I still don't understand. You're not really married, are you?"

"It's legal. It's binding. In Massachusetts, at least. Dan and I are married, just like you and Dad are married."

Betty thought about this for a few seconds.

"Can I ask you a very personal question?"

"Of course, Mother."

"Which one of you is going to do the laundry?"

The boys looked at each other with puzzled expressions on their faces. Dougie wiped his nose with his jacket sleeve again. That would definitely need a washing.

"We still have some things to figure out," said Danny. He wasn't kidding.

"I just wish you would have waited to tell us back at the house. Where nobody else could hear," said Betty.

"Mother, this is a cemetery. We're alone."

"Alone? Most of Dustin is here." Betty nodded at a row of tombstones.

Dougie grinned. "I'm sure they can be trusted to keep a secret."

Betty felt dizzy and unstable, like the earth was moving under her feet. It must have been all the dead Lorettos, turning over in their graves.

Thirteen

Allan Weiss

In the four and a half years Allan had been a pastor, several women had sought his counsel regarding unwanted pregnancies. Much as he tried to maintain an open mind about the matter, Allan was inclined to think of the fetus as an unborn child. One of the women he had slept with in college was militantly pro-life. Before she would consent to intercourse she made Allan watch a film portraying graphic pictures of aborted fetuses.

The film had a lasting effect upon Allan. These many years later he would not have sexual relations with a woman unless she used birth control. As a pastor, he remained wary of sending pregnant women to abortion clinics, let alone accompanying them there. Yet here he was, parked across the street from the Women's Choice Reproductive Health Center on the north side of Pittsburgh. Then again, this situation was different from most. The woman in the passenger seat was bearing *his* unborn child.

Unborn child? What was he thinking? It was just a fetus. An undeveloped mass of tissue. This was a surgical procedure. Minor surgery actually. No one was dying here. No murders were being committed at the Women's Choice Reproductive Health Center.

On the sidewalk in front of the clinic, a large man with a crew cut and bushy goatee, one of several dozen protesters, carried a sign proclaiming, "THIS IS A DEN OF INQUITY."

"I'm scared," said Cathy.

"I'm sure there's a back entrance," said Allan.

A number of the protesters were chanting. It sounded like: "A bore shuns his mother!"

The Health Center was a two-hour drive from Pottersfield, located in a dilapidated neighborhood none of Allan's parishioners would frequent on the off chance any of them were passing through Pittsburgh. Not a wise place to park an unattended Porsche, but Allan planned to stay no longer than necessary.

"Listen, Cathy. It's a safe procedure. It doesn't even hurt." He wasn't sure about that part. It probably did hurt, but certainly not as much as childbirth.

"I don't know," she said. "I'm getting cold feet."

"I understand."

Allan's feet were cold, too. The heater in his Porsche wasn't working properly. One more problem to deal with.

"Do you really think I'm doing the right thing?"

"You told me you wanted to have this abortion, right?"

"I did. And I do. I mean—it seems like the best thing to do. But it's so complicated."

"Of course it is."

She had conceived the time they were together the week before Halloween. Allan had felt unsettled ever since then. He could no longer conceal his true self from his daughter. Now she saw him as the fraud he was. It was also becoming increasingly difficult to conceal his ugly true self from Cathy. Pastor Weiss sincerely sought to comfort her; Allan just wanted this unfortunate predicament to be over.

"This must be hard for you," said Pastor Weiss.

"It is."

"But you don't want to have a baby, do you?" asked Allan.

Pastor Weiss did not want Cathy to feel coerced; Allan kept thinking this should not have happened in the first place.

"No. Of course not. I can't. My father would kill me if he knew I was pregnant . . . You're mad at me, aren't you?"

"You told me you were on the pill." He tried not to sound angry.

"I know. I read one of those medical sites online and it said antifungals reduce the effectiveness of birth control pills. They should have taught me that in the sexuality class I took at college."

"Antifungals?"

"I have a fungal infection under the nail of the middle toe on my right foot."

This was not something he wanted to know. He could not imagine something as hideous as a deformed toenail on someone so beautiful as Cathy. Allan's cold feet were starting to itch. "Fungal infections—are they contagious?"

"Unfortunately, yes."

"Oh hell."

He should have kept his socks on when they had sex. People were lecturing about protecting yourself from venereal diseases. Why didn't anyone warn about the dangers of having intercourse with exposed toenails?

"It's my fault. I'm sorry," said Cathy.

Tears were streaming down her cheeks. She really was a pretty girl. Pastor Weiss handed her a tissue, gently touched her arm, and said, "You can't blame yourself for this."

She dried her cheek with the tissue and whimpered a couple of times. When she peered over at him, Allan immediately sensed the desire in her eyes. If they weren't parked in front of several dozen rabid morality enforcers, he might suggest they engage in a bit of nonsexual genital stimulation, to take the edge off.

"It's okay," said Pastor Weiss.

"Is it murder?" she asked. "That's what those people are saying."

"Of course not," said Allan, more gruffly than he intended.

"I don't want to go to hell for this."

It amazed Allan that intelligent people like Cathy believed in hell as a place of future eternal punishment. Allan had no doubt hell existed. He experienced its agony everyday. $30,000 of credit card debt. Receiving a text message from your daughter calling you "a damn mean liar" because you cannot afford to take her to Disneyland. Looking in the mirror and realizing the handsome man gazing back at you is the biggest fraud you have ever seen. That was hell. You do not have to die to live there.

"You've got to ignore those people. You can't let them make you feel bad."

"What about God?"

What about God? This was one thing that bothered Allan about being a pastor. People were always worrying about God. *What does God want me to do? Will He be mad if I do the wrong thing?* Every time people made decisions they were looking over their shoulders, afraid of divine retribution. The ministry would be a more pleasant profession if it weren't for God.

"Listen, Cathy, God trusts people to make their own decisions about abortion."

"I want to do the right thing."

"So do I, Cath. This is the right thing. You know neither of us can afford a child. You need to get on with your life."

"I could put the baby up for adoption."

Allan knew this was not a valid option. Even if he were freed from financial obligation for the child, people would gossip when they learned that the church youth director was pregnant. What if Cathy accidentally let it slip who the father was?

"There's something you should know," said Allan. "Birth defects run in my family."

What a manipulative thing to say, thought Pastor Weiss.

Stop thinking, thought Allan.

"That's horrible. What kind of birth defects?" asked Cathy.

"My cousin's boy was born with heterochromia iridis."

"That sounds awful."

It did sound awful. Allan knew Cathy would be too embarrassed to ask any further questions.

"Remember—whatever you decide, God's cool with it."

Cathy nodded. That must have been what she wanted to hear.

"There's nothing to be afraid of. Look, I'll go in with you. We're going to walk right past those protesters."

"You're so kind, Pastor. Lots of men would leave a woman to fend for herself."

Cathy had arranged for a friend to take her home since Allan had an appointment back in Pottersfield at noon. He was glad he wouldn't have to sit and wait for her, but he wasn't about to drop her off and go on his way. Partly because he was a kind and responsible man and mostly because he wanted to make sure she actually went through with this procedure. *This painless minor procedure.* The last thing he needed was another child turning up on his doorstep in the middle of August.

"Let's go," he said. Allan handed Cathy five $100 bills.

They had started to cross the street when a familiar-looking stocky man with a receding hairline approached them. Allan noticed he was wearing a blood red clerical shirt beneath his overcoat.

"Allan!" the man shouted. He smiled and waved his hand. "I'm glad you came! Can you believe you and I are the only Lutheran clergy who showed up for this rally?"

"No," said Allan. "No, I can't." Blood rushed to his ears and his heartbeat quickened. He was talking with Pastor Robert Zimmerman from Naptonville, president of the local chapter of Fetuses for Jesus. The man was prone to fanaticism. Allan had heard rumors that Zimmerman once baptized an aborted fetus. He recalled that Zimmerman had recently corresponded with him about something. It couldn't have been about attending an anti-abortion rally, could it?

"I'm disgusted with our peers, Allan. Afraid to take a stand. I see you brought along a parishioner. Got a few of my own." Zimmerman pointed toward a group composed of post-menopausal women and men with buzz cuts. Why were most anti-abortionists people who could not possibly get pregnant themselves?

Allan was trying to think of a way to talk himself out of this awkward situation. He needed a portable teleprompter. Cathy interjected before he had a chance to speak, "Oh no, I'm not a parishioner. I just met Pastor Weiss. I work in the Health Center."

Zimmerman stepped back suddenly and gasped. "Lord, have mercy! You're one of them!" His face was flushed red. Allan could not tell whether it was from the cold or a sudden burst of self-righteous indignation.

"One of who?" asked Allan.

"Don't you realize? This woman is a butcher! She kills children."

"Actually, I'm only a receptionist," said Cathy. She stepped around Zimmerman and passed through the crowd of protesters. One of the men with a buzz cut said, "Hey lady! You don't have to work for the devil! Come to our church and we'll find you a real job."

When Cathy reached the door she glanced back at Allan. Hopefully someone inside would help her through this.

"I trust you set that girl straight," said Zimmerman. "Grab yourself a sign, Allan. I haven't seen anybody go in for an abortion yet. I think we're scaring them off."

Conceding that he had no other choice if he wanted to save face, Allan marched with Zimmerman's army for forty-five minutes before heading back to Pottersfield for his next appointment.

+++

"A Pastor Cam?" asked Allan. "Is that what I think it is?"

He was sitting with Molly and his publicist at their weekly public relations planning session.

"You wouldn't even notice it, Pastor. We'd attach it to your collar. We think this would be a big hit on the website. People are curious about the daily life of clergy. This would give them an inside view into what you do each day."

No doubt about it, Jeffrey Horner was a brilliant publicist. His TV spots had received rave reviews. But a few of Jeffrey's ideas were ill-conceived, and the Pastor Cam was one of them. The last thing Allan needed was people knowing how he spent his working hours.

"We'll run it on a time delay. People are going to love this!" said Jeffrey.

Allan hoped Molly would see the folly of a Pastor Cam. He rubbed his right index finger against the left side of his nose, Allan's signal that she should interject and move this meeting along. But Molly was preoccupied with a letter that she had read several times in the past half hour.

"Look," said Allan, "We can discuss the web cam later. Right now I need your help with something else. The Bishop has recommended that after the holidays I take a brief sabbatical from my responsibilities at NEW CREATION!!!"

"You don't have health problems, do you?" asked Molly.

"No, nothing like that. It's something that happens from time to time."

Molly nodded. A few years before, in the weeks after the former director of entertainment ministries was paid a substantial severance package to resign quietly, Allan had taken a leave of absence to sort out his life priorities.

"Your secrets are safe with us," said Jeffrey.

The e-mail from Bishop Mainlaver's office had been formal and direct. *Allan—In light of recent allegations regarding your conduct in the office of Christian ministry, I recommend that at the start of the New Year you excuse yourself from pastoral responsibilities until such time as I can meet with you to resolve this pesky matter ;-) The Reverend Bishop Leroy Mainlaver*

"Anyway," said Allan, "I'm afraid my leaving for awhile might upset some of our members. People are attached to me." Allan paused and waited for his staff's requisite affirmations.

"Indeed they are," said Jeffrey.

Molly, again distracted by the letter, missed her cue. Allan allowed himself a moment to savor the fact he was respected and beloved.

"Anyway, we need to put the proper spin on my being gone," said Allan.

"How about 'Pastor Weiss is on a pilgrimage in search of more answers to your questions'?" said Jeffrey. "When you return we'll rename the church—NEW AND IMPROVED CREATION!!!"

"I'm afraid things could fall apart around here if we get the wrong interim person to replace me."

"Replace you? Nobody could ever replace you, Pastor Al," said Jeffrey.

"You're one of a kind," said Molly.

"I've got it!" said Jeffrey. "I say we go with a 'Best of Weiss' format while you're gone. We can replay your previous sermons and clips on the big screens. Music and other accoutrements can go on as usual. We'll keep everything the same, except you won't be physically present for worship services."

"But you'll be there in spirit," said Molly. Was it Allan's imagination, or did she look less unattractive than usual? There was a twinkle in her eyes.

"Eighty-eight percent of the live audience prefer watching you on the big screens anyway," said Jeffrey. "They enjoy the close-ups and angle shots. You're a good-looking man. We can make this work."

Allan still had his doubts. Molly was reading that damn letter again.

"Excuse me," said Allan. "We're having a meeting. Would you be so polite as to tell us what's distracting you?"

"She's in love," said Jeffrey.

"Well, I don't know if it's love," said Molly. She giggled. Allan had never heard her giggle. "I've met a man over the Internet."

"Really?" said Allan. "I don't mean to pry but—has he seen your picture?"

"He doesn't need to," said Molly. "I met him through Lutheransin-love.com. They match you based on your interests. You correspond anonymously. It keeps your interaction on a deeper spiritual level. After awhile, if you both agree, you meet."

"Interesting," said Allan. The idea of relating to someone of the opposite sex on a deeper spiritual level sounded like a radical concept. Certainly nothing that would interest him. "Well, Molly," he said. "I wish you luck."

"Thanks Pastor Al. Don't worry while you're gone. We've got everything covered."

+++

Later that night he called Cathy. They had not spoken since their awkward parting at the clinic.

"It went fine," she said.

"That's good."

"You wanted me to do this, right?"

"Of course. We agreed."

"Yeah, we did."

"Thanks for bailing me out with Zimmerman."

"You're welcome."

"Do you want me to stop by? I could come over now."

"No, that's okay. My friend's here—the one who brought me home from the clinic."

"You didn't tell her about me? I mean, my role in this?" *Which role? Sperm donor? Abortion underwriter? Pro-life protester? Flagrant hypocrite?*

"No, I didn't tell him. Doug's too polite to ask."

"You have a man with you? Don't let him take advantage of you."

"Don't worry. He's gay. You know—Doug Mundy."

Best not to see her. Allan knew little about the physical aftereffects of an abortion. He guessed it might be awhile before even a warm-blooded woman like Cathy would be in the mood for some nonsexual genital stimulation.

Fourteen

Gerald Schwartz

"Excuse me," said Gerald, as he cut in front of Dick Weinwright at the dessert table. One more piece of Jane Herberger's German chocolate cake remained and Gerald knew he could not endure the congregational meeting without more food in his stomach.

"Hey there, Pastor," said Dick. "Thought the nativity scene looked good this year. The tinsel on the donkey's tail was a nice touch."

"Hmm," said Gerald, with as much enthusiasm as he could muster.

Every year on the afternoon before Christmas Eve, Dick, Roger, and Leroy combined their artistic talents to honor the tradition of displaying a manger on the church's front lawn. The current arrangement had a best-forgotten history, which Gerald had heard many times. The scene included life-sized molded plastic figures of the baby Jesus, Mary, Joseph, shepherds and sheep, a donkey, and three wise men.

A few years before Gerald arrived, someone noted there was no star above the manger. Thus, Dick, Roger, and Leroy took it upon themselves to make a trek to the Wal-Mart in Naptonville in search of a star. Finding none, they purchased what they deemed to be a suitable replacement—a red-nosed reindeer. After considerable deliberation at the Korner Tap, they devised a way to perch Rudolph atop the manger by contorting two of its plastic legs.

When Gerald first witnessed Abiding Truth's version of the nativity he could not believe Pastor Franklin had allowed this anachronistic rendering of the Lord's birth on church property. He planned to rail against the secularization of sacred Christian holidays in his Christmas Eve sermon.

That was before he learned Santa made an appearance at the end of the service and Irmalee Hackett's repertoire of sacred Christmas music inexplicably featured *Silent Night*, *O Come All Ye Faithful*, and *Frosty the Snowman.* Gerald conceded then that in Dustin, as in most of America, Christmas was foremost a secular event. Even in church.

+++

Gerald sat in a folding chair next to Sophie. He finished his cake as he watched Roger Weinwright attempt to bring the annual congregational meeting to order. Roger was seated next to his wife and eldest son along with the other council members at a long table near the entrance to the basement fellowship hall.

"I better get this thing started, being as I'm President and all."

Roger sported a black and white striped tie, the only one Gerald had ever seen him wear. His usual week's worth of facial stubble had been shaved away. Edna was wearing a tent-sized homemade dress. She sat in a padded extra-wide chair that resembled a throne. Roger was an unskilled mill worker and Edna was an unskilled mill worker's wife. But today, for a few hours, Roger and Edna were king and queen and Abiding Truth their kingdom.

After Gerald fulfilled his pastoral responsibility by opening the meeting with prayer, Roger cleared his throat and glanced at his wife. He turned toward Rogie, who was seated at the right hand of his father. "Time for a report from our treasurer," he said.

Rogie was gawky and socially inappropriate yet fairly intelligent, which Gerald considered remarkable considering his lineage. After clearing his throat and glancing at his mother, Rogie stared down at pages of spreadsheets, which were sprawled across the table.

"The money situation isn't good," he said. "If this trend continues we won't be able to pay our pastor. Unless one of you is planning to die soon and leave your estate to the church."

Rogie snickered, apparently intending this as a joke. With the exception of Edna, nobody even cracked a smile. Several people shuffled in their seats.

"Seriously," said Rogie, "some of our best giving members have started going to other churches. We're running in the red, but as you know I've taken steps to save the church money. Any questions?"

Eleanor raised her hand.

"Thanks for that fine report, son," Roger said. "I'm sure Rogie could explain the details of the money situation but none of us would understand it anyways. So let's move on to the big issue of the day.

"You all know our wonderful sign that was donated in memory of my wife's great-great-grandfather got run over by a coal truck. We on the council's been discussing what kinda sign we should get to replace it. We're pretty much in agreement we should stick with a white sign with black letters just like we always had." Roger fidgeted with his tie and peered over at his wife. "Ain't that right, council members?"

With the exception of Les Cresco, everyone seated at the head table nodded in unison.

"Perhaps one o' you should talk about this since I don't wanta bias people being as I'm President and all." Roger glanced at Dick who turned toward Dorothy who grimaced at Joyce.

"Well, if no one's gonna say anything, guess I'll have to speak," Edna said finally. Gerald sensed this entire scenario had been rehearsed in advance.

Edna pushed her arms against the table like she was about to stand, then settled back into her seat. She reminded Gerald of a hot air balloon that couldn't get off the ground.

"Long ago," she said, "my great-great-grandfather, the very first vice-president of Abiding Truth, placed the very first sign in front of our church."

Edna was beaming as she usually did when recalling the accomplishments of the Moyers family. "Now whenever I make a decision, I always ask myself, 'What would great-great-grandpa have done?' because he was a great Christian. And I always try to do the Christian thing, as you all know.

"I've been praying long and hard about this. The other night I asked God to give me a sign—a sign about our sign. Well, I had a dream. And the Lord has put it upon my heart to share this message with all of you. In my dream I saw our church, standing tall and strong as it always has . . ."

Edna paused and tilted her head back so that she was looking at the ceiling. "There was a new sign in front of our church. And the sign was white with black letters on it. It said 'Abiding Truth Lutheran Church. Time of Service: 9:00 a.m."

Someone gasped. It sounded like Eleanor. For the past five years at Eleanor's initiation worship had started at 10:00 a.m. Edna had recently been lobbying for a change to an earlier hour. Apparently God shared her sentiment.

The meeting progressed.

"White paint is cheaper than black paint."

"If you use white you'll need two coats. With black you only need one."

"You can see black letters on white background better. Why do you think, when you go for an eye test, the sign is white with black letters?"

"Those eye doctors just want to sell you glasses. "

Several people misquoted scripture, the most popular passages being Ezekiel 12:6 and Matthew 12:38. Others stormed out when Roger refused to allow them to speak. According to the church constitution, congregational meetings were to be conducted by parliamentary procedure, but as Roger frequently said, that would make for dull meetings.

Leroy was in the midst of one of his histrionic diatribes when Gerald received word via Betty that Lois Warner had been admitted to the hospital. She required his immediate pastoral services.

"If this church stoops so low as to put up one of them damn black signs—excuse my French—I will start giving my offering to the Methodists!" shouted Leroy.

"Tell her I'm on my way," said Gerald, with uncharacteristic enthusiasm. He could stop by the parsonage for a bit of liquid fortification before and after his visit to the hospital.

It did not happen often, but at the moment, Gerald felt grateful for Mrs. Warner.

+++

When Gerald returned two hours later, Betty said, "It's good you're back, Pastor. The house is split. Your vote might be needed."

Technically, Gerald was a voting member of Abiding Truth. Unless the vote was tied, however, he refrained from casting ballots in matters he considered to be superfluous to his pastoral domain, such as the issue at hand. He returned to his seat beside Sophie after checking out the dessert table. All that remained was an untouched plate of Eleanor's low-fat macaroons that tasted like sand.

"Well," said Roger, "Being as I'm President and all I guess I better call for a vote."

As soon as he said it, Harriet burst through the doorway from upstairs. Immediately Gerald felt short of breath. Rogie and Dick began to pass out ballots along with some other sheets of paper.

"Let's get this over with. I don't have much time," Harriet said, loud enough for everyone to hear. Rogie shuddered and quickened his pace.

Roger said, "While we're voting, The Wife has an announcement to make about the pastor."

Edna cleared her throat. "As you all know," she said, "We formed a committee to check up on our pastor. There have been many complaints in recent months and we decided something needs to be done about it. Isn't that right, Harriet?"

"Every man's work shall be made manifest. 1 Corinthians 3:13," said Harriet.

Rogie shuddered again.

Gerald stood and said, "Excuse me."

As he did so Dick approached him, waving a handful of paper. "Better read this, Pastor."

+++

A List of Things Pastor Schwartz Has Done/Is Doing That The Pastor Of A Luthern Church Should Not Do— According to the Bible and Harriet Redgrave, Who Knows the Bible Really Well

1. Ruined The Prayer At The Wilmore/Sidman Wedding Reception Which is Why the Wilmores' Left Our Church And Now Go To That Church In Pottersfield With The God-awful Music And The Good-Looking Pastor
2. Does Not Ever Visit Lillian Sutherland Who Has Been On The "Shut-In List" For 3 Years Now
3. Acted Snobby To Lillian Sutherland When He Saw Her At Shop n Save
4. Takes Naps' When He Should Be Working—Dorothy Has Proof Of This In Photos She Took At The Parsonage
5. Slept Thru Rogies' Interesting Talk About Why The Church Should Get Automatic Thermostats'—Even Started Snoring—How Insulting!!!

6. REFUSED TO BABTIZE ALFY WEINWRIGHTS' DAUGHTER EMILY—EVEN THO SHE IS A DIRECT DESSENDENT OF ABIDING TRUTHS' FIRST VICE-PRESIDENT! THIS IS NOT RITE!!!
7. Did Not Visit Johnny Moyers Hardly At All Before He Died Even Tho He Was A Church Member
8. Preaches Sermons' No One Can Understand—Most Everyone Agrees About This
9. Said Insulting Things About Church Council In The Newspaper
10. Caused $421 In Flood Damage To Parsonage Because He Let Toilet "Overflow"
11. Always Eats Last Peace Of Pie And Cuts In Line At Church Suppers'
12. Has Bad Breath and Body Odor—Most Everyone Says So
13. Leaves Fly Open In Plane View Of Women And Children—Has Done This Many Times—Maybe You Don't Think This Is A Problem But You Don't Ever Here About Jesus Leaving His Fly Open in Public Do You?
14. Talks About Disgusting Things in Bible Study—S-E-X! Ask Joyce—She Looked It Up On The Internet
15. Seen Buying Girly Magazines' At EZStop In Colton!!!
16. Drinks Lots' And Lots' Of Liquor When Alone In Parsonage—Dorothy Has Proof Of This
17. Wastes Lots' Of Toilet Paper in Church Bathroom
18. Has Gas Problem—Makes It Hard to Sit Next To Him At Council Meetings And Church Dinners'—You May Not Think This Is Serious But Can You Imagine What The Last Supper Would Have Been

Like If Someone Was Braking Wind The Whole Time?

19. Destroyed Mabel Hawthorne's Gob Which Had The Face of Jesus And/Or Elvis On It—Lots Of People Saw It And Said It Was A Miracle
20. Broke Mabel's Favorite "Jesus Is the Light of the World" Lava Lamp
21. Heard Swearing—Saying "G-D" At Vally View—What A Nasty Temper!!!
22. Did Pre-Verted Acts IN PUBLIC With Shut-In Who Lives At Vally View And Has That Disease That Makes You Forget Stuff — We Will Not Name Her To Protect Her Identity
23. Plays Favorite With Shut-In At Vally View Who Lives In Room 128 And Has That Disease That Makes You Forget Stuff—Visits Her More Than Other Shut-Ins' Who Don't Have Lots of Money
24. Acts Snobby To Most Everyone—Thinks He's Better Then Most Everyone Because He Went To Schools' With Fancy Names' Which Most Everyone Has Never Heard Of
25. This Is Just Some Of The Problems—Copies' Of This Have Been Sent To The Bishop—Most Everyone Thinks Pastor Should Be FIRED—We Will Vote On This SOON!!!

+++

With a great deal of effort Edna rose from her throne and addressed the assembled members of Abiding Truth. "As chairman of this committee I took it upon myself to put together this list which is based on many hours of talking to members of our church."

Eleanor was waving her fist in the air. "Nobody talked to me. Why wasn't I consulted?"

"We asked Everyone That Matters," said Edna, bits of her saliva spraying like venom as she spoke.

Milly said, "You didn't ask me."

"Nor me," said Jane.

"Well, it's impossible to get around to all the members," snapped Edna.

Gerald had never seen this coming. This was a semi-organized, maliciously motivated, conspiratorial scheme to destroy his reputation.

"I hate to have to do this because as Most Everyone knows I've been behind our pastor since day one," said Edna. "But we can't ignore the fact our pastor has been shirking his duties and doing some things that just ain't right."

Suddenly it was hunting season and Gerald was the prey.

"Pastor Schwartz is a pervert."

"He's a drunk."

"He's lazy. He doesn't do his work."

"He doesn't even wave when you drive by him."

"That's right! He thinks he's better than everyone else."

The five or six shots of Irish whisky Gerald had consumed at the parsonage were starting to take effect. He felt as though he were floating, viewing this scene from above. He observed a church basement half-filled with tired and angry people. He saw the counter piled high with dirty dishes and a trashcan overflowing with garbage, the crusty remains of dried food on casserole bowls, crumbs strewn across the grimy tiled floor. The kitchen crew would be working long after the Steelers game started and tonight, as they washed and dried, swept and mopped, they would have much to discuss.

He saw a defeated old man in a clerical suit, fighting back tears, bereft of words, berating himself for having failed to see this coming, enraged by the sting of false accusations, plotting a defense for charges that could possibly be construed as true.

He saw his secretary sitting beside the old man with her arm around the pastor's shoulder, heard her saying, "I'm sorry. I should have warned you. I had no idea they'd take it this far."

He was walking then, the snow crunching beneath his feet, the sky an ashen gray. He felt a blast of warm air when he opened the parsonage door, the sofa stiff beneath his back, the muscles in his neck taut and throbbing.

+++

He had to pee. If he did not get up soon he would probably wet his pants. When he lifted himself from the sofa his mouth was dry as dust and he could not find his glasses. The last bottle of bourbon was sitting empty on the coffee table.

The room kept spinning. He was trying to focus now, sitting up on his bed, holding the photo a few inches from his eyes. He had said things he knew he should not have said though at the moment he could not remember what they were. He sacrificed his marriage for this? Only to be humiliated by a bunch of uneducated, inarticulate hillbillies?

After a half hour of torturous writhing, Gerald fell asleep again clutching the photo facedown against his chest. Within minutes, they were walking hand-in-hand along the beach.

+++

He awoke to the sound of the doorbell ringing. It was four in the morning and the doorbell kept ringing. Gerald rolled over on top of the photo but the ringing would not stop.

"Shit," he said to No One in Particular. He staggered into the hallway, down the stairs, through the kitchen. He unlatched the door and pulled it open. He would have turned on the porch light but it had been burnt out since September and Gerald had neglected to replace it.

Allan Weiss loomed before him like a specter, holding a suitcase in his right hand. Now Gerald felt like God was really messing with him.

"Happy New Year, Father. I guess you do sleep with that clerical collar on."

"Huh?" said Gerald. He was still dressed in the clothes he had worn to church. No wonder his neck hurt.

"Man, it's cold here on the mountain," Weiss said as he stepped inside. A gust of wintry air was briefly visible before the door slammed behind him.

"What in the hell are you doing here?" said Gerald. He had not realized how parched his mouth was until he started to talk.

"How can you live in this crap-ass burg? Main Street's a graveyard."

"It's four in the morning."

Weiss reached into his coat pocket and pulled out some sort of electronic device. "4:13:35 actually. But getting back to your original question— I need a place to stay for a while."

"A place to stay? Don't you have any friends to stay with?"

Allan looked like Gerald had slapped him across the face. "You're my friend. My best friend. Aren't you?"

"What sort of trouble are you in?"

"Nothing really. Virginia thought it might be best for us to spend some time apart. You know how marriage is."

"She caught you with that youth director."

"Cathy? No. It was more of a misunderstanding. It was … Kelly."

"Kelly?"

"The associate minister of arts and crafts."

"You are incorrigible."

"I didn't come here to be judged by you." Weiss wrinkled his forehead and pressed his lips together like he was about to cry. His eyes were teary but Gerald supposed that was because he had recently stepped in from the cold.

"I am no one's judge."

"Virginia's been spreading lies about me to The Bishop." Weiss dropped his suitcase on the floor. When he looked up again he was sporting his childish grin. "So she hates me. You're always an ass to someone."

"So I've heard."

Weiss slipped out of his shoes, flipped on the overhead florescent light and headed toward the refrigerator. "Hey, Old Man, what do you have to eat?"

Fifteen

Betty Mundy

At least they were talking. It wasn't the topic Betty needed to discuss, but when your spouse has spoken only a handful of words to you in the past month, you can't be choosy. Besides, it's easier to talk about someone else's problems than your own.

"It was horrible," said Betty. "Edna and Harriet were merciless. They've riled up a lot of members against him. I'm afraid Pastor's going to lose his job."

"When ya gonna vote?" asked Clarence.

"Ash Wednesday."

Pastor Schwartz had done little to help his cause on Sunday. If Betty didn't know better, she might think he was guilty of some of Edna's accusations. When he started yelling at everybody, you could smell liquor on his breath and his fly was open the whole time.

And some of the explanations he gave were a bit unbelievable. He claimed he bought a hunting magazine and *Weekly World Enquirer* at the EZStop. People laughed when he said that. Everyone knows Pastor does not hunt and makes fun of the *Enquirer*. And why would he hide perfectly respectable magazines under his jacket when he left the store?

Then when Dick Weinwright turned to his brother and told that disgusting joke, Pastor muttered something that sounded like a swear word. Of course he might have been praying. Betty wanted to give Pastor Schwartz the benefit of the doubt.

"So the pastor's been doin' some readin' about huntin', huh? Sounds like beaver huntin' to me," said Clarence. He started to laugh, but Betty frowned so severely it stopped him.

"Good heavens, Clarence! You're as disgusting as Dick. That's exactly what he said. And in church! Are all you men a bunch of perverts?"

"Sounds like your pastor is."

"You don't believe all those complaints are true, do you?"

"No, I don't," said Clarence. He had the contrite look on his face he always got when he realized he had said something he should not have said.

"Neither do I."

"Nothin' wrong with a man having a drink now and then. He's no liar or thief. Little standoffish and hard to understand, but that's no sin. And why would he be trying to get it on with Kristina Kirch? She useta be a looker but now she's practically dead."

Betty had heard a few people say they believed Edna's allegation that Pastor was "dating" Miss Kirch. None of them thought he could be attracted to her in her current condition, but Edna had an explanation.

"Everyone knows that woman's rich," she said. "Next thing you know, he'll be trying to marry her so he can wait for her to die and make off with her money."

Clarence kept rambling. "Those women are dumb shits, if ya ask me. What's the church gonna do if they can ol' Schwartz?"

"Edna's got it worked out. That's why we're voting on Ash Wednesday. Irmalee's sister's boyfriend gets done with his construction job that week and said he'd take up preaching on a temporary basis again if we need him."

"He ain't Lutheran, is he? I thought he belonged to one of those half-assed religions."

All the fighting at Abiding Truth did not seem Christian. They could not even decide what kind of sign to put up. Roger had tabled Sunday's vote till spring after all heck broke loose over Edna's list of complaints.

In the four days since the congregational meeting Betty had yet to see or hear from Pastor Schwartz. Dorothy told her she had peeked in the parsonage living room window and saw him pacing around the house in his boxer shorts. Meanwhile Betty had to fend off curious parishioners. "Pastor Schwartz is not feeling well," was her standard reply. But Harriet would not buy it.

"He's not sick!" she bellowed when she stopped by the office on Wednesday for her weekly tirade. "That man is getting lazier by the day. I don't know why I have to waste my time checking up on him."

Betty had worried Pastor Schwartz might get depressed again. Then Dorothy told her that Pastor Weiss was in the house with him. Betty knew the two of them were close friends.

"They better not try to fire you," Clarence said, while helping Betty dry the supper dishes. "Or I'll be knockin' some heads together."

"Now Clarence." Betty knew her husband would not do something violent. Still, it felt good to know he would defend her.

Clarence kept ranting. "I sure as hell wouldn't set foot in that church again." This was not much of a threat since it had been eleven years since Clarence had been to church. "I don't know why ya keep goin' to that place."

"You know what Abiding Truth means to me," said Betty. "That's my great-great-granddaddy's church. But if they get rid of Pastor Schwartz, I don't know. I might have to become . . ." she lowered her voice to a whisper and said, "a Methodist."

January 4, 2005

Dear Mrs. Mundy,

I hope this letter finds you doing well. I've been meaning to write for a long time.

I'm terribly sorry for the way I treated you when Doug and I were together. I said some horrible things about you and the people who live in your town. You probably think I'm an arrogant snob. I realize I have lived a privileged life and sometimes that causes me to say things that sound insensitive.

I've spent my life taking many things for granted. Marrying Doug was one of them. I've spent many tear-filled hours wondering how I missed signs that seem so clear to me now. I'm sad, I'm angry, and I'm grieving the loss of something that will never come to be. I suppose you might have similar feelings. Doug told me what a shock it was to you and your husband.

I've moved back to Philadelphia. I've discovered a wonderful support group, which also has a chapter in Altoona. It's called Families of Lesbians and Gays Support Network. You might want to attend some of their meetings. You'll be amazed how many people have loved ones who are gay.

Please accept my apology, Mrs. Mundy. You are the most wonderful mother a person could have. Doug is so fortunate to be loved by you. I think one of the reasons I said such cruel things about you was because I was jealous of the relationship you have with your son. If everyone had a mother like Betty Mundy the world would be a happier place.

Most sincerely yours, Allyson Jenkins

+++

Betty had read Allyson's letter a dozen times and still choked up every time she came to the end. These were the sweetest words she had ever read. Of course, Dougie had said many precious things to her over the years, but these words came from Allyson Jenkins, of all people. At the time when Betty most needed them.

Clarence refused to talk about Dougie and Danny. He spent most of his time sprawled out on the sofa, mindlessly scratching Spot's back. Marian was mad at Betty for being more open-minded about the boys' situation than she was when, according to Marian, everybody knew Marian was about as open-minded as a person could be. Even Dougie and Danny were upset with her. She hadn't heard from either of them since telling them she did not think it was a good idea to have a blessing service at Abiding Truth.

When he returned to work on Friday, Betty showed Pastor Schwartz Allyson's letter and asked if he had heard of the support group for family members of gay people. He said it sounded legitimate.

"I might have to check them out," said Betty. "I hate driving in Altoona, though. Everyone's so rude."

She had last driven in Altoona when Clarence was attempting to fix the kitchen sink drain and he sent her down to The Home Depot for some piping. She ended up at a red light next to a car driven by a large man with a crew cut and bushy goatee. He had a bumper sticker on his car that said, "Honk If You Love Jesus." She pushed her hand against the horn and waved. The man sneered at her and raised his middle finger, a gesture she suspected was not a sign of Christian unity, not even in Altoona.

"So Pastor, why haven't you done anything with the computer dating form I gave you?" Milly's son had found a dating website on the Internet called Lutheransinlove.com. Betty had downloaded one of their questionnaires and slipped it in Pastor's *IN* box.

Pastor Schwartz was browsing through one of his book catalogues. "Huh?" he said, without looking up.

"I'm trying to find you a wife."

"That's not one of my foremost priorities."

"Milly's son says computer dating's all the rage among single Lutherans. Clarence's niece did it. She used to run with a rough crowd but then she met a clean-shaven Lutheran chiropractor from Ohio. He doesn't have any tattoos and he goes to church every Sunday. Now they're getting married. You don't want to be alone for the rest of your life, do you?"

"Not if I can meet a clean-shaven woman with no tattoos."

Betty removed the dating questionnaire from Pastor's *IN* box and reached for a pencil. Sometimes a man needs help.

"All my single friends are doing this. Milly is, of course. And Sophie too. 'A life without love is like a year without summer.'"

"So I've heard."

"Come on, Pastor. Just answer a few questions. What's your favorite color?"

"You're suggesting I'll find a compatible partner based on my color preference?"

"It's just for fun."

"Gray."

"Come on. Nobody's favorite color is gray." Pastor needed more help than she had imagined.

"Oh," he said, between sips of coffee. "Do you suppose a potential partner might find my predilection for somber tones idiosyncratic?"

"You'll never find a wife if you keep taking like that. I'm going to say blue."

"Betty, I'd rather not do this. I'm stuffy, dull, and if you haven't noticed, not that photogenic."

"Oh, Pastor. You don't submit a photo. This is a Christian organization. Christians don't care how you look."

"That's not what I've heard. If you're determined to play matchmaker, why don't you complete the questionnaire for me?"

"Great idea. I'll show you how to write e-mails after they match you up with someone. It'll be so romantic."

Pastor Schwartz stared out the window. "Seriously, Betty, I have more important concerns at the moment."

It had been snowing for a few hours and now the wind had picked up. All Betty could see outside was a swirling blur of white.

"Nobody's going to fire you."

Betty and Milly had been lobbying on Pastor's behalf. So far, Betty had convinced five people including Irmalee and her husband to support Pastor

Schwartz. Maybe Edna didn't have as much power as she thought. Betty laid the matchmaker form aside for a moment and refilled Pastor's mug with coffee.

If everyone had a mother like Betty Mundy the world would be a happier place. Whenever she thought of that—she couldn't help it—she started to smile.

Betty was still smiling when the phone rang.

"Is Reverend Schwartz there?" said a shaky voice on the other end of the line.

"Yes. Would you like to speak with him?"

"Could you pass on a message? This is Elly Samuel up at Valley View Manor. Tell him we need his prayers."

"I'm sure he prays for you already, but I'll tell him."

"No, no. Something awful has happened. Kirstina Kirch has disappeared."

"Disappeared?"

"Somebody left a door unlocked and the poor woman walked right out of here. She's confused, you know. She disappeared into the woods. Least that's where we think she is. Can't see past your nose with all this snow swirling around."

"Oh my God! She'll freeze to death."

"If she hasn't already. Tell Reverend to pray. I hear he and Miss Kirch are close. I'm sure he'll be worried."

+++

Joyce, whose son worked on the ambulance crew, said when they found Miss Kirch, she was already in a coma. Joyce's son said Miss Kirch was wearing a necklace that froze fast to her skin. When she got to the hospital there was a mark on her neck in the shape of a cross. Joyce thought it was a sign from God.

Pastor Schwartz went to see Miss Kirch at the Mountain View intensive care unit in Altoona, where the flight for life had taken her. He said Miss Kirch's chances of survival were slim. Another resident told Betty she had seen Miss Kirch shortly before she disappeared. She was wandering the hall in a daze, complaining because someone had taken her picture. Betty's mother had been like that, too, when she got older. Whenever she saw someone with a camera, she would cover her face.

+++

Betty tried to look confident. She had never been good at trying to be something she wasn't. It did not help that the building was large and she had no idea where she was going. The meeting was in room 208. Was that on the second floor?

A creepy-looking man had followed her in from the parking lot. She wasn't about to ask him for help. A sign by the front door listed all the organizations that met here each week. She had not known there were so many kinds of support groups. She had heard of AlAnon and AA. But there were also meetings for cancer survivors and grieving widows and widowers. There was a group for domestic abuse victims and even one for something called s-e-x-u-a-l addiction. That must have been where the creepy-looking man was going. She could hardly imagine living with someone who had that problem.

Clarence was bad enough, wanting to jump into bed anytime of day or night since he found the book Marian had given her for Christmas. Betty had asked him several times to accompany her to tonight's meeting. She was getting bold with Clarence, saying things she would not have even dared to think when they were first married.

Before she left for Altoona she said, "You can't go on pretending this isn't happening. I don't care if it makes you uncomfortable. How do you think I feel? Do you even care how I feel? What kind of father stops talking to his son? Don't you love Dougie?"

"'Course I do," said Clarence.

"Then why don't you tell him?"

"Come on, Betty. I can't do that."

"Why not?"

"Guys don't do that."

"Maybe if you had told Dougie you loved him a few times, he wouldn't be so confused."

"What the hell is that supposed to mean?"

"I don't know." She walked out the door then, got in the car, and started driving down the mountain.

Now she was thinking about returning to the car and heading back home. She hoped the creepy-looking man wouldn't follow her. She was still studying the confusing sign when someone tapped her on the back. Betty turned to see a lanky woman with bulging eyes and a bad case of facial psoriasis standing a few inches away.

"Perhaps I can assist you. I'm Vera," the woman said.

Betty stepped back and the woman leaned toward her, extending her right hand. This woman, whoever she was, could use a lesson about respecting other people's personal space. Plus she smelled like she had just come from the gym and forgotten to take a shower.

"The group you are looking for is upstairs," she said. "Take a left out of the elevator. It'll be the second door on your right."

"Excuse me," said Betty. "How do you know which group I'm looking for? I've never been here before."

The woman kept staring at her. "I'm a mother too," she said. "A Mother Always Knows."

"What are you talking about?"

"You're new at this. I can tell. And I can figure out which group people want just by looking at them. Did you notice that man who came in behind you?"

Notice him? Had he come any closer she would have yelled, "Rape!" and hit him over the head with her purse.

"This is his third time here. When he first came two weeks ago I could tell his wife had just died and he was looking for the grief group."

"Grief group?" Betty would have never guessed that.

"You don't need to feel embarrassed," said Vera. "I've been to the support group for family members of gays many times. My uncle swung both ways, if you know what I mean."

Betty had no idea what she meant, but she wasn't about to ask.

Vera said, "I've been to all the groups that meet here, except the one for people trying to kick cigarettes. They get kind of testy."

This woman could not possibly be a gambler, cancer survivor, grieving widow, alcoholic, domestic abuse victim, anorexic, s-e-x addict, and mother of a gay son, could she? And Betty thought *she* had problems.

"You?"

"You guessed it," Vera smiled, revealing a mouth missing a number of teeth. "I'm addicted to support groups. I can't get enough of them. They make me feel so . . . so Not Alone."

"Uh huh," said Betty. She would feel more sympathetic if this woman kept her distance and quit staring at her.

"You'll be happy you did this when the night is over."

Betty turned away and when she looked back again a few seconds later, Vera was gone, though her body odor still lingered. What a strange woman.

+++

Room 208 looked like a classroom. There was a chalkboard on one wall. A large banner decorated with a rainbow hung from another wall. Almost all of the molded plastic chairs arranged in a circle were occupied already. Betty ended up sitting next to a young-looking person with a five o'clock shadow, large breasts and a pierced nose, who was wearing combat boots, a dress, and lipstick. This would not have been Betty's first choice for seating but there weren't a lot of options.

The young-looking person turned to Betty, smiled, and said, "Welcome! I know what you're thinking."

Apparently everyone here could read her mind. Did she look that out of place?

"Hello," said Betty.

"You're thinking—TS or TV? Right? Actually we prefer CD to TV now but you probably already knew that. Go ahead—guess. I'm cool with it."

What on earth was this person saying? What was a TS? She figured it must be something electronic since she already knew what televisions and compact disks were.

"Uh," said Betty.

"Hey, it's all right if you can't figure it out. I like to mess with people. TV all the way, MTF."

"Uh, that's what I would have guessed."

"Yeah, the milk wagons look so real they throw people sometimes, if you know what I mean."

Betty had no idea what he or she meant, but she wasn't about to ask her or him. She needed to get out of here.

"Excuse me," she said, not intending to be rude. She reached into her purse and pulled out Allyson's letter, now tattered around the edges. She hoped it would inspire her to stay.

The room was filled with chatter, a mixture of pitches and tones all blending together in an incomprehensible din. It seemed that everyone was talking to someone else. Except her. Betty wanted to look around to see what other people here were like, but she was afraid they might all resemble the young man and/or woman sitting next to her. Just when she had decided to leave she glanced across the room and saw Sophie Oglesby smiling at her.

Sixteen

Betty Mundy

At first Betty thought the stress of the evening was causing her to hallucinate. A few moments later she and Sophie were standing in the hallway, hugging like two friends who had been separated for years. Except that Betty had just seen Sophie this morning, outside the post office back in Dustin. Twenty-five miles up the mountain, half a world away.

"I see you've meet Denise, formerly known as Dennis," said Sophie.

Betty leaned toward Sophie and whispered. "Is that a boy or a girl?"

"He prefers you think of him as a woman."

"And he's gay? I mean—does he like boys or girls?"

"He's a cross dresser. Dennis—I mean Denise—has male parts, but he—I mean she likes to dress and behave like a woman. And as far as, well—he likes to be with both men and women. Sometimes he considers himself a straight woman and other times he says he's a butch lesbian. That's why he—I mean she—wears those ugly combat boots. It gets confusing."

"Is—is…" Betty whispered, "…everyone around here like him?"

Sophie laughed. "Oh no. Dennis—I mean Denise—is quite unique. Most of the people here have children who are gay. There's a young woman over there whose father is gay. And here comes Lou—he's only 15— bisexual." Sophie smiled at a gangly teenager who reminded Betty of Dougie at an earlier age.

"A couple of transgendered people stop in sometimes," said Sophie. "There's mothers, fathers, siblings. It's a mixed group. That's why we have the rainbow banner. It's a symbol of diversity and gay pride. You know."

"Pride? Isn't that one of the seven deadly sins?"

Sophie smiled, but she did not reply.

"You can't believe how glad I am to see you," said Betty. "I met this crazy woman in the lobby and then I sat next to Denise—I mean Dennis—no, I mean Denise . . ."

"You met Vera?"

"You know her?"

"Everyone around here knows Vera. She's strange, all right. But she's not crazy."

"She kept staring at me. Up close."

"I know what you mean. She gets in your face. And she could afford to take a bath. But once you get to know her you don't notice those things. She's actually kind of refreshing. You know."

"If you don't mind me asking—who is…? Who do you . . . I mean both your kids are married."

"My second husband was gay. I joined this group when he was still living and I've made lots of friends here. So I keep coming back. I feel I can help new people coming in, like yourself."

"Horace was? But you were married."

"We had an understanding. You might remember he used to spend weekends in Harrisburg."

Harrisburg, according to Edna Weinwright, was perversion city. Her second cousin twice removed had a friend who once spent a weekend there and she was terrified the whole time. Prostitutes, drug dealers, and gay bars on every corner. You take Las Vegas and San Francisco and put them together and you've got Harrisburg. Minus the glitzy casinos and scenic ocean views, of course.

"But—how? Why did? Were you? Was it?" Betty took a deep breath to compose herself. She wasn't giving Sophie a chance to answer her questions.

"I didn't know when we got married. He kept it from me for a while. He wanted to fit in. You know. He was a great stepfather to the kids and he liked living in Dustin. So we stayed married."

"So he had a friend in Harrisburg and you—"

"I met my third husband. You may recall we got married rather quickly after Horace passed away."

Three weeks, as Betty recalled. Funeral and wedding in the same month. People had chattered about that for a while.

"How did you find out about this group?" Betty asked.

"Pastor Franklin's wife told me about it."

"Gracie?"

"She used to come to meetings on account of their oldest daughter. You know."

"Really? She was?"

"You knew that, didn't you?"

"No."

"I figured you knew since you worked for Pastor Franklin."

"No, I didn't. Wow. That's really shocking. I suppose I should have known. I hope I didn't ever say anything inappropriate."

"It's all right. You know."

"My son Dougie, he's why I'm here."

"I didn't think it was on account of Clarence."

An image popped into Betty's head then—Clarence sitting at home that very moment, plopped in front of the television, wearing a dress, lipstick, and falsies. She let out an undignified snort. That was about the funniest thing she had ever imagined.

+++

"What's so funny?" Clarence asked.

"You are," said Betty. They were sitting in the living room, snacking on leftover apple cake and hot chocolate.

"What the hell's that supposed to mean?"

"I don't know." They were resuming this conversation where they had left off.

"How was the meetin'?" he asked.

"It was wonderful."

"There's a phone message. Someone called while I was in the can."

"You should have come, Clarence. There was a guy there about your age."

"Probly was Jane who called. I never did listen to it."

"Did you hear me, Clarence? I said there was a guy there who reminded me of you."

"What's his problem?"

"He doesn't have a problem. His daughter's a lesbian."

"Sounds like a problem to me."

"Everyone was normal, Clarence. Well, except for this one kid. But you wouldn't believe how many people have family members who are gay. Did you know Pastor Franklin's oldest daughter was a lesbian? Well, she still is. I think she's out in San Francisco now."

"That figures."

"Seriously, Clarence. You'll never guess who was at the meeting. Go on, guess."

"Edna."

"Edna? Why would she be there?"

"Well, that older boy of theirs ain't ever been on a date."

"Rogie? He's not gay."

"Well, he's kinda weird, ain't he? Figure if anyone else round here's a fag, gotta be him."

"Don't call them that, Clarence. Just say they're gay. That's the proper term. Sophie was there and she said Mrs. Franklin used to come."

"Sophie was there?"

"Remember her second husband—Horace? He was gay."

"Horace?"

"Yeah, remember him?"

"Horace? No, that can't be. Him and my older brother used to pal around."

"Your brother Steve?"

"No, Mike."

"The one who died in the hunting accident?" Clarence had six older brothers, three of whom were deceased, and Betty had never been able to keep any of them straight.

"No, that's Todd. I'm talkin' about Mike. The one who moved to Harrisburg. He died from that strange case of n'monia. Back in '94. Horace wasn't no fag. He was one of the pallbearers at Mike's funeral, 'member?"

"Kind of."

"B'sides, he was married to Sophie. He wasn't no fag."

"The correct word is 'gay'."

"That guy was a bear. Could crush a beer can with his thumb."

Betty rose and headed to the kitchen. "I'm going to check the phone message."

"Could open a bottle with his teeth. He wasn't no fag."

As soon as Betty hit the *PLAY* button on the answering machine and heard the familiar voice, she had an uneasy feeling.

"Betty! Edna here. I'd like to know what you're up to, telling people to vote to keep Pastor on. It's none of your business! You stay out of this. I happen to know a few things about your son I don't think you'd want to get around, if you know what I mean. Like the real reason he broke up with his fiancée. And frankly, as a Christian, I think it's disgusting what he's done. So stop interfering, got it? Oh yeah, thanks for bringing donuts to coffee hour on Sunday. Everyone said they were delicious. Have a nice night. This is Edna. Bye."

Betty was surprised at how calm she felt. She had been preparing for a moment such as this one ever since Dougie told them he was gay. It had helped to talk with Sophie.

Betty called into the living room, "Clarence, come here."

He must have known something was wrong because as soon as she turned around he was there. Betty hit the *REPLAY* button and watched Clarence as he listened to Edna's message. His eyes bulged out and his jaw clenched shut and his face turned so red it looked as though he had been out in the sun too long.

"I shouldn't have played that for you," said Betty when the message was over. It sounded even worse the second time she heard it.

"That fuckin' bitch!" growled Clarence.

"Shh now. Shh!"

"How the hell did she find out?"

Had someone overheard the conversation in the cemetery?

Clarence clenched his fist and Betty could tell he wanted to throw or hit something. He started to reach for Betty's "God Bless This Happy Home" ceramic coaster, but she stopped him.

"Go to bed, Clarence."

"If that bitch says anything about Dougie, I'll fuckin' kill her."

"Now Clarence, remember at times like these we need to ask: what would Jesus do?"

"He'd fuckin' kill her."

"Now, now, I don't think he'd do that."

"He'd cut off her fuckin' hands and pluck out her eyeballs."

"I can't imagine Jesus doing something like that."

Betty recalled there was a Bible passage in which Jesus told his disciples to cut off their hands and pluck out their eyeballs. Surely He could not have been serious. Then again, as the only begotten Son of God, He probably didn't joke around much.

"Edna's trying to blackmail me," said Betty. "She's not going to get away with it."

"No, she ain't," said Clarence.

"She's not going around telling everybody about Dougie and Danny getting married."

"Damn right, she ain't."

"She's not going to do it. Because I'm going to do it first."

"What?'

"Dougie's my son. And I'm going to be the one to tell people."

"Ya can't do that, Betty. Are ya nuts?"

"People are going to find out one way or another. I'm not going to let Edna be the one breaking the news."

"Just do what she's asking. Stop tellin' people to vote to keep Schwartz on. C'mon, Betty, it's not worth it."

"What kind of coward are you, Clarence Mundy?"

Clarence stomped his foot. His shoe made a squeaking sound when it struck the recently waxed linoleum floor.

"I ain't no coward. Damn it!" Clarence reached across the counter and grabbed the ceramic coaster. He raised it above his head, but Betty caught his arm.

"If you throw that, Clarence Mundy, I'm walking out of here. And you'll be making your own supper from now on."

Clarence kept his arm raised for a few awkward seconds. Then he placed the coaster back on the counter. He grunted, stomped his feet twice, left the kitchen, and headed up the stairs.

Betty flipped a switch near the telephone and the overhead fluorescent light in the kitchen went black. She looked out the window above the sink. It had started to snow. They were supposed to get three to four inches tonight.

"Good night, Clarence. I'm sorry," Betty called to her husband. She was still amazed at how calm she felt.

Clarence turned and shouted down the stairwell, "I ain't no coward. And Horace Johnson wasn't no fag either."

Seventeen

Allan Weiss

"Welcome, gentlemen. You're getting to be regulars," said the waitress. She beamed at Allan. The hazy gray aftermath of a trucker's breakfast filled the nearly empty dining area.

"Hey, Father, we've added a new item. You should try it."

"Let me guess," said Gerald, pointing to the handwritten section in his menu entitled *Lighter Fare*. "Might it be the so-called *Dieter's Veggie Platter*?" Other items in the spare overnight addition to the menu included a half-pound steer-burger topped with reduced fat American cheese and a 20-ounce chocolate malt made with two percent milk.

"I assume that's what you want." The waitress kept smiling at Allan. Her nametag said she was *Caroline*.

"How is it that you always know what men want?" said Allan.

Caroline laughed and said, "Experience."

"Come on now," said Allan. "You're much too young for that."

She was attracted to him. He could tell. He could feel her undressing him with her eyes. She wasn't bad looking. Late 20s, not married, probably divorced. Her raspy voice was a definite turn on. Carrying a little extra weight around the midsection. Needed some dental work. This kind of woman was usually good in bed.

It had been thirteen days since Gerald had allowed Allan to set up camp in the parsonage's drafty un-insulated attic. Allan spent his days watching television, responding to emails, or strolling the dreary snow-packed streets of Dustin. Despite the fact virtually everyone in the county knew of him, he could think of no one other than Gerald who would spend more than a few minutes with him. Not even his own children, neither of whom had responded to any of his calls, text messages, or emails.

There were women, of course. But since the start of the year, Allan had sworn off adultery. With the exception of a Siberian monastery, where better than Dustin to remain chaste? Thirteen days and Allan had yet to slip. Another week and he would make it to twenty days—half as long as Jesus once went without eating. Now there was a man with spiritual stamina. If Jesus could fast in the desert for forty days then surely Allan could refrain from sex for that long. Forty days. That was his goal. If he could make it, he could break this habit forever.

"You're always asking for veggies, aren't you?" Caroline said to Gerald.

"Go ahead," said Allan. "Order a steak." Allan peered up at the waitress and winked.

"No," said Gerald. "That's what I had last night."

The longer Allan went without sex the more he thought about it. Even the religious television stations had latent sexual undertones. The shapely chef with the southern accent on *Baking with the Bible* was repeatedly leaning over the stove and flaunting her well-toned Baptist bum. The cute blond soprano who wore a push-up bra and sang *Amazing Grace* on *MidMorning Hymnfest* stared into the camera with seductive eyes and Allan had an overwhelming sense she wasn't wearing any panties. Or maybe it was his imagination.

"You can get pie for dessert if the veggies don't fill you up," said Caroline. "Today we've got coconut cream."

"You hear that?" said Allan. "Lovely Caroline never lets a man go hungry."

She dyed her hair platinum blond. Nothing wrong with that. Crows' feet around her eyes. Maybe she was a bit older than he had first imagined. Caroline stepped closer. Beneath the greasy hamburger smell, Allan caught a whiff of a subtle perfumed fragrance. Natural full lips. She'd go down on him, no doubt. He wouldn't even have to ask.

"I suppose I could order the vegetable platter." Gerald was giving this too much thought. The old man seemed distraught about the possibility of losing his job. Allan could not understand how a brilliant man like Gerald had landed in such a mess. He suspected it had to do with his bad haircut.

"Who's your stylist?" asked Allan, after Gerald finally ordered.

"My what?"

"Who does your hair?"

Gerald glared at Allan as though he had just asked him where he could get a bikini wax.

"Nobody *does* my hair. I cut it myself."

"Yourself?" Allan had heard of people changing their own oil, cleaning their own house, even caring for their own children. He'd never heard of someone cutting his own hair. "How do you do that?"

"With scissors and a mirror." That explained the gash above Gerald's right ear.

"Hopefully not when you're under the influence."

"I never drink to excess." Gerald would get testy if Allan even implied he had an alcohol problem.

"You'd definitely benefit from a makeover. I know the perfect stylist for you."

"I'm not setting foot in one of those beauty salons. They smell like someone detonated a perfume bomb. And the conversation is absolutely asinine. Besides, I despise being touched."

"I'll remember not to hug you."

Gerald eyed Allan warily. Sometimes Allan did feel an urge to hug the old man. This must be what it's like to have a real father. Someone you could banter with. It was a shame Gerald had no children. He was sullen, aloof, and devoid of affection—traits Allan had once admired, then tolerated, then finally overlooked in his own father.

Caroline returned with their food. "Here you go, Father. Happy eating."

"What's that?" asked Gerald, as he stared at a plateful of misshapen breaded food items sitting in a puddle of grease.

"Veggie platter. Today we got cauliflower, mushrooms and pickles. Eat this and you'll be looking as trim as your buddy."

"I work out," said Allan, catching Caroline's eyes with his gaze. "Obviously you do, too."

She leaned across the table, affording Allan a brief glimpse at her cleavage as she placed his meal—a grilled cheese sandwich drenched in butter—in front of him. Caroline had it backward. If they kept eating here, Allan's physique would start resembling Gerald's. God forbid.

+++

It had been two years since Allan had visited The Bishop's district office in Johnstown. The experience reminded him of sitting in the principal's office. Generally, no one went to see The Bishop unless they were in trouble.

Bishop Mainlaver was supposed to see Allan and Gerald as soon as He returned from the restroom. Allan thought fifteen minutes was a long time for someone to be sitting on a toilet, especially when He knew people were waiting for Him. Allan felt like he had been waiting all morning. On the way to Johnstown, Gerald had insisted they stop at the hospital in Altoona so he could pay a pastoral visit to a comatose parishioner, whom he had already seen five times the past week. While Allan flirted with cashiers in the gift shop, Gerald spent nearly an hour with the patient.

Time for a phone call.

"Hey, Molly."

"Pastor Al, what a surprise. I haven't heard from you since—let's see . . . Oh, I guess it has been two hours since your last call."

"Are you teasing me?"

"Seriously, Pastor, everything's fine here."

"Are you sure Sunday went all right?"

"I've told you a zillion times already—everyone's cool with your taking a break. The video we ran on Sunday was a big hit. It was from the series you did on spiritual multitasking. People love that practical stuff."

"Do people miss me?"

"There's no substitute for you, Pastor Al."

"Yeah, but have people said they miss me?"

"I'm sure they have. You're breaking up—"

"What?"

"I'm losing you . . ."

"HELLO— MOLLY?"

"Gotta go. Someone's on the other line."

+++

Finally Bishop Mainlaver emerged from the restroom and led them into His office. The Bishop was an odd-looking man. He was completely bald and His nose was covered with warts that, from a distance, resembled horns. The Bishop's weathered face appeared to change in tone depending on where He was standing. Mainlaver attributed this unusual phenomenon to a melanin imbalance. He wore oversized glasses that emphasized His bulging eyes and made Allan feel like The Bishop was watching his every move. If ever there were a candidate for cosmetic surgery, it was Bishop Leroy Mainlaver.

The Bishop's office was sparse and functional. A framed calligraphic print which read *I have become all things to all people—1 Corinthians 9:22* was prominently displayed on the wall behind His desk.

"Gentlemen," said The Bishop as He sank into his ergonomically designed chair. He slid the chair slightly to the right, then back to the left, and once more to the right, until He was seated exactly in front of the calligraphic print. He raised his eyebrows and stared at Allan. "It delights me you two have become faithful prayer partners. If only all pastors in this district got along so splendidly."

This made Allan feel better. Sometimes he had the impression Gerald did not like him, but The Bishop seemed to think otherwise. And while The Bishop was rarely right about things, He was also seldom wrong.

"I apologize for not meeting with you earlier. I've been out of town for the Lutheran Hispanic ministry conference. Do you realize that Hispanics are the fastest growing ethnic group in America? Yet studies reveal few of them are Lutherans. Those dang-blasted Methodists are way ahead of us on this one. Problem is, a sizable number of lifelong Lutherans don't want Hispanics joining their churches. Why do you suppose that is?"

"Because they're racists?" said Allan. The Bishop stared at him through His oversized glasses. Allan hoped he hadn't answered a rhetorical question.

"Now, now," said The Bishop. "'Racist' is a rather offensive term. Nobody wants to be called a racist. We refer to them as 'ethno-sensitively challenged.'"

"Oh," said Allan.

"Anyway, here we have a conflict," said The Bishop. "Should we encourage Hispanics to join our churches?"

He stared at Allan and Gerald like He expected them to answer.

"Yes?" said Allan.

"On the one hand, yes," said The Bishop. As He did so, He lifted His left hand from His lap and turned it back and forth while staring at it. "I've met a couple of Hispanics. They seem like nice people. The ones I know happen to be affluent, which is a favorable attribute for church members.

"I'm thinking we might do some things to make them feel more included. Such as posting our church restroom signs in Spanish. You don't suppose they'd find that offensive?"

Again The Bishop waited for a response.

"Well," said Allan, "You wouldn't want any hombres in the mujeres bathroom."

"I concur," said Gerald.

"On the other hand . . ." The Bishop lifted His right hand from His lap and examined it in the same manner as He had His left one. "We wouldn't want to offend the ethno-sensitively challenged persons who have been the backbone of this church. They have a legitimate point."

"They do?" said Allan.

"Consider the detrimental effects a mass influx of Hispanic persons might have upon church potluck dinners. Studies show food favored by persons of Hispanic descent is—shall we say—on the spicy side. It could wreak havoc on the digestive systems of our ethno-sensitively challenged members, don't you think?"

Allan said, "They could end up spending a lot of time in the cuarto de baño."

Was it his imagination or was this a strange conversation?

"Yes, yes," said The Bishop "What to do? What to do? Those dang-blasted Methodists are way ahead of us on this one."

"Galldarn those Methodists," said Allan. He hoped The Bishop didn't think he was making light of the matter. "Have I told you how much I like your office?" he said. "It's homey yet practical."

"Excuse me a moment," said The Bishop. He rose and left the room.

"Where'd he go?" asked Allan. "Did I offend him?"

"Cuarto de baño," whispered Gerald.

Ten minutes later The Bishop returned.

"Anyway," He said. "We are here to discuss your troubles. Gerald, I have reviewed the list of allegations against you."

Allan felt momentarily relieved they would be discussing Gerald's situation first. He knew Virginia had contacted The Bishop, but he wasn't certain what lies she had told Him.

"On the one hand," said The Bishop, "the allegations appear trivial, and I know how churches waste time on the trivial."

Gerald nodded.

"On the other hand," continued The Bishop, "a number of these charges are of a serious nature. Halitosis can be quite offensive." When He lifted His hands up toward the light Allan noticed how chapped they appeared.

"The accusations are completely unfounded," said Gerald. He looked tired.

"Oh, yes, Sir," said Allan, sensing this was an appropriate time to interject. "These charges are false. And malicious."

Allan suspected that a few allegations on the list were true. But he and Gerald had agreed to serve as character witnesses for one another, even if it involved lying.

"Gerald, I'd certainly like to help you," said The Bishop. "But unfortunately this is out of my hands. Excuse me a minute." He stood and left the room.

Allan turned to Gerald and whispered, "Why does He keep running to the bathroom? And what's with the hands?"

"Don't you know? He's obsessive compulsive."

"He is?"

"Surely you've noticed this before."

Now that he thought about it, Allan realized every conversation he had ever had with The Bishop had ended abruptly.

"You mean He spends all that time washing His hands? Has anyone told Him He might require psychological help?"

"Of course not. He's The Bishop."

After ten minutes, Bishop Mainlaver returned. "You see," He said, continuing the conversation as though it had not been interrupted, "The congregation will ultimately decide whether or not you remain at Abiding Truth."

Gerald said, "Could you intervene on my behalf?"

"I would certainly like to, Gerald. I am convinced, given your character, you are mostly innocent of the charges against you." Mainlaver leaned across His desk toward Gerald and His complexion grew darker as He did so. "I appreciate your faithful service to our district and the people of Abiding Truth. However—"

Mainlaver tipped back His head. Beneath the overhead fluorescent light His scaly crown became noticeably lighter. "I wouldn't want to offend any of those dear people at Abiding Truth. I don't have to remind you that your parishioners contribute faithfully to help provide my salary as well as yours."

"I see," said Gerald.

"Your future at Abiding Truth is in your own hands, Gerald. I know you're not asking for advice. But I'll give you a few hints to being a better pastor."

The Bishop paused. Allan could tell He had given this speech many times. "Gerald, my friend—never take a stand when you can sit on the fence. Generally, speak out softly and obscurely without affront against wrongdoing when appropriate. If you can't say something good, say something ambiguous. Be firm yet flexible, generous yet thrifty, remarkably ordinary, intimate in a distant sort of way. Have a serious sense of humor. And above all, never listen to unsolicited advice."

Gerald nodded.

"Your friend Allan can give you pointers on spiffing up your sermons. I'm sure if you make a few changes, the good people at Abiding Truth will vote to keep you on."

"You want me to 'spiff up' my sermons?" asked Gerald.

"Add some stories. People love that. Have you heard the one about little Timmy, the one armed orphan boy with cancer?"

Allan thought he saw Gerald roll his eyes.

"I also recommend quoting from that popular *Peleg Principle* book. I know some pastors think it's trite, but people go for that stuff."

"I'm not familiar with it."

Allan was certain Gerald was lying. He had seen a waterlogged copy of the book on the back of the downstairs toilet at the parsonage.

"Please don't be offended, Gerald, but I think you'd also benefit from losing weight. Or at least redistributing what you already have. A decent haircut might help you too."

What did Bishop Mainlaver know about haircuts? Yet one could hardly dismiss His advice, seeing as He had ascended to His prestigious position despite being so god-awful ugly.

"Thank you," Gerald said without moving his lips.

"By the way, have you tried that anti-flatulence medication they advertise during Panther games? It worked miracles for my wife. We even gave it to the dog."

Gerald said nothing. He was sitting so still it felt as though he wasn't there.

The Bishop now fixed His disconcerting gaze on Allan. "As you know, I recently received a letter from Mrs. Weiss." The Bishop rubbed His fingers together but kept His hands beneath the desk. Allan sensed He was straining to keep them there.

"May I interject, Sir?"

"Yes, Allan."

"Before You continue, I want to remind You that under my tutelage NEW CREATION!!! has become the fastest growing Lutheran congregation east of the Mississippi. At a time when the vast majority of mainline churches are steadily losing members." Unlike Gerald, Allan was not about to sit back and watch his career go down the tubes.

"Yes, I'm always bragging about you to the other Bishops. If you don't mind me saying so, your approach to the Christian faith is a bit unorthodox. But we certainly can't argue with the results."

"We also happen to contribute more money to the district office than any other congregation—money which comprises a major portion of Your salary."

"As I am well aware."

"I'm certain You'll agree that were I to be removed from my position at NEW CREATION!!! the backlash against Your office could be debilitating. However, were I to encourage my congregation to increase its monthly contribution to the district office, they would undoubtedly do so."

"I've got to hand it to you, Allan. You make several excellent points. I will take them into consideration as we examine this matter." The Bishop was now sitting on His hands, as though they had minds of their own and needed to be contained. "On the other hand—for formality's sake—perhaps we should review a few of the allegations. Your wife lists three separate incidents of sexual indiscretion in which she alleges you have been involved during the past year."

She was only aware of three? This was going to be easier than Allan had imagined.

"Generally speaking, such behavior is unacceptable for clergy. Ordinarily, if you were found guilty of these offenses, you would be asked to resign from your position. So I must ask you—might you possibly in some general manner or another have engaged in any sort of behavior which might be construed in certain circumstances as inappropriate?"

Allan considered the question.

"Perhaps in some general way. But hey, who's perfect?"

"You need say nothing more. Are any of your parishioners aware of your wife's allegations?"

Allan nodded his head back and forth in a vague sort of way.

"I understand that per My direction you've taken a temporary paid leave of absence from your pastoral responsibilities."

"I have not set foot on the church grounds since the beginning of the year."

"I recommend you continue your leave while I examine the charges against you. I'm certain your congregation will continue sending financial contributions to the district office. The amount of those contributions could indirectly influence the outcome of my investigation in a tangential sort of way. If you understand what I mean."

"Thank you, Sir!" Allan leapt from his chair then stepped back. He sensed a hug would be inappropriate and he certainly was not about to shake The Bishop's overly disinfected hand.

"Keep your nose clean, Allan, and one day you'll be sitting behind a desk in a Bishop's office such as this one." Mainlaver rose and nodded at the framed print on the wall behind him. "I've seen you preach. You've got what it takes."

Allan smiled tentatively. Surely The Bishop was seriously overestimating his abilities. All things to all people? Lately he felt more like nothing to anybody. Besides, The Bishop did not seem to understand that no matter how beloved Allan might become, he would always be an ass to someone.

Eighteen

Gerald Schwartz

Sometime in the past half hour the drizzle had eased, the enveloping fog had dissipated, and the traffic had multiplied. Gerald was so entranced in his own predicament that he had failed to notice the subtly changing environs until now.

After their visit with The Bishop he had closed his eyes, leaned into the plush leather passenger seat, and timed his breathing until the steady squeaking of the windshield wipers became the inexorable pulse of the ocean. He had seen her again this morning. The hospital staff left the two of them alone because he was the pastor and she was going to die. In the darkened room, he prayed at her bedside, clutching her hand in his own.

In the name of the Father and of the Son and of the Holy Spirit. Into your hands, O merciful Savior, I commend your servant, Kristina Kirch. Acknowledge, I humbly beseech you, a sheep of your own fold, a lamb of your own flock, a sinner of your own redeeming.

When he closed his eyes he saw not the withered comatose figure before him but a young woman with sparkling eyes the color of the place where sky meets water on the brightest day of summer. The woman Joseph Franklin once loved, the one Gerald would forever cherish, if only in his imagination.

I've prayed for you, Kristina. What more can I do? You'll be gone soon, and I'll miss our moments together. I could never talk with Margaret like this. Honestly, I can't speak to anyone like this. I hide behind my books, my black suit and clerical collar, my intellectual snobbery. I can't even talk to God without pulling out a pretentious prayer book. Who am I without my collar? Just this failure of a man who never learned how to love . . .

Weiss overcorrected his steering on a curve, jerking Gerald awake. They passed a traffic sign indicating Pittsburgh was seventeen miles away.

"Taking the long way home?" Gerald asked.

"We could use a bit of diversion," said Weiss. "I know this place outside of Pittsburgh. They've got a great buffet."

The unfruitful audience with The Bishop had spiked Gerald's appetite. The only item on his docket for the rest of the day was a late afternoon meeting of the men's upstairs restroom renovation committee, which would do better without his input.

"So Gerald, this vote—when is it?"

"They've scheduled a congregational meeting following the evening service on Ash Wednesday. I preach, preside at communion, administer the imposition of ashes, and then await my fate."

"Ash Wednesday? Do you still observe that?"

"Of course."

"Why?"

"Why? Because it marks the beginning of Lent—forty days of solemn preparation leading to the culminating observance of the Triduum. The heart of Christian liturgical practice for centuries."

"I convinced the council at NEW CREATION!!! to do away with Lent."

"'Do away' with Lent?"

"It's depressing enough in February without carrying on about sin and death. We replaced it two years ago with the Pre-Spring Jesus Fling. We decorate the church with neon lights and mirror balls with crosses on them. It's a bit retro. But it goes over well."

"Retro?"

"Oh yeah. Who am I kidding? Ash Wednesday—that's retro."

"You've eliminated the imposition of ashes?"

"We've also quit burning people at the stake. Seriously, Gerald, I can't believe anyone in the 21st century would participate in a morbid rite where you smear little black crosses across their forehead."

"I suppose you've come up with something better."

"We have an activity where the children get smiley face tattoos on their cheeks."

"If I may be so bold as to ask—where is God in this?"

"God?"

"Yes. God. The Almighty Omniscient One. Creator of Heaven and Earth. Ever heard of Him?"

"You can lay off the sarcasm. You need to understand that for most of history God has played a much too important role in organized religion. Personally, I don't think God is either organized or religious. Organized religion—that's nothing but a fantasy. We take Jesus and turn him into whoever we want him to be. You want him to be an old-fashioned defender of orthodoxy because you're afraid of the ways the world is changing."

"And I suppose you've got Jesus figured out."

"Let's put it this way—I've figured out who most people want Jesus to be."

"Enlighten me."

"People want Jesus to be their friend. Their buddy. They want him to like the things they like, agree with their opinions, overlook their shortcomings."

"Buddy Jesus?"

"Everyone needs a buddy."

"Why is it that you aspire to charm everyone except me?"

"Because I respect you."

Weiss had pulled into a crowded parking lot. A signboard near the entrance announced that the establishment had fifteen kinds of beers on tap, early bird specials, and daily shows till closing.

"Dinner theatre," said Weiss. "My treat."

+++

It took a minute for Gerald's eyes to adjust to the darkened atmosphere and another one for him to realize where they were. They had followed two men in business suits down a rain-streaked sidewalk and through an entrance with tinted glass doors. Weiss had slipped what appeared to be a $50 bill into the hand of a large man with a crew cut and bushy goatee. The man turned and sneered at Gerald as he led them to a table across the room in front of a circular stage surrounded by flashing lights.

Large screen televisions covered every wall and corner of the room. The plush carpeting, linen tablecloths, and oversized padded chairs reminded Gerald of a theater in Atlantic City where Margaret had once cajoled him into sitting through a three-hour performance by an Elvis impersonator.

On the stage closest to them, a few feet away, a young woman with caramel-colored skin, flowing black hair, and a tattoo just above each of her fully-revealed, surgically-enhanced breasts, gyrated in rhythm to a song with garbled lyrics. Weiss, who had been gawking like a 6-year-old at the circus since they sat down, hummed along. Most of the patrons wore sports jackets. Others were dressed in formal business attire. Gerald could not locate anyone else wearing a clerical suit.

"I don't feel comfortable here," said Gerald, trying not to shout yet still be heard over the music.

"Don't get righteous on me. We came here for you," Weiss said.

"I didn't ask you to bring me to a strip club."

"It's not a strip club. It's an adult entertainment center."

"Excuse my semantic gaffe. I want to leave."

"Listen, Gerald—you told me you haven't thought about sex in months. That isn't normal. You need to get out more. Besides, nobody knows us here. We're out of my TV viewing area." Weiss said all this without shifting his gaze from the woman on stage.

"Oh hell."

"We look but we don't touch. I'm a celibate man these days. Think of it as a religious experience. We behold the beauty of God's good creation. See, that one up there—she reminds me of the 23rd Psalm."

"The Lord is her shepherd?"

"Her cup runneth over."

"Those can't be real."

"I don't know. Why don't you ask her?"

When it became apparent Weiss had no intention of leaving, Gerald ordered a pitcher of microbrew. After a trip to the buffet, he settled into his padded chair, which afforded him a perfect view of a television showing highlights from the last World Series. Another screen, nearly ten feet high, featured breaking news from the war in Iraq.

Gerald would not admit it to Weiss, but this place was fantastic. He would not mind spending the rest of the afternoon here. The buffet consisted of one of the best spreads he had ever seen—leg of lamb, beef Wellington, smoked salmon, crème brule, and chocolate torte. This was pure heaven for a man who had subsisted for weeks on Tater Tot hot dish and Jello salad.

+++

When Gerald returned from his second trip to the restroom, the woman Weiss had pointed out earlier stood beside his chair.

"Hey, Gerald," Weiss shouted over the music. "She wants to dance for you."

Gerald had supposed the young woman would leave when he sat down but she continued to stand incommodiously close. Because of the way she had situated herself Gerald could not avoid staring at her breasts which, except for two heart-shaped pasties, were now completely revealed. It had been awhile since Gerald had seen a bare bosom at this proximity. Even Margaret had rarely come this close.

Gerald reclined. The dancer leaned toward him. She smelled like peppermint. Did Weiss expect him to sink to the depths of moral depravity and ogle this woman?

"I've always had this fantasy about seducing a priest," said the dancer. She winked at Gerald.

"I'm not a priest."

"You just enjoy dressing like one?" She smiled flirtatiously. "Whatever turns you on."

"He wants to know if they're real," Weiss shouted over the music.

The dancer giggled as she cradled her breasts in her hands. "Everyone wants to know." She paused and examined her ample bust. "What is real, anyway?" It sounded like a philosophical query, the way she said it.

Her breasts were so close to Gerald's face that he felt like he was being smothered. He would get up and leave were it not for the fact that his penis was now fully erect.

The dancer began to sway her hips. "You're cute," she said. "What shall I call you?"

Weiss leaned across the table and shouted, "He likes to go by the name of Joseph. Isn't that right, Father Franklin?"

The dancer flicked her tongue against her upper lip. "So who do you want me to be?" she said.

Gerald sensed that other patrons were laughing at him. With his clerical collar he must have stood out like a blemish on a fashion model's face.

"I can be anyone you want me to be," said the dancer.

"All things to all people!" Weiss shouted, guffawing like a man who was egregiously pleased with himself. Gerald closed his eyes and covered them with his hands.

Margaret had tried to dance for him. Once. In an effort to revitalize their love life, shortly after their move to Dustin, she had purchased a lace negligee from a mail order catalogue. It was supposed to be packaged in a plain brown wrapper. By the end of the day it arrived everyone who had ears to hear and lips to speak knew about it. Roger Weinwright adjourned the council meeting early that night with a wink because "Pastor's got some business to take care of at the parsonage."

Gerald closed the blinds in their bedroom but felt certain someone was outside watching for Margaret's silhouette in the window.

"Turn off the light," he said.

"Don't you like to look at me?"

"Of course. I don't want anyone else to see you. Turn off the light."

"That defeats the purpose of dressing up in lingerie and dancing, doesn't it?"

It must have. Because after Gerald turned off the light Margaret slipped out of her teddy, threw on a sweat suit, and disappeared into the spare bedroom.

When Gerald opened his eyes he could still smell the peppermint.

"She left?" he asked Weiss, who appeared visibly disappointed.

"You were supposed to play along. I paid her good money to dance for you."

+++

Gerald did not speak until they were nearly half way back to Dustin.

"You humiliated me."

"You need to lighten up. I was trying to help you."

"How officious of you."

"It was harmless adult entertainment."

"I don't want to talk to you."

It was at least another hour to Dustin. Gerald stared out the window.

"Look, I'm sorry. Talk to me, please." Weiss started to whimper like a wounded dog. "Listen, Gerald. When you told me you hadn't thought about sex in months, I actually envied you. I can't even have a conversation with a woman without imagining what she looks like naked."

Gerald struggled to concentrate, distracted at the moment by a sharp pain in his bladder.

"I'm in dire need of a restroom."

"I'm spilling my guts. Is that all you can say?"

"I don't want to be your confessor."

"I want us to be friends, Gerald."

"I don't need any friends. Please, shut up."

"All right then."

A mile down the road, Weiss pulled up to a small brick church. There were no other dwellings in the proximity and no signs identifying the purpose of the building. Half a dozen cars were parked on a stretch of gravel road along the side of the church and lights were visible through the fog-covered windows.

A pimply-faced girl, no older than twelve, met Gerald at the entrance with a piercing gaze.

"Welcome, sir. The adults are in there," she said, pointing to a closed door that appeared to lead to the sanctuary. Gerald heard the screeching of an electric guitar and the steady pounding of a drum.

"I'm in need of a restroom." The excruciating effort of holding in the contents of his bladder had brought tears to his eyes.

"You smell like beer and cigarettes. You smell like my Daddy."

The girl pointed down a set of stairs. Gerald brushed by her, nearly toppling over her, and headed toward the stairs as fast as he could, limping like a wounded deer.

The urinal in the men's room, which stood nearly as high as Gerald did, was not functioning properly. A continuous stream of water gushed down from the top of it with a deafening roar that echoed through the spacious restroom. Gerald stood before it and as droplets of water sprayed onto his jacket, the contents of his bladder spewed into the rushing torrent and were carried away down the drain. Five minutes later he stepped out of the restroom relieved of the load he had been carrying, ephemeral though it may have been.

"Come and see," the girl said when he met her again at the top of the stairs. She headed toward the door that led into the sanctuary. Gerald followed the girl, his senses dulled from too many microbrews.

A dozen people were gathered in the sanctuary, a mix of men and women. The girl appeared to be the only child. The band consisted of four members: a keyboard and bass player in addition to the guitarist and drummer. Though they had stopped playing momentarily a number of people throughout the sanctuary continued to sing.

There was a pulpit but no altar. The words *Speak, Lord, for your servant is listening*, painted in calligraphic style, graced the wall behind the pulpit. Padded folding chairs had been grouped together into two sections. Marks on the hardwood floor indicated where pews had formerly rested.

"I like to dance," the girl said. She moved to the center aisle and began to twirl. She was wearing a pink dress with a large bow on the front and a couple of brightly colored bracelets, which rattled together as she moved. A number of the adults were watching the girl closely and a man with oversized glasses and a gaudy cross around his neck made eye contact with Gerald. Time to leave.

Gerald said, "Thank you for showing me the rest room."

The girl did not acknowledge him. She continued to spin, her arms raised above her head, palms open, her eyes fixed on an indiscernible spot on the ceiling. Her neck was tilted back so that she appeared to be carrying a burdensome weight in both of her open palms. She looked too fragile to be carrying such an invisible load, as though she would soon topple over beneath its force.

The girl had been humming to the song the adults were singing, but now she began to babble like a baby. *Good Lord, she's speaking in tongues.*

Gerald had little experience with Pentecostalists. In his seminary days, he and his orthodox classmates mocked what his favorite professor called "the hysterical affectations of glossalalia." Whenever Gerald heard someone ramble on about being moved by the Spirit he could not help but cringe.

He watched now with cautious fascination as the girl gyrated and babbled incomprehensively. Twirling frenziedly, standing on tiptoes, arms uplifted, droplets of perspiration now forming on her cheeks, her head tipped back, her unblinking eyes fixed on a place only she could see, an ethereal voice rising from the back of her throat, as though God were a ventriloquist and she His dummy. Her nonsensical babbling gave way to a distinctly familiar unspoken language. Familiar to Gerald, at least.

The adults had stopped singing. Most of them were now gathered around the girl. The man wearing the gaudy cross slapped Gerald on the shoulder. "Do you know what Vera is saying, Father?" he asked. "She speaks that phrase all the time. But none of us can understand."

In an instant Gerald recognized exactly what the girl was saying. Over and over she said it, chanting the phrase like it was a mantra. Gerald could scarcely believe what he was hearing. This girl, no more than twelve years old, was chanting in Latin.

"What is it, Father? What is it?" the man asked again.

A woman with a mole the size of a dime above her lip, shouted, "God is speaking! Praise the Lord!"

Were he not intoxicated, Gerald might think he was in the midst of a grotesque dream.

"Tell us, Father. Tell us!"

The girl had begun to cough. She was gagging now, no longer talking, as though the words had become lodged in her throat. The veins in her neck were visible and her lips assumed a bluish tinge. She fell backward suddenly and was caught by a man who had come up behind her.

Gerald must have looked concerned because someone said, "It's all right, Father. She always does that."

Her eyes were glazed over and her lips were trembling, but the girl was breathing normally now.

"What did she say, Father? God sent you here to tell us."

"Yes! Praise Jesus!" said the woman with the mole.

"She spoke in Latin," Gerald said, louder than he intended. He paused and surveyed the church again. "Her subject-verb agreement was incorrect."

"Hallelujah!"

"Please tell us!"

"Yes! Yes! Praise Jesus!"

Gerald glanced nervously at the expectant crowd that had gathered around him. "What she said . . ."

"Come on, Father. We need to know."

"She said . . . 'You is always an ass to someone.'"

Before anyone could respond, Gerald fled from the sanctuary and out the front of the building, where Weiss was waiting, with the car still running, and the stereo blasting.

"That took a while," Weiss said, as Gerald sank into the passenger seat. "Holy shit, Old Man, you look like you've seen a ghost."

Part Three

Winter into Spring

Nineteen

Betty Mundy

After living in Dustin for fifty-four years, Betty felt she knew her neighbors well enough to predict how they would respond to the news about Danny and Dougie. She supposed even lifelong friends like Milly and Jane would stop talking to her. So be it. At least she had Sophie.

Two days after receiving the threatening message, Betty trudged into the church office and discovered Edna hunched over a file cabinet. She was wearing a pair of sweat pants, which were several sizes too small. It wasn't the kind of sight Betty wanted to see first thing in the morning . . . or any time of day, for that matter. The peaceful feeling she had experienced two nights before had dissipated. When Edna turned around, Betty looked her straight in the eye.

"How dare you try to bully me," she said before Edna could speak.

Edna jerked her head back like a boxer surprised at receiving the first blow. "I'm no bully."

"You've threatened to tell everyone about Dougie. That's blackmail."

"If you don't want people to talk about your son, tell him he shouldn't do those sorts of things in public."

What things? Had Edna seen the boys walking arm in arm down Main Street? They wouldn't do that, would they?

"Who have you told?"

"Nobody yet. But if you're gonna keep interfering with my firing of Pastor Schwartz I might have to share what I know with Dorothy." This was akin to saying she was going to stand on the summit of Mount Kiersey and proclaim it with a megaphone until every creature with ears in a fifty mile radius had heard it. *Go Tell It on the Mountain* was Dorothy's favorite hymn.

"What are you doing in here?"

"I'm council vice-president. I have a right to be here."

"Get out of my office!"

"This isn't your office."

"Well, whose office is it?"

"This is a church. It's the Lord's office."

"Then get out of the Lord's office before I pluck out your eyes and cut off your hands!"

"What's got into you?"

"I'm doing what Jesus would do. Now get your you-know-what out of here!"

For once Edna was speechless. She put down the folder she was holding and waddled toward the door. Before she left the office she glanced nervously over her shoulder as though she were afraid Betty might act upon her threat.

Betty could hardly believe the way she was talking. What had gotten into her? Now that she had started down the highway to hell, there appeared to be no turning back. She had taken the Lord's name in vain, stopped praying, and threatened to mutilate the council vice-president. Worst of all, she was starting to doubt the word of God. How could the Bible say homosexuals were sinful when so many kind people felt otherwise?

She and Sophie discussed the matter later that afternoon while driving to Altoona in Betty's car to have coffee. They limited their conversation to the weather and the best way to make pickle relish until they were off the mountain. You never knew when a passer-by might be reading your lips.

"I don't know what to think," said Betty when they were almost on the outskirts of Altoona. "I always figured if I followed the Bible and went to church, everything would turn out fine. But it isn't so black and white anymore."

"Love complicates things. You know."

"Tell me, Sophie—did you ever think Dougie might be gay?"

"Maybe. I never thought it was my business one way or the other."

"What about Horace? Did other people know about him? I mean, I never did."

"I suspect some did."

"And the Franklins' daughter. I still can't believe that."

When Betty thought about the Franklins raising a gay daughter, she started to wonder whether Dougie might be right—that homosexuals are born the way they are and cannot change. Certainly the Franklins would not have permitted their daughter to become a homosexual if they had control over the matter.

"Why didn't I know Audrey Franklin was gay? There aren't any secrets in Dustin—are there?" said Betty.

"That's what they say."

"Then why didn't I know?"

"Maybe there are some secrets in Dustin after all."

"There are?"

"Well, there's those secrets we keep from ourselves."

"What do you mean?"

"There's those things we know that we don't want to know. So we pretend we don't know them."

"Yeah?"

"But sometimes that's hard to do. So we find something else to keep us busy."

"What do you mean?"

"Oh well, it can be anything really. Like television or gossip. Or drinking too much. Even going to church. You know."

"I suppose."

"Then after a while we get so busy we forget we ever knew those things we didn't want to know."

"Uh huh."

Betty nodded and pretended she understood what Sophie was talking about. Neither of them said a word for a few minutes, which was fine since they were at the city limits and Betty needed to concentrate on her driving.

While they were sitting at a red light, Betty finally spoke. "You really loved Horace, didn't you?"

"I did." Sophie had a whimsical expression on her face. For a few seconds, Betty could have sworn her friend looked twenty years younger.

"You're right, Sophie. If I didn't love Dougie so much this wouldn't be so hard for me. Love makes things more complicated."

"It makes them more lively, too. You know."

They stopped at a coffee house where all the patrons were half their age. Betty felt out of place but at least she was almost a hundred percent certain she wouldn't run into anybody she knew there. The girl behind the counter had earrings in both nostrils, above her eyebrows, around her mouth, through her tongue, in her belly button—which was exposed for the world to see—and probably in a number of other places Betty did not want to imagine. They found a cozy table in a secluded corner.

Sophie said she admired Betty for what she was about to do. She promised to support her no matter what anyone said.

"I feel embarrassed."

"Just imagine other embarrassing things that have happened to you. It can't be worse than those. You know."

"I suppose."

Betty recalled the time many years before when she was teaching Sunday School to the Sixth Graders. They were a rowdy group, and a number of the boys liked to poke fun at how proper she was, especially Andy Weinwright, Dick's youngest boy. Fortunately, Andy was absent the day they studied the commandment about not committing adultery.

Then they read the story in the Old Testament in which God makes Balaam's donkey speak out loud, in plain English, just like a real person. Unfortunately, the King James Bible, the only version Sunday School superintendent/ dictator of curriculum Harriet Redgrave would permit, referred to the donkey as an "ass."

Betty did not want to sound prudish, especially when the word was printed right there in the Bible. Still she was sure that Sixth Grade boys, especially Andy Weinwright, would find it funny to hear her say the word "ass" in Sunday school, even if she was referring to a donkey. The whole matter made her so nervous that when she finally taught the lesson she said, "This is a story about how God spoke through Balaam's donkey's ass."

Andy, who had the ability to pass gas at will, started to snicker. "I can speak through my ass, too," he said, before cutting loose.

Though he was in his thirties now, and slightly more mature than he was as a Sixth Grader, sometimes Andy Weinwright still smirked at Betty, and she knew exactly what he was thinking.

+++

They stopped at the mall. Betty decided on a whim to have her hair done in one of those expensive salons where the beauticians are certified graduates of SGCOB. On yet another whim, she bought a flashy sleeveless rayon dress that was totally inappropriate for any upcoming January social functions.

"I feel guilty," she said, standing before a full-length mirror at Boscov's in her new dress. She had decided to wear it home despite the freezing temperature.

Sophie shook her head. "Guilt is only good when you've done something wrong. You haven't done anything wrong. You know."

"I haven't?"

Sophie shook her head again. "You're a wonderful wife and mother. You've raised a son you can be proud of."

"I am proud of him."

"It's okay to reward yourself. You're about to do a brave thing."

"I am," she said, looking herself in the eyes. "It's strange, Sophie. But since this happened, I've been standing up to Clarence more. I know he's the master of the house but he's been no help during this."

"Men aren't nearly as strong as they pretend to be. You know."

"He's so hard to talk to. That's why I appreciate this. What we're doing right now."

"You look wonderful, Betty Loretto Mundy."

"Don't say that."

Sophie was admiring Betty's reflection in the mirror in a way that made Betty feel giddy and gratified and nervous all at once.

"It's true. You look beautiful. You know."

"I do?"

Sophie nodded. Betty knew it was a vain thing to say and she wasn't sure she believed it, but she said it anyway, "I do."

"Now you need a new pair of shoes."

+++

They were on their way out of Altoona when Betty noticed a pet store she had always wanted to check out. Without signaling, she slammed on the brakes—which wasn't easy to do in her new stilettos—crossed two lanes of traffic, and pulled into the parking lot. No one gave her the finger.

"Now what?" asked Sophie, with a devious grin.

Betty said, "I've always wanted a parakeet."

+++

Betty wore her new dress and shoes to the women's guild meeting. She could not remember the last time she had dressed up for any event that was not a funeral or a wedding. A church meeting was hardly on par with the prom or a night of dancing at the Legion Hall in Naptonville. Still it felt good, almost glamorous, to apply a bit of makeup to her cheeks and a dab of Mountain Spring on either side of her neck.

Halfway through supper, Clarence stared at her with a puzzled look on his face like he had noticed something was different but could not figure out what it was. She could hardly blame him for not noticing her haircut. He was still recovering from the shock of having a new pet in the house.

As she headed out the door Clarence looked up from the television and said, "That's the dress I bought at Walmart for your fiftieth birthday, ain't it? Still looks good on ya."

+++

It was a typical meeting. Milly made the coffee. Dorothy got them started with devotions—a delightful reading from *The Peleg Principle.* After Irmalee led a rousing version of *In the Garden*, Edna said a nice prayer for Lois Warner, who was unable to attend because she had come down with a bad case of malaria.

The women played a few rounds of low stakes Bingo, all of which were won by Lillian Sutherland. In the final game they played for a set of flannel bed sheets with the Ten Commandments printed on them, donated by Gert Arnason. The prize included a pillow cover that read *Thou Shalt Not Commit Adultery* which, as Harriet pointed out, might make a husband think twice before straying. A minor argument broke out when Eleanor accused Lillian and Edna of cheating.

After that, Edna encouraged everyone to sign a petition denouncing the American Atheist Society, which was trying to have the word *God* removed from the Bible, according to a television evangelist Edna's mother-in-law had recently watched. Edna made a good point—if those atheists succeeded at taking God out of the Bible it would only be a matter of time before they took over the whole country.

They spent forty-five minutes arguing about whether to contribute $15 to the Greater Dustin Council of Churches Send-A-Kid to Camp fund, then another twenty-five minutes arguing about whether to specify that the money could only be used to sponsor a Lutheran child since those Methodist kids are a bunch of hellions.

About halfway through the Send-A-Kid to Camp discussion, Betty noticed some of the other ladies staring at her. Before the meeting she had received a number of compliments on her dress and haircut, but now Betty sensed people were not staring at her in admiration. It felt more like the way people look at the bereaved during a funeral.

As the meeting drew to a close Betty felt her heart beating rapidly. She noticed her hands were shaking. Had they been shaking the whole time? Was that why people were staring at her? Finally Edna spoke the words Betty had been anticipating all evening. "Does anyone have any announcements?"

Betty stood up immediately. Before Edna had time to acknowledge her, she cleared her throat, glanced at Sophie for moral support, and said, "I would like to announce that my son Dougie is a homosexual. And what's more, he married his cousin Danny, who is also a homosexual."

Instead of leaving, as she had planned to do, Betty sat down again. She was not sure why she did that. It may have been because she was hungry and did not want to miss the key lime pie they were serving during the after-meeting fellowship time. Or maybe she was curious to see how people would respond to her. Or perhaps it was her way of showing Edna that she would not be bullied.

Whatever the reason, Betty realized right then that not walking out at that moment was the most courageous act of her life. Even more courageous than making the announcement about Dougie and Danny, which, of course, was the second bravest thing she had ever done.

Edna glanced at Dorothy, who shrugged her shoulders. "Any more announcements?" asked Edna.

Betty stood up again and said, "In Massachusetts. That's where they got married. Not here, of course."

When Betty sat down a second time, Edna said, "I want to thank Jane for making dessert. This meeting is a-journed. Let's eat."

During refreshment time, Jane and Milly sat next to Betty as usual. Joyce and Irmalee sat across from her. They marveled about the pie for a few minutes. Then they talked about Irmalee's cousin's husband's new snow blower and Joyce's grandson, who was going to Iraq in a few weeks. As they were leaving, a few of the women complimented Betty on her new dress. No one said a word about Dougie.

+++

Betty was not in the habit of entering Pastor Schwartz's office without his permission, but she had to know what people were saying about her, and at the moment this seemed the best way to do so. She knew Most Everyone would linger in the kitchen after the meeting, returning the cups, plates and sugar bowl to locations where no one else would be able to find them. Betty pressed her ear to the heating vent that led to the kitchen. Not that she needed to. Edna's voice carried like that of a drill sergeant—or a preacher.

"If it weren't for us, nothing would get done around here."

"Come on, girls. Let's speed this up. I don't have much time."

"Look at the dust on this counter."

"You can't win the battle with dust."

"You're right about that."

"I thought it was a good meeting, Edna."

"We really could have done without those interruptions. That sort of thing never happened when I was guild president."

"You mean Betty?"

"What kind of mother goes around telling everyone her son's a homo?"

"She's mad at him. That's why she's doing it."

"Of course she is. Cheating on his fiancée with another girl. And knocking her up besides."

"Are you sure he made her get an abortion?"

"I told you—Priscilla saw it with her own eyes. She was there with Fetuses for Jesus. They were marching at one of those abortion clinics in Pittsburgh. And in the middle of the protest Dougie steps out of the clinic with this girl."

"She's sure it was Dougie?"

"She saw it with her own eyes. The girl pretended she worked at the clinic. But Priscilla found out later she was there for an abortion."

"Betty's got to be upset. You know how she feels about abortion being murder and all."

"Well, she ought to be ashamed. It's in the Bible, isn't it, Harriet?"

"For thou hast covered me in my mother's womb. Psalms 131:13."

"Poor Betty wants to be a grandma so bad. And now Dougie and that girl went and killed her grandbaby."

"If God takes your child away that's one thing."

"Oh, don't think about that now, Edna. That was nothing like this."

"Before I formed thee in the belly I knew thee. Jeremiah 1:5."

"When Betty stood up and said Dougie got married to that colored cousin of his, I didn't know whether to laugh out loud or feel sorry for her."

"Same here. Being a good Christian, I kept my mouth shut."

"Nobody would believe something like that anyway. I mean, we've all seen Dougie grow up and come to church every Sunday and go hunting with his Dad and everybody knows he's not like that."

"There's nobody round here like that 'cept Mrs. Schwartz and she wasn't from round here."

"I feel sorry for Dougie. His own mother making up lies about him."

Betty had heard enough. *Lord, have mercy*. This was much worse than anything she could have ever imagined.

Twenty

Betty Mundy

February 2, 2005

Dear Betty,

How delightful to hear from you! I am well these days and enjoying life to its fullest. Beth and Todd both live within a couple hours of me. I see them and the grandchildren—four now! —frequently. Audrey is still in San Francisco with her partner, Ruth. They have been together for nearly twelve years now. I saw them last November and was pleased to learn they are adopting a little girl from China, hopefully before the end of the year.

I understand how difficult Doug's coming out must have been for you, not to mention the shock of his elopement. It's a different world these days. I'm also sorry to learn of the stress you're experiencing because of the effort to force your current pastor to resign.

The people of Abiding Truth were so forgiving after they learned of Joe's indiscretions with Kristina. I suppose it's easier for people to be gracious with their pastor when the church is thriving than when it is in decline. But as you say, no one talks about the matter now that Joe has passed on.

Back to Doug. I am impressed with your openness about your son's sexual orientation. In all the years we lived in Dustin, Joe and I never felt comfortable publicly sharing that Audrey is gay. Things were different then, of course. I still find it disconcerting that Joe was able to confess his infidelity to the congregation yet could not share the simple truth of his daughter's homosexuality. Then, as now, most Christians were more accepting of adultery among heterosexuals than fidelity between homosexuals.

I am convinced that for some people homosexuality is a natural state of being. I believe God loves gays as much as the rest of us, and that God approves of their relationships when they are loving and monogamous. I am so happy my Audrey found Ruth, and I have a feeling Doug and Danny are in it for the long haul too.

I'm glad you joined the support group in Altoona and met my dear friend Vera. It took Joe awhile to accept Audrey's sexuality, so maybe there's hope for Clarence! Don't give up on him.

One more thing—I don't know where your current pastor stands on the matter but I recommend you approach him about blessing Doug and Dan's relationship. It is important the boys make God a part of their lives. I'd love to be a support for you and hope you'll stay in touch.

Much love,

Gracie

+++

February 9th was marked prominently on all the church calendars, but when the day came Betty felt like she was at least a week behind. The arrival of Ash Wednesday meant extra work, including the tedious task of preparing worship bulletins for mid-week Lenten services. The additional paperwork inevitably led to the breakdown of the church's overworked copier, which caused Betty to lose her concentration and make more mistakes than usual. During one particularly stressful year when Reverend Franklin was pastor, Betty had accidentally typed, "Come forward to receive the imposition of asses."

Betty had been mortified but Pastor Franklin laughed when he saw it and said, "My life would be easier were it not for the imposition of asses."

This year worship bulletins were the least of Betty's concerns. Edna and Dorothy had spread the most outrageous lies.

"I don't believe anything they've said about you," Jane told Betty over blueberry pie and coffee. One afternoon, Milly stopped Betty on the sidewalk in front of Bubby's. "Remember how those two told everyone my son had been arrested for selling drugs?" she said. "Not a word of that was true. I admire you for sticking up for Dougie."

So it appeared Betty had not lost any friends. At least not any that mattered. And she and Marian were working things out. Marian had apologized to the boys for her tirade in the cemetery after Betty reminded her that Marian's own marriage announcement had been rather inapt.

As Betty remembered it, Marian had returned to Dustin for the first time in a year to deliver the eulogy at their Papa's funeral while eight months pregnant. She smiled and announced before a church full of gasping Dustinians, "It's okay. I'm married to the father. By the way, he's Black."The more Betty considered what Dougie and Danny were doing, the less harmful it seemed. It still felt strange and confusing but her talks with Sophie had helped. And now this letter from Mrs. Franklin.

Betty had always felt deep respect for Gracie. Though Pastor Franklin and Pastor Schwartz had been to seminary, Betty sensed that Mrs. Franklin was as smart as either of them. Mrs. Franklin read almost as many books as Pastor Schwartz did. After Pastor Franklin's unfortunate affair, she had confided to Betty that she had contemplated divorce but having grown accustomed to a minister's life, she would probably end up marrying another pastor, so she might as well stay with the one she had.

Betty admired how Gracie forgave and supported her husband when he needed her and now she respected her all the more for standing by her daughter. Betty could not argue with Gracie's comment that God should be part of the boys' relationship. She planned to broach the topic of a blessing with Pastor Schwartz as soon as this hullabaloo about firing him was over.

+++

You could always tell who had been to church on Ash Wednesday. Devout Christians proudly displayed their cross-shaped ashen markings and refused to wash their foreheads until they went to bed. As Betty scanned the crowded basement hall she noted that nearly every member of Abiding Truth was here, including a number who were supposedly homebound. Mabel Hawthorne and Gert Arnason, both of whom were peeved at Pastor, sat with Lillian Sutherland—who sported a new permanent, but no ashen cross.

Pastor Schwartz was standing near the kitchen door, talking with Ed Jacobson, who held a can of beer in one hand and a lit cigarette in the other. Apparently no one had the heart to tell Mr. Jacobson that smoking in the church had been banned in 1999.

"Seeing as I'm the President and all, I'd like to call this meeting to order," said Roger Weinwright, while people were being seated. "Now The Wife has a few things to say."

"We're good Christian people here," said Edna, not missing a beat. She glanced at the rest of the council members who were seated with her at the head table and waited for them to nod their heads. "We would never leave our ex-pastor out in the cold. The council has decided to let Reverend Schwartz stay in the parsonage till he finds a new place to live. We'll provide him with a decent severance package, which is mighty Christian of us considering our money situation."

Jane jumped up and did not wait to be acknowledged. "Some of us don't appreciate you referring to Reverend Schwartz as our ex-pastor before the vote is taken."

Edna glared at Jane with the expression she always used when someone challenged her authority. "All I'm saying is we ain't going to let Pastor Schwartz go homeless. All right?"

Betty turned to Sophie and whispered, "I wish we could get this over with." As soon as she said it, Harriet appeared, standing a few feet behind Edna, the ashen marking on her forehead glistening beneath the overhead fluorescent light. She looked paler than usual.

"Let's get this going, Roger. I don't have much time," growled Harriet.

She took one step forward, glared across the room at Pastor Schwartz, and toppled onto the floor. Her head hit the tile-covered cement with such a sickening thud Betty knew immediately she was dead. Someone gasped and someone else screamed and bedlam broke loose as people gathered around Harriet.

"Call 9-1-1!" shouted Leroy. When Betty looked up, he and Dick were kneeling beside Harriet and had turned her onto her side. Leroy had pinched her nose shut and was blowing air into her mouth.

"Let me try!" shouted Dick. He began to push against Harriet's gaunt chest and continued to do so for at least two minutes. Betty heard gasping and whispering but no one in the room was crying or appeared particularly upset.

Finally Dick looked up, with sweat glistening against his forehead. "She's a goner," he said.

"No pulse," said Leroy. He clasped Harriet's withered wrist in his hand, then placed her arm gently on the floor. From across the room Betty caught a glimpse of Harriet's face, enough to see her badly disfigured nose and blood smeared cheeks. Betty felt light-headed and had to turn away.

"Everybody get back!" shouted Leroy. He remained hunched over the body as onlookers strained their necks to peer at Harriet.

Sophie came up beside Betty and squeezed her arm. "She was right. You know."

"What do you mean?" said Betty.

"She didn't have much time."

Dick summoned Pastor Schwartz to come forward and say a prayer.

"Pastor looks okay tonight, doesn't he?" Jane whispered to Betty.

"I noticed, too," said Betty.

"He shaved off his moustache, didn't he?"

"Heavens, Jane, he hasn't had a moustache for years."

"Something's different."

The room grew silent as Pastor knelt next to Dick and Leroy. He cleared his throat like he always did when he was about to preach or pray. *What would he do?* In the past seven years Betty could not recall Harriet saying one nice thing about Pastor Schwartz. Then again, she could not recall Harriet saying anything nice about anyone. Even Chip the parakeet was more pleasant to listen to than Harriet, and Clarence had taught him a few choice expressions.

Usually in situations such as this, Pastor read from his prayer book but now he began to speak unscripted, the way Betty used to pray when she was still speaking with God.

"Father," he said, "You gave Harriet to us and n-now it's time for her to b-be with you. She is . . . w-was a unique woman and—we ask that you b-bless Harriet as she comes to you and joins again with . . . with her husband Harold."

Several people gasped. Immediately Dick grabbed Pastor's arm and said, "'Scuse me for inneruptin' Reverend—but considerin' how Harold beat the crap out of Harriet here on earth maybe she'd best not see him again in the next life."

"Harold beat her?" Pastor Schwartz asked Dick.

"Broke a few bones as I recall," said Dick.

"He nearly killed her a couple times," said Leroy.

"All best forgotten," said Dick.

"That's horrendous," said Pastor.

Harold Redgrave had been gone at least twenty years. He shot himself in the head after supper one night, in front of Harriet and all the children. This was the first time Betty could recall his name being mentioned in public since then.

Pastor Schwartz placed his hand on the back of Harriet's head and prayed, "Forgive her, Father, for she knew not what she did."

+++

Edna decided to continue with the vote because "that's what Harriet would have wanted." The ambulance had come and gone and someone had cleaned up the blood that remained on the floor after they removed the body. No one would stand on the spot where Harriet had died, as though it had become special ground. Sacred or haunted—Betty wasn't sure which.

Edna nodded at Rogie, who promptly began distributing ballots. Betty glanced at hers, which read, *Keep Pastor, Fire Pastor, Circle One.* Apparently Edna had taken the liberty of copying the ballots, since this was the first time Betty had seen them.

As people voted, Betty sensed a strange levity in the room, which seemed inappropriate in light of the fact that someone had just died. She had the feeling that despite all that had happened, everything would turn out for good.

+++

"It's a tie!"

These were the first words Betty had ever heard Les Cresco speak in his official capacity as a council member. He was quiet anyways, and she never knew what he was thinking. He seemed the perfect person to count the ballots.

"That can't be!" Edna shouted. She nodded at Dorothy, who reached across the table and grabbed the ballots from Les's hands.

"He counted twice and I counted, too," said Rogie.

A tie? Now what?

A number of people started talking at once. Roger attempted to restore order by nodding at Edna. She bellowed, her voice rising above the chaotic murmuring. "Listen here. We're forgetting something. Harriet didn't get a chance to vote."

"Hey, that's right!" said Dorothy.

Edna said, "Everyone knows what she thought about this matter. If she hadn't checked up on Pastor Schwartz and found out all he's been doing wrong, we wouldn't be here tonight."

Dorothy said, "It's our Christian duty to show our respect to Mrs. Redgrave. Let her cast the deciding vote."

Chaos resumed. So many people started talking, Betty could barely tell who was saying what.

"Dead people can't vote!"

"She wasn't dead an hour ago."

"We weren't voting an hour ago."

"If we'd started on time like she wanted us to, then she would have voted."

"There's other people who are members of this church who aren't here tonight and they didn't get to vote either."

"But she was here!"

"This whole damn thing is ridiculous!" shouted Leroy, who was standing up and waving his fist, as Joyce attempted to restrain him.

Roger was so preoccupied with restoring order he either overlooked or ignored Sophie, who was standing with her hand raised, waiting to be called upon. Betty thought Sophie looked like a schoolgirl who knew the correct answer while everyone else shouted out wrong ones.

"Being as I'm President and all, I hereby command everyone to shut up!" roared Roger. Finally he looked at Sophie and acknowledged her.

Sophie stood and waited for Leroy, Dick, and a couple of others to cease their bickering. She spoke quietly, "There is one person who's here tonight who didn't get to vote. You know."

Sophie looked toward the kitchen where Pastor Schwartz had been lounging in the shadows. There was an awkward pause. Roger sat there with his mouth wide open. All the color drained from Edna's face. She reminded Betty of a wild animal who had been caught in a trap.

Jane leapt out of her chair and sashayed into the kitchen, where she handed Pastor a blank ballot. The only time Betty could remember Pastor voting at a congregational meeting was when they were deadlocked over whether to place the Reverend Franklin Memorial Plant Stand on the left or the right side of the narthex. Betty recalled that Pastor Schwartz voted for the right side, where it was immediately placed and remained until it mysteriously moved to the left side six months later.

Pastor emerged from the kitchen. He held up the ballot and stared at it curiously.

Sophie tapped his arm and said, "It's been in your own hands all this time. You know."

Pastor glanced down at her. "What's that?" he asked.

Sophie smiled, but she did not reply.

Pastor looked out at the room and turned his head the way a person would if he were standing at the top of the mountain and taking in a panoramic view of the valley. Then he turned toward Roger and said, "Mr. President. I cast my ballot in favor of terminating my tenure as pastor of Abiding Truth. I assume this will become effective immediately, with the aforementioned severance compensation package in place."

What was he saying?

"You resignin', Pastor?" asked Roger

"No… I've just been fired."

"Are you sure?" asked Roger.

Edna elbowed her husband in the side and said, "Well, we sure are sorry to see you go."

Before she thought to stop herself Betty leapt from her seat and shouted, "No Pastor! You can't! We need you."

Pastor ignored Betty's outburst. "This being Ash Wednesday, it is appropriate I publicly acknowledge my transgressions." He wrinkled his forehead and stood perfectly still for a few seconds. Nobody said a word. Then he smiled slightly, and it reminded Betty of the way he used to smile, when he had first moved to Dustin. "I'm trying to say—I deserve to be fired. I've been an ass to all of you."

Dick bellowed, "Holy shit! That's the first thing he's said in seven years I can understand."

Pastor Schwartz couldn't leave. If he left there would be no one at Abiding Truth to bless Dougie and Danny. Irmalee's sister's boyfriend surely wouldn't do it.

Betty stood and said, "No, Pastor! You can't quit! Not yet."

"He's got to be out by Sunday," said Edna.

"Says who?' said Jane.

"Irmalee's sister's boyfriend will be here to lead church on Sunday," said Edna. "Council decided he'd take over when Pastor got fired."

"You mean we're without a pastor till Sunday?" said Jane.

"It's just a few days," said Edna.

"We can't be without a pastor," said Jane.

"Poor Harriet's died and her kids will be coming into town for the funeral and need some pastoral comforting," said Betty. She doubted Harriet's children would return for the funeral. If they did, they would certainly need more than pastoral comforting.

Edna looked at Pastor and said, "Would you mind staying on 'til Saturday? I'm sure you'll want some time to wrap things up."

Roger and Rogie stood up and headed toward the door, while Edna rambled on about how there were no hard feelings and Pastor could stay in the parsonage as long as he wanted. While she was talking, Dick tapped Betty on the shoulder. He handed her a small handwritten card. "From Roger and Edna," he said.

Your invited to the babtism of Emily Weinwright at Abiding Truth Luthern Church this Sunday Febuary 13 at 9:00 AM.

When Betty looked up she saw Jane waving a card of her own in the air and shouting, "What's this about church starting at 9:00?"

"That's right," said Edna. "Council's decided to change the time. Like it says on the new sign Roger and Rogie are putting up right now." She turned so she was looking directly at her sister across the room and said, "White sign with black letters."

Twenty-One

Gerald Schwartz

How much could happen in three days? If all went as planned, Gerald would conclude his beleaguered pastorate by bringing communion to homebound members of Abiding Truth one final time. He would provide pastoral care to Lois and Miss Kirch at the hospital. He would commence the process of vacating his office and help Betty to prepare for the tumult to come.

As he lumbered up the stairs Gerald detected the distinct aroma of Weiss's favorite cologne. He heard a rustling sound coming from his bedroom. Was Weiss in there, snooping through Gerald's personal possessions? He felt too fatigued for an argument.

When Gerald entered his bedroom Weiss was standing over Gerald's bed, frantically tucking in bed sheets. He was wearing only dress socks and a pair of briefs. Near the dresser stood a completely naked woman whom Gerald recognized as a waitress from the Highland Café. Gerald blushed and looked away. This was far worse than he had anticipated.

"What are you doing?" Gerald asked, surprised at how calm his own voice sounded.

"It was cold in the attic," said Weiss, as though that explained everything.

"You had sex in my bed?"

"Well, you sort of interrupted us—"

"Good God, Weiss! What the hell were you thinking?"

"Thinking?"

Now painfully cognizant of the ignominy he was enduring, Gerald clenched his jaw and tightened his fists, unable to contain his smoldering rage, which he had managed to suppress through two worship services and the congregational meeting. He glared uncomfortably into Weiss's eyes. Between the naked waitress, Weiss's turquoise-colored bikini briefs, and what appeared to be an electronic sexual device lying on the dresser, there were not many other places he dared to look.

"What kind of depraved pervert are you?"

"You don't understand, Gerald. It's not like that. I went 40 days without sex. I made it."

"And you celebrate by desecrating my bed?! What the hell is your problem?"

"There's no problem, Gerald. That's my point. I can go without sex whenever I want to. I proved it." Weiss spoke with a tone of unsuspecting innocence, sounding more like a child who didn't know any better than an emulated spiritual leader.

"You've proved nothing."

The waitress had scrambled into the hallway and was furiously pulling on her pants.

"I'm sorry about the bed, Gerald."

"Out!"

"How did—?"

"Out of the house! Now!"

"What do you mean?" Weiss still seemed unaware he had done anything wrong.

"Gather your belongings and leave. Get out! I never want to see you again."

"What? Where will I go?"

"Go to hell. Just leave!"

"No, Gerald. You don't understand."

Gerald reached for the closest object, which happened to be Miss Kirch's photo, sitting as usual on the bedside table. He flung it at Weiss's head. It hit the wall and cracked the plaster. The frame shattered and shards of glass showered onto the floor.

Gerald stumbled across the room and opened his closet door. *This day could not be much worse.* He slipped out of his shoes and reached for a hanger. "Holy shit!" he shrieked, jumping backward with a start.

In the darkened closet stood another young woman whom Gerald did not recognize, clad only in a brassiere and panties. She held a video camera.

"Sorry to scare you, Father," she said. "Guess I better get going."

After all the houseguests had put on their clothes and departed, Gerald slid into his living room recliner and waited for the lump in his throat to subside. Only Gerald and his demons now. He started to sob and did not stop until well after the bottle of bourbon was empty. *Too much emotion for one night.*

+++

"I'm sorry, Pastor. It's probably past your bedtime. But after all that's happened today I really need to talk to you."

Gerald glanced at his watch. It was quarter to ten. He could not remember opening the door and inviting Betty into the house. But she was sitting on the divan in his study, and unlike others she surely would not have entered the parsonage unbidden.

"I need you to do this. I know you won't want to. But if you don't, nobody will."

What a strange day it had been. For fifty-nine years, time had been a reliable constant in Gerald's life. The earth rotated on its axis in predictable increments, day after night after day, as certain as gravity and inertia and all the immutable laws of God's universe. But today something had gone astray. This was indubitably the longest day of Gerald's life.

He had risen before dawn, before the blackness of night gave way to the shrouded gray translucence of yet another February morning. Weiss had coaxed Gerald to accompany him down the mountain to Pottersfield, ostensibly to go out for breakfast.

After they ate, Weiss drove Gerald across town and parked in front of an establishment named Hair-riet's Hair'Em, which sounded like the sort of place Weiss would frequent.

"No," said Gerald, before Weiss had spoken a word.

"You have an appointment. You need to look sharp for your meeting tonight."

Five minutes later Gerald was settling into a hydraulic salon chair as the perky stylist asked, "How do you want your hair done, Father?"

"As expeditiously as possible," said Gerald. He tried not to make eye contact with the frumpy old man in the mirror before him. On the wall he noticed a framed diploma from Spooner's Grove College of Beauty, nearly twice as large as the ones he had received from Johns Hopkins and Princeton.

+++

"I see," said Gerald. If Betty knew he had not been listening she did not appear to care.

"So, I'm wondering if—well, I wasn't planning to do it so soon but it'll have to be before Sunday because you won't be my pastor after then. If you wouldn't mind," Betty's voice became so soft Gerald had to lean forward to hear it, "would you do something to bless the boys."

"Pardon me?"

"Like you do for a marriage. In the church. Dougie wants it to be in the church."

"You're asking me to preside at a gay wedding?"

"Not a wedding, exactly. A prayer. A blessing. Don't you have something in your book for this?"

Gerald was certain his well-worn copy of *Minister's Prayers for Every Imaginable Occasion* contained nothing of the sort. It was published in 1974 when such an occasion was not imaginable.

"Betty, I believe I've already articulated my position on this matter. I intend to support you. I wouldn't want to alienate your son, but you're asking me to violate my principles."

"Your principles?"

"I do have some."

"Are you saying I don't have principles, Pastor? That Dougie and Danny don't have principles?"

"What I meant—"

"Listen, Pastor." Betty spoke much louder than usual and clenched her hand in a fist. "Those boys didn't have sex 'til they were married. They pray together before they go to bed every night. Those boys love each other. I don't understand it and I don't know if it's right or wrong. But I know they're good boys."

"I don't doubt what you're saying. I'd like to assist you. But how can I invoke God's blessing upon a situation which I can not in good conscience condone?"

"Con-done?"

"What I mean—"

"Listen Pastor. I don't know what 'con-done' means. But I know you blessed Harriet. I saw it with my own eyes. And I'm sure there's nobody in Dustin who con-doned Harriet. Including yourself."

Gerald nodded, recalling his mid-morning conversation with Harriet. Unilateral verbal assault might be a more apt description. She had tracked him down at the parsonage after he had returned from Pottersfield.

"Between you and me, Reverend," said Harriet. "I'm voting for you to stay. That boyfriend of Irmalee's sister is a crackpot. Last thing we need is him messing with things around here, preaching his end of the world garbage.

"Don't get me wrong. As far as I'm concerned, you're doing a lousy job. But right now you're the best we've got."

Another classic Harriet Redgrave compliment.

"There's something else you need to know, Pastor. I went to see my cardiologist and he told me I'm a walking time bomb. I could go at any minute. But as long as I'm alive, I'll make certain you stay our pastor. You've been around long enough to know your fate is in my hands. 'If any man's work shall be burned, he shall suffer loss: but he himself shall be saved; yet so as by fire.' 1 Corinthians 3:15."

What the hell was that supposed to mean?

"I'm ready to go whenever the Lord wants me. And when I'm gone, I don't want a funeral. If those kids of mine can't be bothered to see me while I'm alive, I don't want them coming back to see me dead. When my time comes, you will speak a blessing over me and be done with it. Something from your heart. You'll owe me that much for saving your job."

Harriet paused, apparently to provide Gerald an opportunity to express his gratitude. As usual, in her presence, Gerald could not think of anything appropriate to say.

"I'm ready to go, Reverend. Nobody else needs to know this—but I miss my Harold. 'Behold, I shew you a mystery; We shall not all sleep, but we shall all be changed."

"1 Corinthians 15:51," said Gerald.

Later that day, at the noon Ash Wednesday service, Gerald pushed a thumbfull of burnt palm branches mixed with olive oil onto Harriet's forehead and proclaimed, as the liturgy decreed: "Remember you are dust, and to dust you shall return."

Those were the last words he spoke to her.

+++

"So you agree then?" asked Betty. Gerald noticed she was attempting to glare at him in a menacing fashion. She was not very good at it.

"I'm sorry, Betty. Could you please repeat that?"

"I said if you can bless one of the meanest people who ever lived, but you can't bless my dear son and my nephew—my son-in-law."

"Yes?"

"Well, then you're an even bigger you-know-what than you said."

"Than I said?"

"Don't make me say it. That word you used to describe yourself after you resigned tonight."

Betty continued to glare at him. She was getting better at it. She spoke flatly now, with the authoritative tone of one whose demands would not be denied.

"You will do it, Pastor Schwartz. Because you owe me. Because I stood up for you when you wouldn't even stand up for yourself. You will do it. Saturday afternoon at four. Sometimes you've got to do things even when you're not sure they're right."

No doubt he could compose some sort of generic blessing litany for the occasion without violating his conscience.

"Are you intending this to be a public event?"

"We'll keep it small. Of course, other people are going to know about it."

"But when Dorothy and Edna hear about this, they'll—"

"They'll do what? Fire you? As long as you're pastor you have authority to do this. They might control everything else that goes on around here, but what happens in the sanctuary is up to you.

"As far as I'm concerned, those women can do nothing to hurt me more than they already have. Besides, both of them love Abiding Truth. They won't make this public because it would hurt the church's reputation . . . Oh Pastor, I still don't understand why you decided to leave. Now that Harriet's gone, your job would have been a lot easier. I know mine's going to be."

"I suspect Harriet would have become one more ghost to haunt me."

During his thirty years in the ministry, Gerald had presided at well over a thousand public liturgical functions. But this was a first. His final pastoral act. The last would be a first. A gay blessing service.

Twenty-Two

Gerald Schwartz

REBEL PASTOR SPARKS RALLIES

This reporter recently gained "exclusive information" that an area clergyman intends to perform the first "gay wedding" in the greater Naptonville area. The tiny borough of Dustin is home to less than one thousand residents, but if Reverend Gerald Schwartz has his way, it will soon become one of western Pennsylvania's most "infamous" communities.

Though "homosexual marriage" is not legal in Pennsylvania, Schwartz intends to "preside" at a "service" involving a local gay couple, whose identities are not being revealed in order to maintain their privacy. Schwartz is the pastor of Abiding Truth Lutheran Church, where the "ceremony" will be "performed" on Saturday, February 12.

This reporter contacted Reverend Norman Schoffenheimer, President of the Mount Kiersey chapter of "Christians Against Decadence." He stated this was the first he had heard about the planned "wedding." Schoffenheimer later said, "I have contacted the national office of our organization in Washington D.C. They have agreed to send a number of members to protest this abominable act. Frankly, liberal activists like the so-called 'Reverend' Schwartz disgust me."

This reporter has also learned that an organization called the "Families of Lesbians and Gays Support Network," which has an active branch in Altoona, is planning a counter rally in Dustin on Saturday.

An area resident who did not wish to be identified said, "I can't believe this is happening in Berkson County. If people want to do stuff like that, they should move to San Francisco or Harrisburg."

Reverend Schwartz has not yet been reached for comment.

+++

"I see you're going out with a bang, Pastor."

Mabel Hawthorne slid her copy of *The Naptonville News* from Gerald's hands and placed it on the dining room table, where a cat promptly sat on it. Gerald was making a determined effort to conceal his outrage from Mrs. Hawthorne, hoping to protect their already tenuous relationship from further damage.

"As usual, I have been misrepresented by the press."

Gerald feared Mrs. Hawthorne would interrogate him about his participation in the blessing service but at the moment she seemed unconcerned.

"Personally, I know a number of gays, Pastor. There's Dirk—he's a nurse's aide at Sunshine City Hospital. And Chad and Ricardo—they're a couple. I've seen them kissing a few times but they don't show any of the real steamy stuff.

"Chad has the most beautiful brown eyes, which you don't notice until the close-up shots. And then there's that lady on the Burger Shack commercials. You can tell by those boots she wears that she's one of those lesleyans.

"I have nothing against any of those people, mind you. If they want to get married to each other, I say 'go ahead.' This world is going to hell in a handbasket anyway. They'll find out soon enough that living with someone 'til death do you part is no bed of roses—as you are well aware, Pastor.

"Not that I don't miss my Charlie now and then. 'Course he was always leaving the milk out. And he made the most irritating clicking sound with his tongue whenever I was trying to watch my story . . ."

For the first time in several months Mrs. Hawthorne had not greeted Gerald at the door with the declaration, "You're the man who gobbled up my fortune."

She had been unsuccessfully attempting to replicate the face of Christ in her most recent batches of gobs. The previous month she had showed Gerald a hamburger tater tot casserole, which had settled in the dish in such a way that it vaguely resembled Noah's ark if you stared at it under the fluorescent kitchen light for at least three seconds.

"Let the lesleyans get married. Just so they don't get carried away. When they try to play professional football and operate heavy machinery, that's where I draw the line.

"Anyway, since this is your last visit I thought I could finally tell you about the time I almost drowned in Meyer's Creek back when I was four years old."

+++

Betty's eyes were swollen, her face streaked with tears, and her hair unkempt. It appeared that she had neither slept nor showered for a while.

Gerald had not expected to see her in the office this early. He had come here because he needed to start packing his books and because the parsonage felt hauntingly empty at six in the morning now that Weiss was no longer around to aggravate him.

"There's twenty-eight messages on the voice-mail," said Betty. "I'm sorry I got you into this, Pastor. The story got picked up by one of those syndicates overnight. Jane told me it's all over the Internet."

"I'm on the Internet? Can they do that without my permission? Is there someone I can contact to have my name removed?"

"It doesn't work that way. Jane said her son Googled your name this morning along with the words "gay" and "wedding" and over 8,000 links came up. Some of them have a picture, but they must have got something wrong because it's a photo of Pastor Franklin. Guess *The Naptonville News* never updated their files."

Betty clicked on the mouse on her desk and the floating head-of-Christ screen saver gave way to a smaller version of the menacing photo of Pastor Franklin that had oppressed Gerald for the past seven years. Gerald generally avoided looking directly at computer screens, as though one peek would lead down a perilous path onto which he best not venture. But now his eyes were drawn to the place where his own name appeared alongside the words "gay crusader" and "shameless liberal activist." Apparently, there were no secrets on the Internet. Plenty of misinformation, but certainly no secrets.

"You said Dorothy would keep quiet about this."

"Do you think this happened because of Dorothy? It's Dougie's fault. He called *The Naptonville News* yesterday morning and said he wanted to put an announcement about the blessing in the paper.

"This might sound funny coming from me, but Dougie's naïve. He thinks this is some kind of ideal world where everyone will accept what he and Danny are doing. Those people in the press don't care who they hurt."

Gerald felt increasingly apprehensive about participating in the blessing in light of the unexpected media attention. He had become an unwitting pioneer for a cause he did not believe in. *The Reverend Gerald Schwartz—western Pennsylvania's foremost advocate of same-sex marriage.*

"I'm going to do it," he said.

"I'm serious, Pastor. You don't have to."

"At 4:00 p.m., Saturday. It's on my schedule. I'd like to think that like your son, I am a man of principles."

Betty smiled in such a manner that Gerald sensed she had caught the irony of his statement. She and he had this in common with Dougie—they were naïve, a requisite quality among prophets and saints.

+++

Four cups of coffee. Eleven fully packed and sealed cartons of freshly dusted theological tomes. For seven years Gerald had made the pastoral study his second home, but today he was seeing the place in a new light.

Tucked into the back of one of his desk drawers Gerald had discovered a tattered note containing Dorothy's familiar scrawl. *Pastor Franklin—I'm bringing it to your attention that you have not been visiting all the sick and homebound like you should. Also you have been sleeping when you should be working. If you read your Bible you'll see Jesus never did things like this. Signed, A concerned member.*

Gerald had never considered that Joseph Franklin might have endured criticism. In the past seven years he had heard much about his predecessor's legacy. Yet it was only now, as he prepared to leave his pastorate, that he realized he and Franklin had more in common than he had imagined.

Between packing boxes and emptying his office Gerald had listened to all twenty-eight voice-mail messages. Somewhere between the Baptist preacher with a lisp who spewed scripture like venom and the bisexual activist from rural Kansas came a message from a nurse at Mountain View. Kristina Kirch had passed away peacefully around 3:00 a.m. Friday morning. Arrangements had been made with Aschenbrenner Funeral Home to remove Miss Kirch's body.

"I thought you'd want to know," said the nurse. "You're a dedicated pastor. Spending hours with somebody who couldn't talk back. That must have been hard."

The nurse had it wrong. There is nothing easier than talking to someone who does not reciprocate, which undoubtedly accounts for the popularity of prayer.

+++

As Gerald stepped out of the front door of the parsonage shortly after nine, Edna pulled up in front of the sidewalk in her husband's dilapidated pickup truck. The passenger side window was cracked open wide enough for Gerald to hear Edna's voice over the roar coming from the truck's rusted muffler. "Hey, Pastor. I gotta talk to you."

Edna had driven by the parsonage at least three times while he was shooing away the well-groomed man who had emerged from a white van with the words *TV 7—Altoona's Favorite News Source* splashed across the side.

Gerald tentatively approached the truck. "Get in! I gotta talk to you," said Edna. "You're still my Pastor, right?"

Gerald paused with his hand on the passenger side door handle. Edna's voice sounded less harsh than usual. Now that she had successfully ruined his life, she appeared to be assuming a conciliatory tone. Was she planning to apologize for what she had done to him?

Against his better judgment, Gerald pulled himself into the truck. As he searched for the seat belt Edna stepped on the accelerator and the rear tires spun on a patch of ice before the truck jerked forward.

When they passed Abiding Truth, Gerald noticed a second sign in front of the church—a black one with white letters announcing the 10:00 a.m. service.

Edna did not ask Gerald where he was headed. Clearly she had her own destination in mind as they sped out of town on the old Post Road, which led into the wooded bluff north of Dustin.

What was Edna up to? Every time she shifted gears she grunted as though depressing the clutch and moving the lever required all of her energy. She stared out at the road, which Gerald noted was becoming narrower and steeper with each passing mile. They were surrounded on both sides by forest. Trees bordered the road's shoulders so closely that their upper branches met and formed a foreboding arch through which the truck passed.

"You want to discuss my participation in Douglas Mundy's blessing service?" asked Gerald.

"No, I don't."

"It's a favor for Betty . . ." Gerald stopped himself. He did not owe Edna an explanation.

"She's been good to you. She stood by you. Like a secretary's supposed to do."

Edna continued to speak in a soft tone. Gerald struggled to hear her over the truck's persistent roar. "I hope you understand I never meant you any harm, Pastor. I know God's given you special powers. I know you can forgive people all their sins."

"All Christians ought to forgive each other."

"But you're special, Pastor. Right? If you say someone's forgiven then they really are. Look, I need to tell you somethin'."

Edna pulled the truck onto the shoulder. They were deep in the woods now, in a place where Gerald had never been. Mount Kiersey was covered with unimproved capillary roads such as this one, which were traveled mostly by hunters. Edna seemed to be familiar with the road, yet Gerald sensed she, too, was entering previously untraversed territory.

"This is somethin' I never told anyone before. I know you don't tell secrets 'cause God will strike you dead if you do."

"I took a vow of confidentiality."

"You seem that way. Confidant, I mean." Edna looked down and closed her eyes. What did she see in that place hidden to all except her and God? Gerald sat nearly motionless and stared at a stain on his trousers.

"I, well, you know, I had a baby girl 'tween Rogie and Alfred. Vera. My little girl. She's buried up in the cemetery. I—I lost her. And she weren't even baptized, poor thing."

"I'm sorry. I cannot imagine—"

"We had the date set. Pastor Franklin was gonna do it and we'd already sent out the invitations. She weren't but three weeks old and—"

"You're worried about whether she's in heaven." Gerald had tackled this topic more times than he could recall. The salvific nature of baptism had been a popular late night topic in seminary.

"She's gotta be in heaven. Right, Pastor?"

"Martin Luther wrote—"

"How could a sweet little baby like that not be in heaven? It's—it's me. I'm the one who's going to hell. I—"

Edna started to tremble.

"I—I killed my baby." She shifted in her seat and the entire truck started to rock. Tears streamed down her puffy cheeks. Gerald assumed the *I'm not the least bit shocked by what you're saying* expression he had learned in his pastoral counseling class at seminary. It had been awhile since he had needed to use it.

"I killed her, Pastor. It—it wasn't really my fault, you know. I was so tired and she wouldn't stop crying." Edna was writhing in her seat like she was enduring some great internal pain. It reminded Gerald of a parishioner he had once seen trying to pass a kidney stone.

"She kept crying, and I must have gone out of my mind. I picked her up and I shook her. I shook her. I kept shaking her. The—the coroner didn't check things out too closely. They didn't. In those days. I killed her, Pastor. I kept shaking her. Shaking her. She haunts me. I'm goin' to hell. And I—I didn't mean to. My baby, my own little baby. I'm goin' to hell, Pastor. "

In seven years, Gerald had never seen Edna shed a tear. She had never appeared the least bit vulnerable, though sometimes during worship he would catch her staring at the portrait of Jesus that hung above the altar and sense that beneath the jiggling jowls and self-righteous façade there hid a troubled soul.

Edna's trembling had become so pronounced Gerald feared she was on the verge of a seizure. She pulled a tissue from her pants pocket. She wiped her face and emitted a high-pitched noise which sounded to Gerald like a cross between a cough and a snivel.

This was the most horrifying confession he had ever heard. He could not bear to endure another word of it.

"I absolve you," said Gerald.

What else could he do? She was clearly repentant, tortured by demons which made his own nightly angst a comparatively minor irritation.

"What are you saying?"

"God forgives you."

"Are you sure?"

"Yes."

Edna stared out the windshield at the road in front of them.

"I want to see her again. My baby."

"I believe you will."

"Are you sure?"

"Yes."

"Thank you, Pastor."

For a brief moment the lines on Edna's forehead melted away, her expression softened, and Gerald saw her, not as she was, but as the vulnerable young mother she might once have been.

"Thank you," she said again.

Then, clenching her fist around the steering wheel, she gritted her teeth, and the deep furrows on her forehead returned.

"Excuse me," she said as she reached across Gerald's lap and opened the glove compartment. She pulled out a handgun. Gerald jolted when he saw it. Edna rested the gun in her lap with her hand on top of it. He should have anticipated this. Having secured her forgiveness, Edna would kill her unsuspecting confessor and dispose of his body in a remote location.

"I know you keep secrets," said Edna. "But if you ever tell anyone, I will hunt you down and shoot you dead." Edna rubbed her thumb against the barrel of the gun. Gerald did not doubt she knew how to use it.

Could this be the same woman who, moments before, had been blubbering like an inconsolable child? This was the bluffing, bullying Edna he had come to know and despise. She would not kill him. Not if it meant an eternity in hell on two counts of murder and no chance of reuniting with her child.

Gerald peeked at the gun out of the corner of his eye.

"I tell no secrets. You spread no gossip. You owe Betty an apology," he said flatly. He reached for the gun, procured it from Edna's lap unchallenged, and returned it to the glove compartment. It unnerved him how cold it felt against his hand.

"I always try to do the Christian thing," said Edna.

"You're a better Christian than I'll ever be," said Gerald.

Neither of them spoke on the way into Dustin. *Why now?* Gerald kept wondering. *Why did she confide in me now, after shouldering this burden all these years?*

When he stepped out of the truck in front of the parsonage the answer came to him in an instant. *Because he was leaving. Because Edna would not have to cower before the man in the pulpit week after week, mortified he knew her secret.* Gerald would soon depart from Dustin and bear away her unspeakable sin.

Twenty-Three

Allan Weiss

He knew it was a dream even as he dreamt it because she was not the woman who had fallen asleep beside him. She knelt before him, like a saint in worship, staring up at his face. She smelled like peppermint. "I can be anyone you want me to be," she said. When Allan looked into her eyes he saw that her forehead had been marked with a pasty gray cross.

Like a kaleidoscope the shapes and colors of the woman's face blended and blurred and when a new visage emerged from the swirling chaos she was Cathy.

In the flash of a second, Cathy came and left without a word and a new face appeared. And another. Then another. Caroline, the waitress to whom he had never said a proper goodbye after the debacle at Gerald's parsonage, and Mrs. Harrison, who he wished could be his mother, and the former director of entertainment ministries, whose name he had momentarily forgotten. Then Missy from summer camp and Eleanor with braces from art appreciation class and Krissy and the rest of the Eastwood Junior College dramatic dance team, all six of them, one by one, and the girl from Alexandria who said she was twenty but probably was closer to twelve.

Some were blond, most were brunettes, and one had dyed her hair with green Kool-Aid. Another had skin the color of caramel and a few had freckles and the girl with braces wore sunglasses that covered most of her face and a couple were laughing and another was crying and he didn't know why and their eyes were blue and brown and green and one a shade he couldn't quite describe and another had a scar above her eyebrow and one had lips that quivered when she kissed him and they kept changing and melding one into the other.

And every one of them had a cross of ashes on her forehead.

When finally the myriad faces were gone, Allan's mother stood before him, smiling the way she had that day at the zoo, two days before she died. He reached for her hand, which was cold to the touch, so chilling he commenced to shiver.

Allan awoke with a start. The bedside clock read 7:02. Thick drapery covered the only window in the room, concealing so much outside light it could have been either morning or evening. Kelly was still passed out on the bed beside him, leaving Allan to ponder his problems alone. He was always alone—no matter how many women were in the bed beside him.

Fortunately, Kelly had been intoxicated during their attempt to make love the night before. Three attempts in three days now and not once had he been able to achieve an erection. Not even with Caroline and her friend. What the hell was wrong with him? Had all that time in Gerald's parsonage rendered him impotent? Was there something in the water up there in Dustin?

He didn't know how much longer he could stay here. Kelly would never make him leave, but he could barely stand the suffocating stuffiness of this one-bedroom apartment. Altoona was a half-hour drive from Pottersfield and Allan's ubiquitous local media presence assured that someone would inevitably recognize him coming or going.

The day after Gerald had banished him, Allan finally violated The Bishop's decree to avoid setting foot in his church while on sabbatical.

"You look great!" exclaimed Molly when she saw him, but the way she said it made Allan sense that she did not really mean it. Of course, he looked great. He always looked great. But perhaps he did not look as great as usual. Perhaps he was losing his ability to conceal what was inside him, and if he looked like he felt then it was no wonder Molly sounded insincere. Or had she always been so disingenuous?

"I'm ready to return," said Allan.

"No need for that yet," said Molly. It had been nearly a month and a half since she had seen him, and she could not be bothered to take her eyes off her Blackberry. "We've already planned the next four weeks."

"Without me?"

"Au contraire, Pastor Allan. You have such a commanding videographic presence. You really should have gone to Hollywood."

"But wouldn't people rather see me?"

"Of course. People love seeing your magnified image on the twenty-foot screens. There's more of you to love."

"I mean the real me. Flesh and blood. Shake my hand. Pat me on the back. That sort of thing."

"People miss you, Pastor Al."

"That's not what I'm asking."

"People love you. But you have to realize your audience is part of the media generation."

"What are you saying?"

"These are people who best relate to images. They watch Dan Rather on the nightly news, and they love him. They feel like they know him personally. If they met him in real life, they probably wouldn't have a clue what to say to him. But when they see him on the screen, they feel like he's their buddy. It's the same with you. Do you understand what I'm saying?"

"Unfortunately yes."

"BTW, Jeffrey's come up with a great idea for a new enterprise."

"That's what we pay him for." Allan hoped Jeffrey's latest brainchild did not involve use of a pastor cam.

"You know that tract of land bordering the west side of the parking lot? He wants to buy it and develop a combination water park/ baptismal pool. He thinks we should call it 'Holy Waters.'"

"Tell me more."

"Well, everyone likes what we've done with our communion buffet, but we've received complaints about boring baptisms. Imagine how fun it would be to commemorate your spiritual renewal by sliding down a 60-foot long funnel with a forty-five degree drop."

"Sounds great."

"Jeffrey's working on the financing. We're thinking when you come back—and believe me, we're all looking forward to your return—maybe we could redefine your pastoral role a bit. We're playing with the pastor-as-lifeguard image."

"Lifeguard?"

"I bet you look great in Speedo water shorts, Pastor Al."

+++

Kelly's refrigerator was even more poorly stocked than Gerald's. She appeared to live on Lean Cuisine and Diet Pepsi. And vodka. She and Gerald had that in common. Allan was drawn to alcoholics like a fly to a spider's web. What the hell was wrong with him? It was about his father, of course.

Ever since Gerald banished him, the last day with his father keeps coming back. He closes his eyes and it's there before him. Ocean City. Noonday sun. The scent of Coppertone melds with the mouthwatering aroma of hamburger grease on the boardwalk. His hands feel sticky with sweat and the remnants of a raspberry Slush Puppy. Reggae music blares from a loudspeaker and children are screaming on the Tilt-a-Whirl and right here in front of him a hawker taunts, "Bet you can't hit the bottle, skinny."

His father walks with him, his paper cup of lukewarm Coke mixed with whisky, and it's embarrassing the way he's staggering and talking too loud, ogling the women in bikinis—"Hey, Al, look at the rack on that one."

Off in the distance he sees it, rising against the bright blue sky.

"Please, Dad, can we ride the Ferris wheel?"

"Damn it, kid, you're old enough now to go by yourself."

He has never been on the Ferris wheel. His mother once told him when you reached the top and looked out at the ocean on a clear summer day, if you found the place where the sky meets the water and stared at it long enough, you could actually see the face of God. His mother had seen the face of God many times.

Your mother was a nutcase. All that religious crap didn't do her any good. She killed herself just the same.

It would be nice to have someone to ride with, a friend at least.

'Round and 'round he goes and every time he arrives at the top all alone, Al stares out at the ocean and prays to catch a glimpse of what his mother had seen. Yet no matter how much he squints and blinks he cannot detect the face of God. In his excitement, he loses sight of his father.

When the ride was over, Al searched up and down the boardwalk until finally he arrived at the police station. How could his father have abandoned him? Had he been so drunk that he had forgotten his son was with him? What kind of father does that? They found his body in a car outside a bar on the north end of town. They said it was a heart attack.

+++

After a cursory Google search on *erectile dysfunction*, Allan checked his email. When his homepage at www.christianclergynews.com opened, Gerald Schwartz's name flashed across the screen beside a grainy pre-digital picture of someone else. Allan was stunned. He left the old man alone for a couple of days and he managed to get himself into more trouble. Allan had not realized Gerald was an outspoken advocate of same-sex marriage. They had never broached the topic in their conversations.

Gerald Schwartz was a man of substance, a man who stood for something—everything a true father should be. And now Allan had ruined their relationship, disappointed the man he most admired. *Why can't I put someone else's interests before my own for once?*

A bit of online research revealed that a contingency of fanatics was planning to descend upon Dustin this very day. Allan had spent forty days in that sleepy burg, and as soon as he left the place started to hop.

He put away his computer and turned on the television because he was bored and there was nothing else to do. He flipped through the channels until he found something that could hold his attention for more than five seconds. Pastor Weiss was preaching on the local cable access station. Now here was someone Allan could watch forever.

Pastor Weiss was wearing a Gucci dark gray dotted pinstripe wool three-button suit with an Erenegildo Zegna diagonal-striped silk tie. The suit fit snugly enough to accentuate his well-toned deltoids. He was the kind of man Allan would find attractive were he attracted to men. He spoke with a baritone voice which filled the room. It almost sounded like a song the way he was speaking.

But what most impressed Allan about the preacher was the way he looked into the camera with the decorous confidence of a man who commanded the respect of everyone who sat before him. Yet at the same time it felt like this man was speaking directly to you, and to nobody else, that he was delivering his message because he knew how much you desperately yearned to hear it, almost as though he could read your very thoughts, and see deep into your troubled soul. Your soul, above everyone else's.

"God has a plan for YOU. Today YOU will do something truly amazing." Pastor Weiss proclaimed it with so much conviction that for a moment Allan almost believed it.

In the background, Allan saw Cathy, sitting on the stage behind Pastor Weiss, her face beaming, her eyes twinkling like they were the first time they met. He should call her. *A bore shuns his mother.* Allan flipped off the television. He needed some fresh air.

+++

When Allan stepped outside, the noonday sun struck his eyes with such a glare he had to turn his head. As he did so, he saw someone standing in the alley near the garbage bin, staring at him. In the shadow it was difficult to determine whether it was a man or a woman, but Allan knew he was being watched.

"Pastor Weiss," called the stranger, in a woman's voice. She was nearly Allan's height—six feet tall—and when she stepped closer—much too close—he saw she was ugly enough to be Molly Rogers's older sister. She smelled like the garbage bin she had been standing beside.

"Good morning," said Allan.

"I'm on to you," she said.

"Pardon me?" Allan did not like this woman. She was probably psychotic. He stepped back against the side of the apartment building. The woman stepped closer.

"You need help," she said.

This woman had stepped out of a dark alley smelling like rotting table scraps and now she was acting the part of a therapist? "I need to be going," he said, as he tried to step around her.

She grabbed his shoulder and breathed on him. "You're much more charming on television."

Allan was miffed at the insult but saw no purpose in wasting his masculine allure on this eccentric.

"God bless you, ma'am."

The woman would not let him past her. She placed both of her grimy hands on his head so that he was forced to look at her acne-scarred face as she spoke.

"I had a brother like you. Everyone said he was a ladies man. Women wanted him. Men envied him. But deep inside, he was miserable. Problem was, he didn't know how to love anyone."

Allan removed her hands from his head and retreated toward the door from which he had originally come out. "Thanks for sharing."

"That's what you've got to do, Pastor Weiss! You've got to love someone!" she shouted as he escaped into the foyer.

Kelly was awake when Allan returned to her apartment. Her face was gaunt and her eyes bloodshot. She did not look like the kind of woman with whom he would want to have sex.

"Geez, I can't remember anything. What day is it, anyway?" said Kelly.

"Saturday. There's a crazy woman in the alley."

"You smell like garbage. You must have met Vera."

"You know her?"

"She's a snoop. She's not so bad once you get to know her."

"You're kidding."

"Nah. She and I go to AA together sometimes down at the community center. Man, I've got a wicked headache."

Kelly rolled her head back, then leaned forward and vomited on the floor. Allan had to get out of here. Maybe Gerald would take him back. Even if he wouldn't, Allan suspected something was going to happen on the mountain today that a prominent publicity-seeking man would not want to miss.

Twenty-Four

Gerald Schwartz

According to his extensive record, Gerald had visited Lois Warner 287 times during his seven-year pastorate in Dustin, and that did not include the numerous occasions she cornered him after Sunday worship fretting over her latest ailment. A great number of these visits took place in the emergency room of the Mountain View Medical Center. Most of them occurred right here, however, at Mrs. Warner's kitchen table, which, as usual, was partially covered by bottles of medication.

"How are you?" Gerald asked, as he sat down across the table from her. He had let himself in since her vertigo was acting up and she dared not stand unless absolutely necessary.

"It's a good thing I've signed my will, Pastor. You won't believe what I've come down with."

"Probably not."

"I scarcely believe it myself, and frankly I'm embarrassed to tell you."

"If you feel uncomfortable, you need not share it with me, Mrs. Warner."

"It's not the sort of thing a woman generally talks about with a man."

"You need not tell me."

"But you're my pastor. For another day, anyway. You need to know."

"You'd be surprised how many things I don't know. And how many more I wish I didn't."

"I haven't told anyone. Except for the lady Methodist pastor. She said a nice personal prayer for me."

"That should suffice."

"Oh yes, I also told my pen pal in Japan and I've got a few of those TV evangelists praying for me. You can never have too many prayers."

"Sounds like you've covered all the bases."

"Are you sure you don't want to know?"

"Yes, Mrs. Warner."

"It's extremely embarrassing."

"Then by all means, keep it to your self."

"I have Chlamydia, Pastor."

Gerald snorted, failing in his attempt to suppress a laugh. "Chlamydia? You can not be serious."

"Why do you think that's funny? It hurts like the dickens when I pee."

"Mrs. Warner, are you aware Chlamydia is a sexually transmitted disease?"

"Well, how else do you think I got it? It's no secret Ed Jacobson and I have become lovers. We've been having unprotected sex."

Lois Warner was 75 years old. Ed was well into his 80's. *What was there to protect?*

Gerald pondered a proper pastoral response. Typical replies he had learned during the seminary refresher course, *Counseling Sexually Active Non-married Persons*—statements such as, "It only takes once to get pregnant"—did not seem appropriate, given the circumstances.

"It's purely recreational, Pastor. It's not like we're planning to get married."

One more day. Actually 14 hours, 12 minutes, and 37 seconds, if the clock above Lois Warner's kitchen sink was correct. Then the likes of Lois would become the entrusted responsibility of Irmalee's sister's boyfriend.

+++

On the way home from Mrs. Warner's house, Gerald waited at the intersection of Maple and Main while a caravan of a half-dozen recreational vehicles with Maryland license plates rumbled down the street, headed in the direction of the church. One of them was emblazoned with a bright red heart-shaped sign scripted in calligraphic letters which read *Christians Against Decadence*. The presence of these self-righteous outsiders immediately solidified Gerald's resolve to participate in the blessing ceremony, apostate though he be.

Not yet ready for the impending confrontation, Gerald turned in the other direction. He drove two blocks and parked his Buick in front of the Aschenbrenner Funeral Home, where Miss Kirch's remains were being kept until they would be taken down the mountain for cremation in Altoona. Gerald had phoned Mr. Aschenbrenner and requested the pastoral privilege of private prayer over the body in the open casket. He had no intention of praying. He merely wished to return to Miss Kirch that which was rightly hers.

He had removed the photo from its shattered frame and carefully rolled it into a tube. The brittle paper upon which it was printed tore slightly in the process. No matter. The photo would be destroyed imminently. Ashes to ashes.

"This is the second one in a week that isn't having a service," Mr. Aschenbrenner's assistant said when he met Gerald at the door. "Makes your job easier."

He led Gerald to a preparation room in the rear of the building and left the pastor to perform his duties. Gerald approached the casket tentatively. He avoided looking at the corpse's face as he lifted the stiffened arm and slid the rolled photograph beneath it. He did not want to remember Miss Kirch like this.

Gerald noticed that though Miss Kirch still wore a ring on her right hand the familiar necklace with the Celtic cross was missing. He stepped away from the casket and surprised himself by speaking. "Thank you," he said.

His voice sounded muffled, as though it had been engulfed by the palpable aura of death that lingered in this place. He had conversed for hours with Kristina in her comatose state, as the nurse had said, "to somebody who couldn't talk back." But this was different. It felt like he was talking to Nobody. It felt a lot like prayer.

+++

Gerald took a large bite of the coffee cake Sophie had brought him. He was grateful for familiar company. Sophie estimated there were now approximately several dozen protesters and counter-protesters marching in front of the church. She said a number of them had wandered onto the property marked *NO TReSP—AsSING!* across the street, where they were promptly chased away by a shovel-wielding Lillian Sutherland, who moved with considerable dexterity considering her homebound status.

Sophie said Roger had appeared in front of the church and informed the crowd that he, as President of Abiding Truth, had the authority to call the police and would not hesitate to do so. Dorothy had taken it upon herself to stand watch at the front door of the church. She promised to call Roger, who went home to watch the basketball game, should anyone disobey his decree.

"I hear Betty's trying to find you a wife," said Sophie, as she slid another piece of cake onto Gerald's empty plate.

"She supposes she can find someone who complements me."

Betty had persisted in her matchmaking efforts, having uploaded Gerald's anonymous personality profile on the Lutheran dating website. Gerald had yet to reply to the e-mail Betty had printed for him from Lustylutherbabe231.

"I compliment you," said Sophie. "I try to compliment everybody. It's a good thing to do. You know."

"The cake is delicious," said Gerald.

"This is good—what you're doing for Betty."

"She has been faithful to me. I feel obliged. No, that's not it exactly."

"Sometimes you've got to do things even when you're not sure they're right."

"You told Betty that, didn't you?"

"I try to encourage her."

"Sin boldly, but believe and rejoice in Christ more boldly still."

"What's that?"

"Martin Luther."

+++

Shortly after one, Gerald made his first public appearance in nearly fifteen years adorned in an outfit other than one of his seven black clerical suits. Disguised as a commoner and fortified by anonymity, bourbon, and the fact he no longer gave a damn about much of anything, he slipped out the back door of the parsonage, rounded the corner toward the church, and passed the antsy bevy of strangers on his way to the post office.

Judging from the scowls on their faces and the messages conveyed on their signs, the majority of uninvited guests appeared to be vehemently opposed to the so-called "gay wedding." However, Gerald soon realized none of the protesters were able to identify which persons were involved in the "wedding," since Betty's son and nephew had never been named by media sources and Internet photos of Gerald were actually those of Pastor Franklin. For once, no one in Dustin was talking.

"Does Pastor Schwartz live in that house?" asked a middle-aged woman who was wearing too much lipstick and eyeliner. She was pointing toward the parsonage. A large man with a crew cut and bushy goatee stood beside her, holding a placard that read *Leviticus 20:13*. He sneered at Gerald.

"The pastor's not home," Gerald said. He was enjoying the warmth and comfort of his plaid flannel shirt.

"He disgusts me," said the woman. "A man of God ought to know better."

"Well," said Gerald. "You're always an ass to someone."

On his venture to the post office, Gerald witnessed a number of out-of-towners piling into Karen's Korner Bar. He also noted considerably more traffic than usual at Bubby's. If it was Gerald's fault outsiders were overrunning the town, he could also take credit for improving the local economy.

+++

He was certainly no believer in psychic phenomena, yet Gerald could not determine what had caused him to pick up the telephone at the precise moment he did. Upon returning to the parsonage, he decided to call Betty to confer about a plan for entering and exiting the church without confrontation. He had turned off the ringer and quit listening to his voice mail since being inundated with unsolicited calls in the days before.

When Gerald picked up the receiver and started to dial Betty's number, a familiar voice greeted him on the other end of the line.

"Are you there? Hello? Hello. I'm calling for Gerald Schwartz."

Gerald had not spoken with Margaret for over a year, but her demeanor sounded so informal and immediate it seemed as though she had never left him. Like she was calling him at the church from the parsonage telling him to come home for supper.

"My God, Margaret, why have you called? Did someone die?"

"I just read about what you're doing up there. When I saw your name in the paper, I was shocked. And I felt like I had to call you."

"Where are you? Are you still living with Althea?"

"No. We broke up."

"What do you mean—you broke up?"

"We're no longer lovers. We've decided to go our separate ways."

"You were lovers?"

"Good God, Gerald, what did you think we were—fishing buddies? Surely you knew about Althea and me."

There was a lengthy pause as Gerald attempted to inwardly digest what he had heard. Edna Weinwright had been right all this time? He reached into his desk drawer and pulled out a fifth of bourbon.

"Gerald, are you there?"

"So you are a—a lesbian then?"

"I'm bisexual, Gerald. I spent thirty-three years with you—remember? Listen, I just called to—"

Gerald was not listening.

"So you find Althea attractive?" Gerald certainly did not find Althea attractive. Her oversized bicuspids and tangled jet-black locks of hair reminded him of a gorgon.

"Gerald. I'm sorry about the way we ended."

"The last time we spoke you hung up on me. You said—"

"I know what I said."

"You said—"

"I said I couldn't understand why you wouldn't go down on me. At least Althea did that much."

"Althea?"

"Listen, the reason I called—"

"Women can do that? To other women?"

"Rather well, actually. Good God, Gerald, you're acting like a dolt. For thirty-three years you were embarrassed to talk about sex and now you're carrying on like a horny adolescent. I didn't call you to talk about cunnilingus. Can't we let bygones be bygones?"

Cunnilingus?

"Gerald? You there?"

"Umm."

"Listen, I'm sorry I insulted you. I just called to say, well, I'm proud of you. Taking a stand. I don't know what's happened in the last year. You've obviously changed. I suppose we've both changed . . ."

Cunnilingus? "Go down on me" equals cunnilingus. That's what she had wanted all those years? He had a degree from Princeton. How could he not have known this?

"Maybe I shouldn't have called. But I just wanted to let you know you have my support. And if anybody tries to protest or criticize you, don't let it get to you. You've always been too sensitive about criticism."

Cunnilingus. A bit exotic perhaps for a man with Gerald's proclivity for puritanical lovemaking. Yet he surely would have made a determined effort had he known.

"Margaret?"

"Yes."

"May I inquire about one additional matter of a sexual nature?"

"Am I speaking with Gerald Schwartz?" He could hear Margaret smiling on the other end of the line.

"Hypothetically speaking, if I had been willing to, as you say, 'go down on you', would you have stayed in the marriage?"

Margaret laughed in a manner that sounded neither derisive nor amused. "Hmm," she purred into the phone, which was her usual response when giving a matter considerable thought.

"Well?"

"No, Gerald."

"No?"

"No. But it certainly would have made the last years more tolerable."

Gerald had spent enough time with Margaret to know she did not intend this last remark as a joke. The few times during their marriage he had asked for her opinion she had always been certain to give it. Now, for the first time he could remember, he wished he had asked her more questions.

Twenty-Five

Betty Mundy

Betty had imagined the Abiding Truth sanctuary would be the appropriate place to finally settle matters with God. But when she sat down in the front pew and peered up at the stained glass picture of Jesus she could not bring herself to look Him in the eyes.

Then she remembered the woods near Summit Park. It had been years since she had ventured back there. Over time, The Miracle she had experienced in those woods had become so magnified in her imagination that they had become a sacred place for her, to which she returned only when she felt worthy to stand in God's presence. As a good Lutheran, that was not often.

When she arrived at the park, Betty felt more ornery than holy. She ventured toward the rock that had been struck by lightning. It was covered by nearly a foot of snow. Betty would have fared better with skis or snowshoes. She was wearing a pair of poorly insulated boots, which sank in the snow and made it difficult to walk more than a few feet without gasping for breath because of the effort it took to lift her legs.

She stopped about a dozen feet from the rock and peered into the woods, close enough to hear how quiet they were, hushed by the snow. It reminded her of the eerie silence that had filled the forest moments before the lightning struck this very spot nine months and a day before Dougie was born.

Betty had partially memorized what she wanted to say. She had been anticipating this moment for weeks and feared it would be awkward, like the time forty-some years before when she had cracked the crystal vase on the table in the sunroom and finally confessed to her mother. But it was not at all like that. Talking to God again was more like hopping on her bicycle or diving into the creek after a long winter.

Dear God, I'll get right to the point. I'm not sure whether You approve of what Dougie and Danny are doing. I thought you were against it. But after talking with Sophie and Mrs. Franklin and those other people in Altoona—I don't know anymore.

I've been thinking about this a lot, and I don't mean it in a mean way. But if You're going to punish those two sweet boys just for falling in love with each other then frankly, I'd rather be in hell with them than in heaven with You. Maybe You see things differently. But I am a Mother. And by now You ought to know that Nobody stands between a Mother and Her Child. Not Even You.

In the past month, Betty had confronted Harriet, Edna, and Dorothy. She had stood up to the men in her life—Clarence and Pastor Schwartz. But now she had committed the most brazen act of all—she had told off The Man Upstairs. Betty stepped toward the rock and placed her hands on it like she was touching a sacred relic. She half believed God was about to strike her dead. They say lightning never strikes the same place twice and Betty had never known there to be a thunderstorm on the mountain in February, but she figured if the Almighty had been insulted and wanted to zap her from the face of the earth He would not hesitate to break a few laws of nature to do so.

She remained there for what she estimated to be ten minutes. The temperature was dropping and she had lots to do back at the house. She figured ten minutes was enough time for God to reply. She headed toward the parking lot.

+++

Betty returned home to find Clarence peering into the parakeet's cage, dressed in his only suit and tie. He had shaved, parted his hair to the side like he used to do when he was still working, and trimmed his nose hairs for the first time in six months. Despite the gravy stain on his lapel and the fact his trousers were several sizes too small, Betty thought he looked rather dapper. The last time he had worn his suit was the last time he had been inside the church, fifteen years before when his brother Mike died—which must have also been when the mishap with the gravy occurred.

She and Clarence had talked through the matter as much as they were able. He had been interacting civilly with the boys, which was all Betty could reasonably expect of him. He had never been one to show affection to his son, other than the occasional slap on the back accompanied by the universal paternal salutation, "Stay outta trouble, ya hear."

Betty was beginning to understand what Sophie had meant when she said, "There's those secrets we keep from ourselves." Clarence had decided to live as though he did not know Dougie and Danny were gay. He had made it clear that, as far as he was concerned, Pastor Schwartz was asking God to bless the boys as they prepared to move to Boston. It would be like the farewell service the Methodist pastor had for the Morrison brothers before they shipped off to Iraq. That's what he told his buddies at the Buckshot Club.

Betty could hardly believe her ears when Edna had called earlier in the morning to apologize for the false rumors she had spread about Dougie impregnating a young woman and then accompanying her to the abortion clinic. She said Priscilla had not been wearing her glasses that day and must have gotten the details wrong.

Edna said nothing about Dougie and Danny's relationship. Other than Sophie and Pastor Schwartz, nobody in town brought up the subject, which Betty sensed was the way it would be from now on. It was not a topic people felt comfortable broaching. So be it. There were plenty of other things to talk about.

+++

"Who the hell are these people?" said Clarence as he and Betty made their way from the parking lot to the church's front entrance.

"I hope they didn't say anything nasty to the boys," said Betty. Clarence had parked between Danny's VW and Marian's Lexus.

The strangers stood along the public sidewalk about 100 feet from where Betty and Clarence were walking. They had divided themselves into two groups, the larger of which stood near Edna's white sign while the other congregated closer to Eleanor's black one. People from each group were shouting at one another. Betty recognized two women from her support group holding a rainbow-colored flag. She immediately felt a rush of gratitude but she sensed this was not a good time to thank them.

Betty stared straight ahead at the church entrance and whispered, "God help us." Out of the corner of her eye, she noticed a large man with a crew cut and bushy goatee who was sneering at them. Above his head he held a sign with a message so shocking she gasped when she saw it. It said *GOD HATES FAGS*. Betty was overcome with a burst of rage so strong she clenched her fists and had to fight off the urge to charge at the man headlong and knock his sorry butt to the ground.

Two women standing near the man with the sign began to harass them.

"Are you the parents?" shouted one, who wore bright red lipstick.

"You oughta be ashamed," said the other. She pointed her finger at Betty and Clarence.

Betty tried to avoid looking at the women. But the one with the red lipstick caught her eyes and immediately Betty felt like the main attraction on one of those TV talk shows where the audience members berate the guests for sleeping with their daughter's boyfriends or torturing puppies.

Dorothy met them at the door. For once Betty was glad to see her. Denise, formerly known as Dennis, had spotted Betty and came racing toward the church to meet her. Dorothy allowed Clarence and Betty to slip by her while preventing Denise from proceeding any further.

"Hello, ma'am," Denise said to Dorothy, in a voice much deeper than Betty remembered. "It's so refreshing to see your church welcomes gay people."

"Our church doesn't welcome anybody," said Dorothy. "Now get out of here before I call the police!" She eyed Denise's protruding breasts and five o'clock shadow. "What are you, anyway?"

Safely inside the church, Betty caught her breath and glanced around the narthex. Everyone else was here. Dougie, who owned at least ten times as many ties as his father, had opted for an argyle sweater and cords. Danny had on a nice pair of jeans. Marian, still shivering beneath her mink fur coat, stood with Dougie near the guest register. Betty did a double take when she saw Clifton emerging from the men's restroom. He looked much better in a suit than Clarence but just as out of place—whether it was because he was an atheist in church, a Black man in Dustin, or the father of a gay son, she was not sure.

When Dougie saw Betty he came over and hugged her. "I love you, Mother," he said.

The gentle caress of his wispy hair against the side of her neck momentarily brought her back to her happy place, and she knew again that he would always be her little boy.

"I'm sorry, Mother. I had no idea it would come to this."

"We'll survive. Those people will leave sooner or later."

They assembled in the sanctuary. The boys stood side-by-side facing the altar. Pastor Schwartz stood in front of them like he usually did for a wedding, dressed in his white alb with the purple stole he wore during Lent. The rest of them sat together in the front-most pew, which was used only for special occasions.

Clarence surprised Betty by grasping her hand and resting it on his knee. Perhaps being in church reminded Clarence of their wedding day, when he clung to her with his sweaty palm like their hands were glued together. Or maybe it was because he had read the chapter on romance in the "Foreplay for the Faithful" section of that book Marian had given her. Either way, it cheered her.

Pastor started by welcoming everyone. Immediately it became clear that despite what the crowd outside believed, this was no wedding. There was no marching down the aisle, no music, no fainting and/or pregnant bridesmaids, no drunk uncles ogling the bridesmaids, no groomsmen making snide comments, no "here comes the bride." No kiss, thank God, no sweaty hand holding except for Clarence, no overpriced bouquets of flowers, no cute little flower girl being coaxed down the aisle by her mother. None of the usual distractions.

The service was over in two minutes. Pastor Schwartz prayed for God to bless the boys' relationship, but he didn't explain what he meant by that. During Pastor's prayer, she briefly peered up at the stained glass window behind the altar. If Jesus disapproved of what was happening, Betty could not tell.

As they all were standing to leave, the door in the narthex opened and in stepped Pastor Weiss. Betty had not seen him for several days. Dorothy reported that he had moved out of the parsonage on Wednesday night after two women came by in need of pastoral care.

Pastor Weiss stood in the open entryway between the sanctuary and the narthex. He called, "Hey, Gerald."

Pastor Schwartz must have seen Pastor Weiss, but he did not acknowledge him. He headed instead toward the sacristy, the closet-sized room to the right of the altar where he usually changed in and out of his liturgical garments.

The rest of them made their way out of the sanctuary into the narthex. They had planned to gather at the Highland Café for the Saturday evening all-you-can-eat spaghetti and meatball supper, which started at 4:30. Usually Clarence made sure they arrived no later than 4:25 so that no one else would eat all the all-you-can-eat spaghetti before he did. But with the crowd outside, he seemed in no hurry to leave.

Betty returned to the sanctuary to invite Pastor Schwartz to join them for supper. He was talking with Pastor Weiss and as Betty approached she immediately sensed she was interrupting an unpleasant conversation.

"Listen, Gerald, I'm sorry about what happened," said Pastor Weiss. "How can I make it up to you?"

"You can't," said Pastor Schwartz.

"Please, I need your forgiveness. How can I make amends?" said Pastor Weiss. He looked up and flashed a quick smile at Betty. He was such a good-looking man. Betty was going to invite both of them to supper, but given the tone of their conversation, she sensed that might not be a good idea.

She headed back to the narthex where Marian met her. "Do you smell smoke?" she asked.

As soon as Marian said it, the door from outside burst open. Dorothy peered inside the church, her eyes open wide in terror. She cupped her hands around her mouth, and shouted so loud it would echo in Betty's head for days, "Get out! They've set the church on fire!"

"Oh my God!" shrieked Marian.

"Holy shit!" said Clarence.

Betty looked up and saw a cloud of smoke descending upon them from the rafters.

"It's the bell tower!" Dorothy shouted. "Someone snuck in there! Get out now!"

Clarence grasped Betty's hand and yanked her arm so hard she heard it snap. Before she knew what was happening he had pulled her across the narthex and toward the door. When the cold air slapped her face, a jolt of maternal instinct coursed through her body like she had just been struck by lightning.

"Dougie!' she shrieked. "Where's Dougie? Where's Danny?"

When she looked around she was already outside and the boys were standing beside her. A number of locals had mingled with the crowd of strangers. Most of them were gaping at the bell tower, which was now partially obscured by a thick plume of black smoke.

Somebody screamed, "Is everyone out?"

Betty stared at the bell tower. She saw flames now, and felt acid rise from her stomach. She heard the church bell ringing. *Somebody's Up There. Cindy Haverford. Smoking again. She must have set the church on fire. Charlie Cresco's up there with that boy he met at church camp.*

Clarence had been holding her arm, but she pulled away from him now. Before she realized what she was doing, she was back in the church. "Pastor Schwartz! Pastor Weiss!" she shouted.

Betty peered across the narthex and through the open doorway that led into the sanctuary. She stared up at the area above the altar, hoping to catch a glimpse of Jesus. A gray cloud of smoke obscured the entire chancel. Momentarily disoriented by this unimaginable sight, Betty stepped back and stumbled into the Reverend Franklin Memorial Plant Stand. She could not remember whether it was on the left or the right side of the narthex and she could no longer see the door that led outside. Before she had a chance to panic, she heard a voice behind her, "This way! Follow me."

She turned and saw Pastor Weiss, looking calm and dignified. He reached for her hand and they made their way across the narthex and toward the door, where Pastor Schwartz stood, still wearing his alb and stole.

They stepped outside and Betty glanced over her shoulder for what she knew would be her final glimpse of Abiding Truth. She strained her ears, hoping to hear the familiar siren indicating that help was on the way, but all she heard was the church bell ringing. She was standing on the cement steps which led to the church entrance with Pastor Schwartz to her immediate right and Pastor Weiss to the other side of him. As her eyes adjusted to the outside light she saw the large man with the crew cut and bushy goatee standing beside the white sign, about fifty feet away. He was scowling and pointing a gun. It was aimed directly at Pastor Schwartz's head.

"No! Gerald!" shouted Pastor Weiss as he leapt forward with his arms in front of him. All at once Betty felt the force of both men's bodies falling into her own. She heard the clank of the metal hand railing as the back of her head struck against it. She smelled the sweet aroma of cologne. The sour stench of bourbon. She knew a gun had been discharged but she did not hear the shot because the bell was ringing too loud.

There was no bell in the tower and it kept on ringing. A crowd had gathered around Pastor Weiss. Someone propped a jacket beneath his head. His eyes were closed and the color had drained from his face. Pastor Schwartz knelt beside him, his face nearly as ashen as Pastor Weiss's.

Betty turned in a daze. She felt Dougie's hand on her shoulder, propelling her forward.

"Over here!"

"What happened?"

"Goddamn it."

"God help us."

"Where's the guy with the gun?"

"We've got to get away from the church. Too much smoke."

"Weiss. Allan, you're forgiven. I forgive you."

"Move it! Keep moving!"

"Everybody away from the building."

"There was only one shot."

"Pastor Weiss! Stay with us! Help is coming."

"He jumped in front of you, Pastor. I saw it all with my own eyes."

"Hold my hand."

"That man—he was aiming for you. Pastor Weiss jumped in front of you."

"Are you all right, Mother?"

Betty feels Dougie's hand in her own now. She closes her eyes and in her mind she can see a familiar happy place, where everything is as it should be. Dougie draws closer. She feels his breath as he snuggles against her chest, smells the peppermint candy he's been eating, and the Play-Dough on his fingers. He's been digging in the dirt again, as boys are apt to do. The rain comes down, so hard it cascades in a waterfall from the porch roof where the downspout is broken, and it spatters against her bare arms as dozens of goose bumps spread across her skin and she pulls him closer so her ear is against his chest and she can hear his heart thumping and off in the distance she sees a rainbow stretching across the mountain and the beat of his heart is a church bell ringing and she knows what she has known since the moment she became conscious of the miraculous life within her. This child is different. He is God's own gift. She pulls him close and holds him tight. A Mother Always Knows.

Twenty-Six

Betty Mundy

Sophie said maybe everybody in New York City felt like this after September 11th. Abiding Truth Lutheran Church was nowhere near as tall as the World Trade Center but now that it had been reduced to a pile of debris, it left a hole in the hearts of the residents of Dustin as big as Ground Zero. Even the Methodists said they felt sad about it. And the impact of one murder in a town of several hundred residents is no less than the sacrifice of thousands in the nation's largest city.

The story made the news, of course. It would be chronicled forever on the Internet. But as Sophie had predicted, the reporters left town after a few days, moving on to chase the next sensational tragedy. "They don't really care about us. You know," she said.

On Sunday evening, after the fire was finally extinguished, Pastor Schwartz gave a speech to the members of Abiding Truth. They met in the Buckshot Club because it was the only place in town large enough to accommodate them other than the Methodist Church. Despite expressing grief about the fire, none of the Methodists had offered to share their building.

Pastor prayed and talked, but Betty did not consider what they did in the Buckshot Club that evening a worship service. She did not feel the least bit holy sitting in a grimy place used primarily for the purpose of drinking, cussing, and telling dirty jokes. Irmalee's sister's boyfriend never showed up, and people didn't know if it was because he had heard about the fire or whether he never intended to come in the first place. Irmalee said maybe he had been raptured, whatever that meant.

The church was a total loss. By the time the fire department arrived, flames had engulfed the entire north side of the old clapboard building. Fortunately, Pastor had removed most of his books from his study before the fire started. Betty lost a few possessions, including her favorite book about little Timmy, the one-armed orphan boy with cancer.

Pastor Schwartz addressed his former parishioners. Betty could not imagine how awful he felt. No one expected him to say anything. But after seven years as their pastor, Betty supposed he felt a responsibility to comfort them. He spoke softly and somberly, and for once, people could understand him.

"Abiding Truth, as we have known it, no longer exists," he said. "But the church is more than a building. With your insurance benefits, you should be able to construct a new church under the able leadership of your next pastor."

People started shuffling when he said that. Pastor kept talking and the second time he mentioned insurance, Rogie stood up and said, "I hate to interrupt but—don't you remember?"

"Remember?" said Pastor.

"That we stopped paying our insurance premiums on the church property last summer."

"We did?"

"Maybe I forgot to tell you. But everyone else knows, don't you?" Rogie looked around. People were nodding their heads.

Betty recalled the decision to forego paying premiums was never officially voted on at a meeting. It was decided informally at the annual picnic in the parking lot, sometime between the three-legged race and the marshmallow toss, when most of the congregation was there. Except for Pastor, Betty now remembered. He had been called away suddenly during the wheelbarrow relay to visit Lois Warner in the emergency room.

"We needed to save money," said Rogie.

The decision seemed sensible at the time. For 118 years the bell-less tower of Abiding Truth had soared above Dustin as a visible reminder that God and His people do not change. The destruction of the church was unimaginable.

Pastor asked, "Does this mean I won't receive my severance package?"

Rogie sat down, and nobody said anything for a few seconds. Finally Pastor said, "I suppose that's a rhetorical question."

After Pastor's talk they had fellowship time like they always did on Sundays before the church burned down. Jane made coffee and Eleanor, who had abandoned her diet after gaining ten pounds since Christmas, brought butter cookies and chocolate gobs. But it didn't seem like Christian fellowship with the flashing neon Bud Light signs on the walls and Leroy sneaking behind the bar to top off his coffee with "Buckshot sauce."

"I can't believe it's gone," Jane said. She, Milly, and Betty were sitting together in a corner table that was covered with something sticky.

"It's horrible," said Milly.

"Such violence," said Betty, between sniffles.

"Used to be all the criminals stayed off the mountain," said Milly.

"It's getting to be like Harrisburg around here," said Jane.

"I can't believe it," said Milly.

"Poor Pastor Weiss," said Betty.

"There's never been a murder in Dustin. Not ever," said Milly.

"Well, none that was intentional," said Jane.

"Shh, now," said Milly. They all looked across the room at Edna, but she was too busy talking with Rogie to notice what anyone else was saying.

+++

In the days that followed, numerous stories about Pastor Weiss appeared in local and national papers. But the only article Betty saved was the simple obituary from *The Naptonville News* two days after the fire.

The Reverend Allan A. Weiss, 35, innovative and beloved pastor of NEW CREATION!!! in Pottersfield, died unexpectedly and courageously on February 12, 2005. Devoted husband of Virginia nee Abingdon and loving father of Trinity and Kevin. Further survived by his dearest friend and mentor, the Reverend Gerald Schwartz of Dustin. "No one has greater love than this, to lay down one's life for one's friends." John 15:13

Donations may be given in honor of Reverend Weiss's ministry to support construction of the Pastor Allan Weiss Memorial Holy Waters Baptismal Fun Park on the NEW CREATION!!! Campus.

How did Pastor Schwartz feel, knowing he was alive because of what Pastor Weiss had done? Betty did not dare ask such a personal question, but she could tell it had affected him deeply. At the memorial service for Pastor Weiss he turned to her with tears running down his cheeks. He whispered, "I lost the best friend I never knew I had."

The night after the memorial service, Betty saw Pastor Schwartz at the Altoona community center, and she knew why he was there. She wasn't sure whether she should approach him. She wanted to encourage him in his effort to stop drinking but did not want to embarrass him.

Then Betty noticed that Vera had cornered Pastor Schwartz. She had her hand on his shoulder. He looked like he was trying to find a polite way to escape Vera's suffocating grasp, which was how most people looked when they first met her.

+++

Life went on after the boys moved to Boston. Leroy, who had some experience operating heavy machinery, rented a demolition backhoe and razed what remained of the church, which made Betty feel better in an empty sort of way. A vacant lot was less offensive than a charred clapboard shell.

The fire had not damaged either of the signs and Leroy left them both standing. Someone had draped a rainbow colored flag over the black sign, but no one removed it. At the end of February a blizzard covered the flag with snow and ice and caused it to freeze fast to the sign.

Since the fire and shooting, Betty had been troubled by deep thoughts and unanswered questions. She knew better than to share them with Clarence and Pastor Schwartz was preoccupied with his own matters. She thought about talking to Marian, but Betty was afraid her sister would laugh at her distressing ruminations. One afternoon, three weeks after the fire, Betty and Sophie were sitting at their favorite table in their favorite Altoona coffee house, sipping cappuccinos served to them by their favorite excessively pierced waitress, who preferred to be called a "barista."

"I keep wondering," said Betty. "Was it a punishment from God?"

"God didn't have anything to do with it."

"Are you sure?"

"God didn't start that fire. God didn't shoot that gun."

The police had found the man who set the fire and shot Pastor Weiss a few hours after he fled the scene, hiding inside a casket at the Ashenbrenner Funeral Home. Betty knew he was locked up, but every time she saw a man with a crew cut and bushy goatee her heart skipped a beat. She had never noticed before how many men have crew cuts and bushy goatees, especially in Altoona.

"None of this would have happened if I hadn't made Pastor Schwartz do the blessing."

"You didn't make anybody do anything. You stood by your son. It's not your fault other people are hateful. You know."

She knew Sophie was right. Still Betty had spent so many years feeling guilty about everything—from burning Clarence's toast to paying too much for a new broom—that it was hard for her to believe this was not God's punishment.

"Do other people blame me?" Betty asked, as Sophie nodded at the barista for a second cappuccino. She knew Sophie would be honest yet kind.

"Nobody blames you. Look at how we've been helping you out. Do you hear whose idea it was to take up that special offering for you? Most Everyone's."

"You're kidding! I can't understand why those women are suddenly being nice to me."

"It won't last. You know."

+++

It felt strange, not going to church on Sundays. And it was Lent, besides, when you were supposed to go to church more than usual to feel bad about your sins. But Betty did not need to be in church to feel bad. Jane and Milly started attending services at the Methodist church. A few others drove down the mountain to NEW CREATION!!!, which was showing videos of Reverend Weiss's sermons until they found a new pastor.

But Betty did not go anywhere. One Sunday she and Clarence sat around playing canasta in their bathrobes, which seemed downright decadent, especially at ten in the morning. Another Sunday, Clarence made Betty get out the book Marian had given her for Christmas. He blushed a bit when he suggested they might want to attempt the particular activity described in detail and illustrated far too graphically on page 87.

"Oh good heavens!" she said. "Not during Lent!" Secretly she felt grateful that Clarence was becoming adventurous in middle age and promised they could try it some Sunday after Easter.

As far as Betty could tell, Pastor Schwartz was not attending church anywhere, either. She did not ask him about it. She called if she went more than a day without seeing him, to make sure he was all right, all alone in the parsonage.

+++

Easter came and went, though in Betty's estimation it did not seem like spring—partly because it came early, at the end of March. Six inches of snow still covered the ground. Yet Jesus could have made a personal post-resurrection appearance in Dustin and it still would not have felt like Easter.

By mid-April most of the snow melted and daffodils were blooming all across town. Betty had started her new job as an administrative assistant at the button factory in Naptonville. The pay was better than what she had made as a church secretary, but it took awhile to adjust to a different routine.

She was at the post office in Dustin before work one morning when a man in an expensive-looking suit came in and said he was a lawyer from Pittsburgh. He asked for directions to Abiding Truth Lutheran Church. He said he had stopped at the video store and the owner sent him across town to a vacant lot with two signs in front of it indicating there was a church nearby, but he could not find one.

Leroy, who was loitering in the post office lobby as had become his habit now that the church had burned down, said, "Our church is invisible. You can't see it unless you're a member."

Betty thought that was humorous, considering the dire mood around town over the past two months. Since the tragedy, people around Dustin had been more suspicious of strangers than usual and well-dressed lawyers from Pittsburgh were about as welcome as the devil himself.

The man said he was serious and needed to talk to the pastor. Leroy said there was no pastor but he was on the property committee of the invisible church, which was a harder job than a person might think because whenever something broke you couldn't see what it was to fix it. The man stormed out of the post office, growling that he was too important to waste his time speaking to imbeciles.

Apparently the lawyer later found Pastor Schwartz, and turned out to be as important as he had claimed because he represented the estate of Kristina Kirch. That's what Pastor Schwartz said when he addressed the former members of Abiding Truth at a specially called meeting at the Buckshot Club.

"Miss Kirch has bequeathed the entire amount of her estate to Abiding Truth Lutheran Church, subject to one condition."

Edna jumped up a second before her sister did.

"How much did she leave us?" asked Edna.

"How much did she leave us?" asked Eleanor.

"Attorney Fredericks estimates Miss Kirch's net worth at somewhere between three and four million," said Pastor Schwartz, looking at neither Edna nor Eleanor. Betty noticed he had lost some weight.

"Three million!" shouted Edna, turning toward Dorothy.

"Four million!" shouted Eleanor. She glanced at Milly and Jane.

Betty felt an invisible line forming down the middle of the room, and when she looked around she realized everyone was sitting in approximately the same place they would be were they in church.

Roger stood up and said, "Seeing as I used to be the President and all—" But Pastor Schwartz cut him off.

"Miss Kirch has bequeathed the entire amount of her estate to Abiding Truth, subject to one condition," he said. "That the funds be disbursed according to the sole discretion of the pastor at the time of her death."

"That's a lot of money," said Edna.

"This time we'll be able to afford a bell," said Eleanor.

"As the former President—" said Roger before Pastor Schwartz cut him off again.

"Apparently Miss Kirch was aware of the divisive nature of Abiding Truth," said Pastor Schwartz, his voice rising above the others.

"A bell?" said Edna. "The last thing our church needs is a bell."

"With a freely hanging clapper!" said Eleanor.

"Therefore, though some might deem it autocratic—"

"I'm still President and all, ain't I?"

"This time we're building the church out of bricks."

"Limestone. Bricks are ugly."

"Hey! My house is made of bricks."

"A freely hanging clapper?"

"By pastoral decree, I hereby designate that funds from Miss Kirch's estate—"

"We'll need air conditioning."

"Carpeting in the narthex."

"At such time as they are received—"

"Not that awful mauve color we used to have in the nursery."

"Why ain't nobody listening to me?"

"…be donated in their entirety to the Pastor Allan Weiss Memorial Holy Waters Baptismal Fun Park. Good night. I need to adjourn this meeting. The Pirates game is on."

Like a ghost then, Pastor Schwartz was gone.

"Red," said Edna. "Narthex carpeting ought to be red."

"Whoever heard of a limestone church?" said Eleanor.

+++

One afternoon in the second week of May, exactly three months to the day of the fire, Betty returned home from shopping to find Clarence, Spot, and Chip watching a rerun of Pastor Weiss preaching on television. As soon as he saw her, Clarence flipped the channel quickly, like he usually did when she caught him watching pornography or an infomercial for incontinence aids. She knew he was being sensitive. The last time Betty tried to watch Pastor Weiss's show she had burst into tears during the opening credits and rushed from the room.

"It's okay," she said now. "I'd like to watch that with you."

"Really?"

She sat down next to Clarence on the sofa.

"Have you been watching this when I'm not around?"

"Sometimes. I always liked the way that guy talked. Didja get a chance to say goodbye to Pastor Schwartz?"

"I gave him a big hug and a peck on the cheek. He was never much for hugs, though. I told him to remember that whenever God closes a door, He always opens a window." Pastor had found an apartment back in Baltimore, and with money from the sale of the parsonage he would have enough to live on for a while.

"I s'pose," said Clarence.

"I hope he keeps up with his email letters from that computer dating site."

Clarence did not reply. He was listening to Pastor Weiss.

"You know what they say— 'a life without love is like a year without summer.'"

"Uh huh," said Clarence. His eyes were glued to the television set. He reached for the remote and turned up the volume.

"I'm talking to You right now," said Pastor Weiss. "And I want to tell You something my father used to tell me. He said, 'It doesn't matter who You are. It doesn't matter whether You're rich or poor, whether You're young or old, where You were born or where You went to school. Whoever You are — You're always an asset to someone.'"

That Pastor Weiss was a good-looking man.

When the show was over Clarence snuggled up to her and placed his hand on her knee. It did not seem right somehow but watching Pastor Weiss made her feel amorous. He must have had the same effect on Clarence.

"Hey Betty, I was thinking maybe—"

"Yes?"

The way he was smirking she knew what he wanted. Still she liked to hear him ask for it.

"Ya know. Page 87. Last time was kinda fun. I never . . ."

"You never what?"

"I never seen ya react like that before."

Clarence was grinning like the Steelers had won another Super Bowl. Betty grasped his hand and held it against a place on her body that a few months before, she would have been hesitant to touch herself.

"Don't think we should be doin' it in fronta Spot and Chip."

Clarence turned off the television and rose from the sofa. Then, like a gentleman, he helped Betty to her feet. Spot peered up at them indifferently.

"Let's try the spare bed this time," said Clarence, still grinning as they made their way, arm in arm, toward the stairs.

"Why, Clarence Mundy," said Betty, "you look like a man who's going to have his cake and eat it too."

It amazed her these days, the words that came out of her mouth.

Epilogue

Summer

Gerald Schwartz

He had traversed these treacherous roads so many times during the seven years he lived in Dustin that his travels around Mount Kiersey, like his sermons and hospital calls on Lois Warner, had blurred into one insignificant memory. But today, as his Buick crawled up route 49 behind a sluggish coal truck Gerald felt like he was ascending this mountain for the first time.

He was spotting landmarks that had previously escaped his notice, including the rusting railroad trestle south of Colton and the advertisement for the extinct Pinkly's department store painted onto the side of a dilapidated barn across from the turnoff for Simonton Road. Surely, they had always been there. Why was he first observing them now? Gerald sensed it was more than a matter of being sober and undistracted by pastoral tasks.

Even as he dawdled around his familiar haunts in Baltimore, Gerald felt keenly aware of a simple truth he had long taken for granted—he was alive. And as Gerald frequently pondered with unabashed giddiness, his once battered ego had been bolstered by his recent email correspondence with lutheranlady0513.

The temperature in Baltimore had been hovering in the 90s, but the sign outside the bank in Spooner's Grove indicated a pleasant reading of 74 degrees. Gerald turned off the air conditioner and rolled down a window for the final three miles before his first stop of the day.

Betty had kept him abreast of Dustin's latest developments, so he knew what to expect. Yet, like meeting an ex-wife's new love interest, there was no way to emotionally prepare himself for the site he beheld as he passed Ray's Salvage lot and rounded the final corner of route 49 into town. Where the bell tower of Abiding Truth had stood majestically for 118 years there rose an unmistakable icon—golden arches.

"Oh, Pastor, it's so good to see you!" said Betty, when Gerald stepped onto her porch. "You look so different without your pastor clothes on. And you've lost weight, too!"

Through the screen door he heard the rumble of the television and saw a silhouette of Clarence sprawled out on the sofa. Betty ignored Gerald's extended hand and grasped him in a suffocating hug. "I'm going to be a grandma!"

Gerald must have stared at her blankly after he exclaimed the customary, "Congratulations!" because Betty smiled and said, "You're trying to figure out how, aren't you? The boys are adopting. Gay people can do that now.

"The birth mother is one of Dougie's friends. That girl I always wanted him to date—Cathy. She's just had a baby and she's not married and she's going back to college and anyway, she's arranging for Dougie and Danny to adopt her son. They call it an 'open adoption.' The father's out of the picture, not that it's my business to judge that sort of thing."

"Congratulations," Gerald said again.

"I haven't seen him yet, but Dougie says he's really cute. He's got two different color eyes."

"Congratulations!"

"I'm sorry, Pastor. I'm rambling on like Mrs. Hawthorne. When you have such big news of your own. You're on your way to see her, aren't you?"

"Mrs. Hawthorne? Not if I don't have to."

Betty laughed. "You know who I'm talking about. It's amazing who she turned out to be. It's a miracle really."

"Ironic, I suppose."

"See, I told you to keep at it. If at first you don't succeed…."

Gerald's first computer-generated match, Lustylutherbabe231, had lascivious inclinations. She was followed by Lutheranmiss517, who insisted that baseball was a frivolous waste of time. Mamaluther012 had troubling syncretic tendencies and in Gerald's opinion would have fared better in a Unitarian Universalist dating service. Lovelylutheranlass93 had never heard of Helmut Thielecke and luthergal!000 thought the book of Leviticus was in the New Testament.

As an unemployed 59-year-old with a propensity for flatulism, Gerald understood that he could not afford to be excessively discriminating, but anonymity had cultivated in him a heretofore untapped sense of adventure and transformed him into a serial Internet matchmaking profile reader. He worried that he might become addicted to finding fault in all potential matches—until he opened his first email message from Lutheranlady0513 and immediately knew she alone was the one he wanted to meet.

"So now you're going to have your first official date. How romantic!" said Betty.

Aware that he was blushing, Gerald said, "Have you become a Methodist yet?" Gerald's seminary roommate, whose theology was suspect, had once said, "Everyone becomes a Methodist in the end."

"Oh no," laughed Betty. "My great-great-grandfather would roll over in his grave. Milly and I go down to NEW CREATION!!! now. My grandson is getting baptized at the new water park once it's finished."

"I see."

Despite the fact his final pastoral act involved contributing several million dollars to finance a frivolous and arguably sacrilegious venture, Gerald still had a pastor's sensibilities. Giving away Miss Kirch's fortune was an irrational and indefensible decision. But it wasn't nearly as irrational as stepping in front of a bullet to save a man who five minutes earlier had told you to go to hell. God bless Allan Weiss. The water park would be a fitting tribute. And a sizable portion of Miss Kirch's bequest would adequately provide for Weiss's widow and children.

"Edna thinks her granddaughter's going to be the first to get baptized at Holy Waters, but it's going to be my grandson. Dougie's got connections at that church. You know, Pastor, now that we've got a McDonald's nobody's mad at you anymore about giving away that money."

"That's good to know."

"It was a unanimous decision to sell the land. It was the first thing Edna and Eleanor have agreed about since their mother died."

"Blessed be the fries that bind." Gerald knew he best avoid sarcasm, since his ex-parishioners had provided him with a generous severance package.

"They put that place up in less than three weeks. Everyone in town loves it, even the Methodists."

"Maybe I should stop in for a Whopper."

"No, Pastor. They serve Big Macs. You're getting your fast food denominations mixed up."

+++

Hundreds of flowers bloomed in the front yard—a virtual sea of red, orange, and yellow. Planters of marigolds hung from the porch roof and a brightly decorated sign proclaimed *God Bless All Who Enter Here.* Gerald drew in his breath and knocked on the door before he had a chance to reconsider.

He could hear his heart pounding. He felt like a schoolboy anticipating the appearance of his prom date. He checked to make sure the zipper on his fly was closed.

For several weeks they had been corresponding, covering a plethora of topics with a refreshingly intellectual perspective, from death to dieting to the complicated nature of human sexuality. Lutheranlady0513 seemed too good to be real—well versed in Hellenistic mythology, she also knew Brooks Robinson's lifetime fielding percentage.

For a while, he worried it was merely anonymity that enabled their intimacy. Gerald spent hours composing his emails on his new computer. He cautiously edited his words. Face-to-face conversation allowed little room for error. *Extemporal discourse is not my forte,* he had written in an early email message. Then he pressed and held the delete key, replacing his statement with a less pretentious admission—*I am a bit awkward in person.* That was before he had discovered Lutheranlady0513's identity. Before he had realized that, should deeper conversational topics elude them, they could talk about friends and acquaintances they had in common.

In his hands he clutched a box of petit fours from his favorite Baltimore bakery. He had memorized how he would greet her, but before he could ponder the anticipated moment in more detail, the door popped open and there she was, smiling shyly. A face he had come to know well.

She had gleaming blue eyes the hue of that place where the sky meets the ocean on a sunny summer day. Around her neck she wore a finely braided silver chain with a small Celtic cross pendant attached to it. It was not what Gerald had expected to see.

"My God!" he exclaimed, which was not what he had planned to say.

"Yes."

"My God—it's you!"

"I am Grace."

"You're Grace Franklin?"

"Yes."

"I'm—Gerald Schwartz."

"I guessed that."

"You—"

She took his hand in her own. "Well, Gerald Schwartz. You are a bit awkward in person."

"Thank you."

"It's strange to finally see what you look like. You're a good-looking man. I like your haircut. I hope you're not disappointed by what you see."

"N—no. Not at all."

Gleaming blue eyes. The color of the place where the sky meets the ocean. At least forty years had passed, yet there was no mistaking who she was.

"I know you were insistent that we not send each other photos but curiosity got the best of me. I looked you up on the Internet. I thought maybe there would be a picture of you. The only ones I found were actually photos of Joe—which is ironic to say the least."

Regaining his composure, Gerald said, "You are the most beautiful woman I've ever met."

"That's quite a compliment." She smiled. At three a.m. when the demons rose up from the darkness, he would close his eyes and picture that smile. "I like this idea of getting to know each other from the inside out. Too many judgments are made on the basis of appearance."

"I—I'm sorry I was slow to compliment you earlier. I'm a bit overwhelmed."

"You're forgiven then." She said it in such a way that it sounded like a true absolution, one that would cover a multitude of sins. "Welcome to Greensburg. I understand you stopped in Dustin on your way here."

"Yes. I did do that."

"Betty keeps me abreast of the news. I hear Dorothy Moyers has become a Methodist. God help the Methodists. She's already sending anonymous complaints to that poor pastor. And my dear friend Sophie's found a partner on the Internet. Seems to be a popular way to meet up these days. And Betty's a grandmother! I'm sure she talked your ears off about that."

"Indeed."

She had aged in such a way that each wrinkle magnified her beauty, her hair had become a silver crown, time's effect on her body had not caused her glory to fade but served to ground and soften her. She was a few years older than Gerald but he could not help noticing that she looked considerably younger than Margaret.

"I hope it's the necklace you're staring at."

"It's—"

"There's a story behind this necklace." She caressed the cross between her thumb and forefinger as she spoke. "It was taken from me by someone you knew well."

"Kristina?"

"After the affair, she had a breakdown. She broke into the parsonage one night and stole a number of my possessions. At least I had always suspected it was she. A week ago, I received this in the mail. She bequeathed my own necklace to me."

"Hmm." Grace caressed the cross with her hand, the hand he had imagined holding in his own, its warmth an assurance he was not alone in the world. Not Alone.

"She also took a favorite photograph of mine. From my days in Ocean City—where I'm hoping we might go if things work out between us."

"That would be nice." Over her shoulder there is the ocean, an eternal blanket of blue.

"I'm still hoping my photo will show up. Why someone would steal something like that is beyond me."

"It does seem rather strange."

"Please come in. I've made you dinner."

She stepped inside and nodded for Gerald to follow.

"Thank you," he said, without moving.

"Could you make sure the door closes properly behind you? I'll open a few windows to let in some air."

He was still standing on the porch, clutching the box of petit fours. He checked to make sure the zipper on his fly was closed.

"Are you coming in?" she called.

"Yes, I am."

This was starting out more awkward than he had imagined. Gerald had no idea what to say next. But after thirty years in the ministry he knew this for sure—when Grace invites you in for dinner you would be a damn fool to turn Her down.

1126199 FIC EPPL $14.95

CPSIA information can be obtained at www.ICGtesting.com
Printed in the USA
BVOW060943270212

283813BV00001B/7/P

9 780984 010905